RISING DAWN

THE WATCHERS TRILOGY, BOOK 3

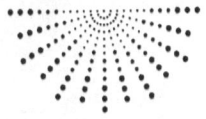

CHRISTINE POPE

DARK VALENTINE PRESS

RISING DAWN

ISBN: 978-1-946435-04-0

Copyright © 2017 by Christine Pope

Published by Dark Valentine Press

Cover design by Christian Bentulan

Ebook formatting by Indie Author Services

CHAPTER ONE

As far as world-changing conversations went, the one that took place between Lucius Montfort, my vampire captor, and my brother Jackson didn't last for very long. Just as he had acted with my mother a few minutes earlier, Lucius remained on his best behavior, telling Jackson that he wished he could have had the opportunity to work with my late sister Vanessa, and that the world would suffer for having lost her talent so soon. Then he offered Jackson a grave smile and excused himself to go across the room and speak to a woman with a severe bob and oversized earrings, someone I recognized as one of the other investors from the reception that followed my sister's fashion show. In fact, there were quite a few people here at this funeral reception who had attended the other event as well, although their overall demeanor was much more subdued.

I wished I could let out a sigh of relief that Lucius was otherwise occupied for the moment, but I knew I couldn't...not with my brother standing right there. He'd be sure to notice.

After Lucius was out of earshot, Jackson turned toward me and lifted a quizzical eyebrow. "You want to talk about it?" he asked.

"Not really," I replied. I could tell he was asking about my relationship with Lucius, not my reaction to Vanessa's death. Since Jackson and I had never been terribly close, due to the nearly twelve-year gap in our ages, I didn't feel like now was the right time to be sharing confidences. Besides, it wasn't as if I could tell him the truth, let him know that I was with Lucius only because the man I actually loved would be dead otherwise.

And that revelation wouldn't even include trying to explain that Lucius Montfort wasn't truly a man at all, but a centuries-old vampire who had his own nefarious reasons for wanting to make my brother's acquaintance.

Once again Jackson lifted an eyebrow. His hazel eyes—the eyes all of us siblings shared—were too sharp, as if he realized something was off, even if he couldn't quite put his finger on it.

"Mom seems to approve of him, despite the disappearing act you pulled this past week."

"Well, of course she'd approve of him," I said, and took a sip from the glass of chardonnay I held. "He's rich and handsome and lives in Linda Vista. I suppose it might be marginally better if his house was here in San Marino, but still, Linda Vista's no slum, is it?"

"No," Jackson agreed, but I could tell from the way his eyes narrowed slightly that he was surprised by my response, which, I had to admit, wasn't exactly the way a woman who was supposed to be madly in love with her partner would have replied to his comment.

I needed to watch it. As angry as I was with Lucius, and as worried as I might be for Silas, I couldn't let those emotions color my words or actions. For now, I had to pretend that I was besotted with Lucius, as much as such a subterfuge might disgust me. Luckily, I had a lot of practice pushing my emotions away to deal with later. No doubt a psychologist would have told me that wasn't healthy behavior, but there wasn't much I could do about it at the moment.

And I should probably be careful with the wine. I was already on my second glass, and I had a long evening ahead of me. Slipping out before nine at the very earliest would look terrible, and no doubt earn me a dressing-down from my mother the next time I saw her. In general, she tried to save those sorts of recriminations for in-person interactions.

"Sorry," I said. "That's not really what I meant. Lucius is...well, he's amazing. But you know how Mom can get under my skin."

"Yes, I know." His eyes slid away from my gaze, clearly distracted by someone across the room. "I didn't know the lieutenant governor was going to be here."

"Maybe Mom didn't say anything because she didn't know for sure." Although Jackson was too polite to act as if he wanted to slip away and talk to someone a bit more important than his little sister, I could tell he wanted to end the conversation so he could go speak to Lieutenant Governor Neal. "It's fine, Jackson," I added. "I'll be fine. Go talk to him."

"You're sure?"

"Yes." I didn't quite make a shooing gesture, but Jackson seemed to believe what he saw in my face, because he said he'd talk to me in a little bit, and then went ahead and walked over to the spot by the fireplace where the lieutenant governor was deep in conversation with two women I recognized from my parents' country club.

That seemed to be my cue to escape. I took a quick note of Lucius' position, saw that he was still speaking with several of Vanessa's former investors, and decided it was okay to make a break for it. Not out of the house altogether—that would probably put the vampire master hot on my trail—but toward the back of the house, where the covered patio offered a welcome sanctuary away from the crowds in the living room and family room and dining room.

The patio was much quieter. In fact, at first I thought it was completely unoccupied—until I saw the party lights strung overhead glinting on my sister-in-law's blonde hair. She was sitting at a table near the edge of the patio, where you could get a clear view of the swimming pool in the yard. The water shimmered blue-green in the gathering dusk, but I didn't find anything terribly inviting about it, not with how overcast and gloomy the day had been.

Then I noticed that Bethany's youngest daughter, Taylor, and Griffin, Bethany and Jackson's only son, sat at the table by her, both of them doing their best to demolish the plates of food she'd set in front of them. My oldest niece, Addison, lay on a chaise longue off to one side, her eyes closed, as if she was taking a nap. Even from where I stood, I could see how pale she looked. Had the memorial service upset her that much? I'd never gotten the impression that Addison—or any of Jackson and Bethany's children—were that close to Vanessa.

How could they be, when they'd spent half their lives away from Southern California? Even when they were staying at the house in Claremont, they never got to see much of their aunt. Her hectic schedule precluded any kind of family visits, except a Christmas here and there.

"Bethany," I said softly, and my sister-in-law startled, and then appeared to relax slightly as she saw who had addressed her.

"Hi, Serena." Her voice sounded very tired, which surprised me. Bethany had always been one of those types who seemed able to handle anything the world threw at her, which made her perfect as a politician's wife. Again, I found myself wondering if the tragedy of Vanessa's death had struck her harder than I'd expected. To tell the truth, the two of them had always chafed on one another, just a little bit. Or, to be more accurate, Vanessa's abruptness had annoyed Bethany on several occasions, although my sister-in-law was too polite to complain about Vanessa to me or anyone else in the family. I'd seen the irritation in her eyes, though.

"Is it okay if I sit down?" I asked, and Bethany nodded.

"Of course. It's been kind of a long day for the kids, so I thought it would be better to have them eat their dinner here." Her gaze flickered toward the French doors that led into the family room and back toward me. "You know, just so I wouldn't have to worry about Barbara hovering, worrying whether they were going to spill something on her rugs."

Oh, yes, I knew all about my mother's continual fear that someone would damage her pristine house. Sometimes I wondered how I'd managed to grow up without major obsessive-compulsive issues, considering the way I'd been raised. "I totally get it," I said as I pulled out a chair and sat down. "Hey, Griffin, hey, Taylor."

My nephew and niece looked up from their sandwiches long enough to mutter, "Hey, Aunt Serena," through mouths full of food before they returned to their determined chewing. If I'd acted like that as a child, I would've gotten an earful about how it was rude to talk with your mouth full, but Bethany had never been as strict as my mother, and I could tell that she was especially distracted now, for whatever reason. Maybe she wasn't as thrilled about Jackson running for President as she'd let on?

Then I glanced over at Addison, still apparently asleep on the chaise longue. I noticed that a barely touched plate of food sat on the little wrought iron table next to her. Bethany clearly caught that look, because her mouth tightened, and she reached for the glass of water sitting next to her.

"Is—is Addie okay?" I asked.

Bethany's lips parted. Then, to my surprise, she closed them just as quickly, and shook her head. "No," she said. "She's not. She's...." To my surprise, I saw tears glittering in her blue eyes.

Clearly, something was going on here that had nothing to do with my sister's murder. "She's what, Bethany?"

A long silence. Bethany's gaze rested on her sleeping daughter, then flickered over to her other two children, both of them happily eating, not paying any attention to our conversation. Then, the words barely more than a sigh, "It's leukemia."

"*What?*" I blurted, the word coming out much sharper than I'd intended. "I'm sorry," I went on, this time in a softer tone of voice. "Why didn't Jackson tell me?"

"He didn't want to make a big deal out of it. Also, we talked to Addie very seriously after she was diagnosed, asked her if she wanted her daddy to postpone running for President. She said no. She said she didn't want to stop him from helping people." Bethany reached up to wipe the moisture away from the corner of her eye—a careful, practiced gesture, as if she knew exactly how to get rid of any pesky tears without harming her makeup. "Pretty amazing for a nine-year-old, I think. Anyway, we have an appointment at UCLA on Monday. We weren't getting much help at Johns Hopkins, but there are some cutting-edge research trials going on at UCLA right now, so...." She stopped there. "Anyway, we're hopeful."

"I'm so sorry," I said. "Have you told—"

"Not yet," Bethany cut in. "Jackson didn't want to worry your parents. They have enough to deal with right now. We're just taking it one day at a time and praying for a miracle."

I nodded, hoping that something of my mute sympathy might communicate itself to her. How awful that they should have to go through this. Addie had been a bright, lively girl the last time I'd seen her, which was in August before the family had returned to Washington. During the service, I'd noticed that she seemed somewhat tired, but I'd attributed her weariness to a combination of sorrow and jet lag. Now, though, I understood that the problem was much, much worse, her very blood attacking her.

Her blood.

The thought made me go cold all over, even though gas heaters had been set out here on the patio to combat the chilliness of the early spring evening. I sent another quick glance at my sleeping niece, taking in the pallor of her cheeks, a thinness I should have noted earlier, but probably had overlooked because of my own grief and worry.

And I thought of the visions that had haunted me, of my brother clearly in some sort of collaboration with Lucius, exchanging the secrets hidden within vampire blood for immortality, or at least a damn good imitation of it. At the time, I couldn't figure out how my upstanding brother would ever allow himself to get tangled up with someone like Lucius Montfort, but now I began to understand...and to fear.

Jackson wouldn't sell out his own people for personal gain, but what if the antibodies contained inside vampire blood could somehow provide the cure for Addison's illness? What lengths would he go to save a beloved child?

I wasn't sure I wanted to know the answer to that question. As I'd told Lucius, my visions didn't always come true...but they had a pretty damn good success rate. Never had I wanted to be wrong more than I did in that moment.

But I could be wrong. It was entirely possible that the people at UCLA would be able to help Addie, in which case my visions were off the mark. If modern medical science couldn't cure her, though...what then?

How desperate would that make my

brother? And could I even blame him? I writhed inwardly, knowing that this frightening development would most likely only bind me closer to Lucius, to his ruthless ambitions.

"We're hopeful, though," Bethany went on, obviously not noting my abstraction, wound up in her own worries as she was. "We've heard really promising things about the clinical trials they're holding right now. But we need to get Addison over there so they can evaluate her, see if she's a good candidate for their program."

"I'm sure it'll turn out fine," I said. I tried to make my voice as reassuring as I could, but I didn't know how successful I was. This day had been stressful enough, and now....

"Ah, there you are," came Lucius' voice, and I looked away from Bethany to see the vampire come through the French doors and walk over to the patio table where my sister-in-law and I sat. "I was wondering what had happened to you."

Since Bethany was looking up at him, her expression frankly curious, I couldn't do much except make the necessary introductions. "Bethany, this is Lucius Montfort. Lucius, this is my sister-in-law Bethany, and these are her children—Griffin and Taylor, and that's Addison taking a nap there on the chaise longue."

He smiled pleasantly at all of them, but I could see the way his gaze tracked over to

Addie, how his eyes narrowed for just a fraction as he took in her wan appearance. "It's very nice to meet you, Bethany. It's rather crowded inside, so I can see why you might want to take refuge out here."

"Yes, this is sort of a big gathering for the kids to handle," she said, smiling as well. The tense, worried woman I'd seen just a few moments earlier was now gone, replaced by the practiced friendliness of a politician's wife. "Since there aren't any other children here for them to play with, I figured it was best to have them be out on the patio where they wouldn't get underfoot."

"Very sensible," he agreed. Then he looked over at me. "Serena, I have that breakfast meeting tomorrow, so I thought perhaps we should go now."

Of course there was no breakfast meeting— Lucius Montfort hadn't eaten breakfast in several hundred years—but I didn't contradict him. I guessed he was using this "breakfast" as a ploy so he could get me away from the reception. After all, he'd accomplished his primary goal, of meeting my brother. No doubt he was tired of making small talk with people he didn't know, and wanted to retreat to the sanctuary of his gothic mansion in Linda Vista.

I shot an apologetic look at Bethany, even as

I got up from my seat. "Of course, Lucius. I'd forgotten about the meeting. Are you going to be okay out here, Bethany?"

"Sure," she replied. "Although if you see Jackson, could you send him over?"

"Absolutely." Another smile, and I waved at the kids. Since Taylor and Griffin had gotten to the dessert portion of their meals and were busy devouring some very messy cream puffs, I wasn't even sure they noticed me leaving, but it would have felt strange not to offer them sort of acknowledgment as I made my goodbyes to their mother.

"I already let your parents know that we needed to leave early," Lucius murmured in my ear as he guided me through the crowd inside. "They're occupied now, so it will be easy enough to slip out."

"I'm not going to bail on my own sister's funeral reception," I began indignantly, only to feel him take my elbow in a grip of iron.

"I'm afraid I must insist," he said.

Since I knew I couldn't make a scene in front of everyone, I gritted my teeth and let him lead me to the front door. As we went, I looked from side to side for my brother Jackson, but I didn't see him anywhere. Damn it. I could only hope that Bethany would understand I hadn't fetched him for her because he'd made himself scarce, not because I'd avoided helping her out.

How my vampire companion had managed it, I didn't know, but the big charcoal-gray Mercedes was already waiting for us outside the front door, the brown-haired semivive driver holding open the rear passenger door for us. Lucius helped me in, and settled himself on the seat next to me. A moment later, the car pulled away from the house, moving toward the gates that would let us return to the outside world.

"Your niece," Lucius said abruptly as the car glided away and headed west toward Linda Vista. "What's wrong with her?"

No way in the world was I going to tell him about Addison's leukemia. He would see that as a certain opening, an easy way to gain Jackson's confidence. On the other hand, I had to watch my lies. I had to make sure he still believed me, still thought I was now on his side. "She's just tired," I said. Luckily, since we sat side by side on the rear seat, I didn't have to look him directly in the eyes as I told him that lie. "Bethany said she had a touch of the flu back in D.C. before they came out here to California, and she still hasn't quite shaken it off."

"No, that was not the flu," Lucius said. He reached over to take my hand, cold fingers wrapping around mine. If anyone had been watching us, they might have said it was a gesture of reassurance. I knew better, though, knew from the way his grip tightened that he meant it very much as a threat. I held myself still and made sure not to react. He already had enough power over me. "We vampires...we can catch the scent of your blood. If you're healthy, it's warm and appetizing, like a well-marbled steak. That child, though...her blood smelled more like meat gone rancid."

It would have been nice if I'd known about that particular detail before I launched into my lie. Unfortunately, there wasn't much I could do about it now. "It's probably just the meds they put her on. I don't know."

The cold fingers clamped down on mine, and I had to force myself not to wince. "Serena."

Only he could turn my name into such a threat. I swallowed, and glanced out the window. Not that I could see much; by that point, it was full dark outside, the houses slipping past us ghostly and insubstantial, save for the brief illumination of solar lights or other landscape fixtures. "She has leukemia," I said flatly.

"Ah." The syllable was little more than an exhalation. Then he smiled. For some reason, his canines looked particularly pointed right then. "That could be useful."

"She's a child, Lucius!" Right then I didn't

care if he was offended by my tone. Yes, I
wanted him to think my loyalties now lay with
him, and I was forced to continue this charade
until Silas was free of Lucius' clutches, but I also
refused to let myself act like a complete monster.
It would have been even more suspicious if I
hadn't made some effort to defend my niece.

"A sick child," he said, voice mild, obviously
not at all ruffled by my rebuke. "One whose
illness could be easily cured."

"How do you know that for sure?" I shifted
so I was turned slightly more toward him,
although the seatbelt stretched across my chest
prevented me from facing him full on. "You told
me that the benefits of the antibodies in vampire
blood hadn't actually been proven, that it was all
conjecture."

"Very well. I don't know for sure, but I
strongly believe that your niece's illness, since it
is a disease of the blood, is something that would
not present much of an obstacle." His head
tilted, and he gave me a considering look. "How
long will your brother and his family be in
California?"

"I'm not sure," I replied. It was nothing more
than the truth; they hadn't told me that much about
their plans. "I know that they're going to UCLA on
Monday to see some doctors there. Something

about a clinical trial, but Bethany didn't give me any real details. I would assume they can't stay out here for too long, since Congress is still in session. Their spring break isn't for another month."

"Hmm." Lucius was silent then, but his expression was so neutral that I really couldn't guess what might be passing through his brain. "It's probably better if I speak to your brother before he sees the specialists at UCLA. You will need to arrange a meeting for tomorrow evening."

"Just like that."

"Yes, just like that. You are his sister—the only sister he has left. Surely he will make time for you."

Once again I was reminded that it had been a very long time since Lucius had been mortal, had interacted with true friends or family. This wasn't like setting up a hair appointment, for God's sake. I didn't know if Jackson had plans to come back and see my parents the next day, or whether he had some sort of activity planned for the kids while they were here in Southern California. Recalling Addie's pale face and limp form, I guessed they probably wouldn't be headed out to Universal Studios or the beach, but they could still have decided to go to the movies or a local park or something.

"Maybe," I allowed. "But I don't know for sure."

"Call him."

"Now?"

"Yes."

"He's going to think that's kind of strange, me calling him not even fifteen minutes after I left the reception."

"Tell him you looked for him but couldn't find him. With that crowd, such an explanation will be plausible enough."

I should have known that Lucius would continue to counter me at every move. Fine. This hill wasn't worth dying on.

As he watched, I got my phone out of my purse, unlocked the screen, and went to my contacts list. I touched the phone icon on Jackson's listing, then waited as the phone rang. And rang. Of course he wouldn't answer it; he was at a funeral reception for his late sister. No doubt he'd turned off the ringer.

Sure enough, the call went to voicemail. All too conscious of Lucius Montfort's eyes on me, I said, "Hi, Jackson. It's Serena. Look—um, Lucius and I were talking, and he'd really like to meet with you in private to discuss a few things. Would tomorrow evening work, around six-thirty? Or later, after dinner, if that's better for you. Just let me know." I ended the call there and slipped the phone back into my purse. "Was that okay?"

"Yes, that should do very well. But if he doesn't call back within the hour, then try again."

"I'm going to sound desperate."

"That might work to our advantage. He'll want to know what's so important."

I couldn't argue with that statement, so I gave a noncommittal lift of my shoulders. By that point, we had reached the Linda Vista neighborhood where Lucius' house was located. A few minutes later, we pulled into the driveway. The car stopped under the porte cochère on one side of the house, and the semivive who'd been driving came around back to open the door for us.

He helped me out first, while I did my best not to shudder as I placed my hand in his. True, the man's hand felt normal and human enough, but I knew his mind was not his own, had been enslaved to Lucius Montfort's will God knows how many years earlier.

We went in through the side entrance. My watch told me it was only a little before nine, and yet I was bone-weary. I wanted nothing more than to collapse into bed, but it was far too early for that. Besides, I knew I was going to have to confront Lucius about the living arrangements here before matters progressed any further...and

I had a feeling he wasn't going to be very happy once he heard what I had to say.

He led me into the small salon, and poured a snifter of Armagnac for both of us. While I really didn't want the strong alcohol, not after all the wine I'd drunk at the reception, I didn't argue. I merely took the snifter from him and allowed myself a very small sip.

"Lucius," I began, then hesitated. This was something I needed to hash out with him, but right then I didn't know how to broach the subject without sounding confrontational, or like I didn't want to be with him. Yes, both of those things happened to actually be true, but....

"What is it, Serena?"

"It's—it's about this." I made a waving motion with my free hand, as if to indicate the house around us. "I can't stay here with you."

At once his dark brows pulled together. The icy gray eyes narrowed slightly. "What are you saying, Serena?"

"I...." As much as I hated to do so, I forced myself to go to him and slip an arm around his waist. He felt rigid, body stiff with annoyance. "It's just...no one in my family is going to think it at all in character for me to be moving in with you like this. Even our 'mountain getaway' was kind of a stretch. But...I'm just not that kind of person. I mean, I didn't even move in with my fiancé, and we'd been dating for years and were supposed to get married."

Lucius didn't respond right away. Then he took my hands and unwrapped my arm from around him, held me out at arm's length. His eyes scanned my face, cold, unblinking. "People change."

"Not that much. Especially...especially after living like a hermit for the past three years." Did I dare try to kiss him? I didn't want to, that was for sure, but would that sort of caress soften the cold suspicion that had settled over his features, or would the gesture merely appear desperate to him? No, better not. I did tighten my fingers around his, though, before I said, "It would look better to them if I was back home. And really, there's no risk involved. Brian is right next door and can keep an eye on me during the daytime. Once the sun goes down, well...he can drive me over here. You'd see just as much of me. But that way I'd avoid rousing my family's suspicions."

Another silence. All I could do was continue to look up into his face and hope that I appeared perfectly innocent, was only doing what I could to make sure our little relationship didn't seem completely out of character.

Then he bent and kissed me, the Armagnac giving his lips a sensation of false warmth. I submitted because I had no choice but to allow the embrace. At least it was only a kiss. He hadn't yet pressed me for anything else.

"I don't like it," he said after the kiss had concluded, and I had to force myself not to stiffen in response, which would only let him see how much I wanted this, needed a few precious hours away from him each day so I might retain some semblance of a normal life. "And yet...I understand why the arrangement would make sense. I must have your family's trust if I am to succeed."

As if on cue, my phone rang. Lucius nodded at me, giving his permission, and I pulled it from my purse and checked the screen. Jackson.

I tapped the phone to accept the call. "Hi, Jackson."

"Serena. I got your message. It sounded urgent."

"Well, I suppose I was disappointed that I'd forgotten to mention it to you when I was at the reception. Are you free tomorrow evening?"

"Actually, yes, because Bethany is taking the kids to visit her mother in Redlands. I had planned to do some work I'd brought with me, but it's fine if you and Lucius want to come over." A small pause, and then he added, "You want to tell me what this is about?"

Not really, I thought. However, I only

replied, "I think it's better if we discuss it in person. Does seven o'clock work for you?"

"It's fine." He still sounded somewhat mystified, but at least he wasn't asking too many questions.

"Okay. We'll see you then." I ended the call and glanced up at Lucius. "We're all set."

"Excellent. I will call for you at six-thirty tomorrow, and we'll proceed to your brother's home from there."

Call for me? I stared at him, startled, then began, "You mean—?"

"Yes," he said. "I think you may be right. No point in creating a situation where people might ask too many questions."

"No, we wouldn't want that," I said, maybe a little too quickly. I could only pray that none of the relief I was experiencing showed itself on my face.

"Let us go get your things together, and I'll have Brian come to pick you up."

"I don't have to go right away—" The last thing I wanted Lucius to think was that I looked forward to fleeing as soon as possible, even if it happened to be the truth.

"No, I think this is better. After an event such as your sister's reception, it only makes sense that you would be tired and would want to go home early."

"I suppose you're right."

"I know I am."

He kissed me again, and I responded with an almost-natural amount of fervor. Let him think what he wanted. Right then, I supposed my gratitude flavored that kiss somewhat. I didn't know what was going to happen next, but I did know one thing.

I was going home.

CHAPTER TWO

THE DOOR TO THE CELLAR OPENED. THIS TIME, Silas could tell right away that the person who stood there was Michael St. John, one of the vampires Lucius had "made." His longish dark hair was slicked back from his face, and he wore a charcoal gray shirt and no jacket, which seemed to indicate that he was staying in for the evening. Maybe.

"You've decided to let me go after all?" Silas asked.

"Yes, that's it." The sarcasm was so thick in St. John's words, you could practically see it drifting on the air. The vampire came farther into the room, and Silas noticed that he carried a bulky bundle of blankets. "I thought you might want these."

Actually, Silas did want them; the cellar was

chilly and somewhat damp. He could bear the discomfort if he had to, but a few blankets would make his confinement infinitely more tolerable. "Isn't that sort of thing going to get you in trouble with your master?" he inquired, jerking his chin toward the bundle St. John held.

"Doubtful," the vampire replied. He came closer, then dropped his burden on the floor next to Silas. "He's not really the type to get his hands dirty. Now that he knows he has you safely locked up down here, he's probably not going to pay much attention to you. He'll have his semi-vives feed you, just because if you die on him, there goes Serena's cooperation, but I can guarantee that he's not going to be paying you any visits anytime soon."

Well, that was something. Silas reached for one of the blankets and settled it around his shoulders as best he could with the heavy manacles hampering his movements. "And he doesn't care that you're playing sister of mercy?"

"He's got better things to do with his time."

Including spending as much time in Serena's company as possible. The mere thought made Silas want to grind his teeth, but he didn't see the point in letting Michael St. John see how much the current situation pained him. "Such as?"

"He hasn't said anything to the rest of us, but

I can tell he's excited about something. I suppose he'll let us in on the big secret eventually. Right now he's off at the funeral reception for Vanessa Quinn. I figured it was a good time to bring you these blankets."

The mental image of the vampire out in public with Serena, acting as if he had a right to be with her, made Silas want to grind his teeth. Because Michael St. John was watching him closely, no doubt looking for any signs of irritation, Silas did his best to remain impassive. "And I thank you for them. You aren't worried that your vampire buddies Leticia or Tristan might notice something?"

"They're not here. It's nighttime…they're hunting." The vampire shrugged. "Or rather, they're out planning a hunt. Anyway, it's just me and the semivives. And you."

More than ever, Silas wished he had the strength to break through the manacles that held him in place. With only St. John here at the mansion, he would have stood a fighting chance —if only he were free. Unfortunately, he knew that, strong as he was, he couldn't destroy the bonds which held him. Not even in *gula* form. These things were heavy enough to keep an elephant in place. In fact, Silas had to wonder whether Lucius Montfort had procured them from a local zoo.

"You're sure you don't want to let me go?" He asked the question in a lazy tone, already sure of how Michael St. John would respond. Still, Silas had to try. It was clear that the younger vampire disagreed with his master on a variety of topics.

"Pretty sure, yeah. I don't think you're worth the trouble that would cause for me. Anyway, have a nice night."

He turned and let himself out, locking the cellar door behind him. Silas slumped against the wall, the wool of the blanket he'd wrapped around himself providing a bit of protection from the cold stone.

It was something. A small gesture, but one he knew neither Tristan McVey nor Leticia Carver would have bothered with. Sometimes the smallest trickle became a flood. Silas had to pray that would be the case here, because at the moment, Michael St. John was his only hope.

$\sim$

Home. I set my purse down on the dining room table, repressing the urge to fling my arms wide and do a happy spin. But there was no way I could abandon myself that much.

Not with Lucius Montfort watching me.

He stood in the middle of my living room,

brows pulled together. Was he trying to figure out why I would willingly return to such cramped quarters after being compelled to stay in his splendid mansion for an entire week? Maybe. But at least I'd given him a story he seemed inclined to believe, and so right then I didn't really care much what he might be thinking.

The condo felt warm and stuffy after being closed up for so long. I went to one of the windows, unlocked it, and opened it a crack. Not too much, because the air outside was cool and damp, but just enough to freshen things up a bit.

"Well, this is it," I said, somewhat lamely. "Would you like some water? I think that's about all I have on hand."

"No," he replied at once. "I will be going soon. But I thought we should lay some ground rules."

"Sure." My voice hadn't faltered, but inwardly I couldn't help wondering what kind of fresh nightmare he planned to inflict on me.

However, he didn't seem to notice any reluctance in my expression. He went on, "Brian will get you at dusk every evening and bring you to my home. You will stay until at least midnight. Understood?"

"Yes." Since Lucius had already hinted at

that sort of arrangement, I wasn't too taken aback by the request.

"You will also not go out during the daytime, except to meet with members of your family as necessary. I will make an exception for them, because I don't want them to become suspicious, but you will not have lunch with your friend Candace or with anyone else."

I wondered how he knew about Candace, since I was fairly certain that I'd never mentioned her to him. A stirring of unease went over me. The last thing I wanted was for my best friend to get dragged into this mess. I didn't know what I could have done to prevent Lucius from learning about her, though—with his lackey Brian next door to helpfully provide whatever information his master required, I didn't have to look too far to locate the source of that particular intelligence.

"Of course," I said calmly. "It's not as if I had some kind of fabulous social life anyway. And half the time, Candace's work keeps her so busy that she doesn't have a chance to even get out for lunch."

"Good," Lucius said. "Then let us hope that she is very, very busy at work, and won't make any social requests of you. Do you have any work of your own coming up?"

I honestly didn't know, because I hadn't had

access to my phone until he returned it to me yesterday. Even then, I'd been preoccupied enough that I hadn't gone looking through the backlog of emails. "Well, I have the one client who postponed. He hinted that he was going to try to get his manuscript to me next week, but he's so flaky that I'm just not sure. And I'll have to see if anyone contacted me for work this past week. I didn't exactly have a chance to check my email."

If Lucius heard the undercurrent of accusation in my tone, he didn't acknowledge it. Smoothly, he replied, "You can check now. It would be good if you had some work. It would make things seem more normal, so to speak."

"I'll do what I can."

At those words, he came closer to me, reached out and touched my hair. By then I'd trained myself not to flinch, to even smile slightly as he touched me. "I'm sure you will. I will leave you to settle in now—and remember that Brian is next door."

That was all he said...all he needed to say. With his servant basically underfoot like that, I'd have a hard time trying to make an escape, or attempting any activities that didn't fit in with Lucius' "guidelines." Anyway, I was going to be very careful, because I didn't dare do anything that would raise his ire, not while he still had

Silas as his prisoner. Having to play meek made my blood boil, but for now I had to work with the hand I'd been dealt.

"But you're going to get me tomorrow night, right?" I asked, hoping I sounded completely guileless. "That is, to pick me up on the way to Jackson's house?"

"Yes, of course."

"Good." I smiled up at him, and he bent and kissed me again.

I had to respond, put my arms around him and hang on to him, trying my best to act as though I truly was saddened by the need to keep up appearances that had led to me returning home. Did he buy the act?

It seemed so, because he stroked my cheek and said, "It won't be so very long, my dear. And then once I've spoken with your brother, we'll have taken the first step into a world where you and I won't have to live separate lives, where at last I'll be able to walk in the sun with you."

"I can't wait."

His lips brushed the top of my head, and he murmured, "Neither can I. Until tomorrow evening, Serena."

He went to the door and I let him out, then locked up behind him and set the alarm system. Could locked doors and house alarms keep out vampires? I didn't know—although I guessed that Lucius could come in whenever he wanted, since I'd already invited him inside—but it would have looked strange to him if I hadn't engaged my usual security measures.

But at least he was gone, and I was finally, gloriously alone. I wanted to hug every chair, every pillow. That wouldn't have been a productive use of my time, however, and so instead I settled for taking some of my bags upstairs, and then getting my laptop plugged in to recharge it so I could check my emails. Yes, I could have done the same thing on my phone, but I knew I'd have a lot to plow through, and it would be easier to do that on an actual computer.

While the laptop was getting some juice, I unpacked my belongings and put everything back where it was supposed to be. I noticed, however, that my notebook and sketchbook, which had been conspicuously missing from my bedside table and my office area, hadn't been included with the items Lucius sent home with me. Clearly, he'd kept them, but to what purpose? Did he still think there were messages hidden within those sketches and those accounts of my earlier visions, even though I'd never been able to construct a coherent narrative from them?

Maybe. I had to admit that I hadn't been given the chance to go back and look at them after I'd experienced the visions that had upset me so much. It was possible I would have seen clues that allowed me to fill in the blanks. Whether there was any chance of getting the notebook and the sketchbook back from Lucius…that I really didn't know. Possibly after he'd met with Jackson, he'd be feeling mellow and more disposed to indulge some of my requests.

I had no idea how that meeting was going to pan out, either. Jackson was a very down-to-earth person, all about the here and now, and what he could do to effect sensible change. Right then, I wasn't sure I wanted to imagine his reaction to Lucius telling him that he was a vampire. Or maybe Lucius wouldn't be that blunt. He'd have to be, though, wouldn't he? Otherwise, the rest of his proposals wouldn't make much sense.

Well, I supposed I'd find out the following night. In the meantime, I'd been given a bit of grace, a little time to regroup and get myself back together. And I had to figure out some way to get word to the Watchers, the shapeshifting gargoyle society that kept an eye on the vampires, let them know where Silas was being held. They'd be able to break him out, surely. Once he was free, I wouldn't have to pretend with Lucius anymore. Silas and I could work together to defeat him.

First things first. I settled myself at the laptop, opened it up, and waited to see how much of my life I'd missed during the previous week. A whole lot, it seemed, although nothing that couldn't be fixed with an apologetic email explaining why I'd dropped out of sight.

Except for the emails from Candace. She tended to communicate that way, just because the asynchronous nature of the messages allowed her to get to them when her erratic schedule allowed for it. There were five emails from her, time-stamped Monday and Tuesday, when they'd suddenly stopped—probably because she'd at last seen the news stories about my disappearance, and realized I wasn't around to answer her.

Did I dare feed her the same bullshit story I'd given my family, that Lucius and I had fallen madly in lust with each other and had disappeared to his compound in the San Bernardino Mountains? I supposed I really didn't have much of a choice, since if I tried to come up with something more plausible, she'd figure out soon enough that my excuses didn't line up. And I honestly didn't know whether the news had run anything about my sudden reappearance—I guessed that my parents must have said something to the Pasadena P.D. once I'd rematerialized, just so they could call off the search, but I didn't know whether that information had been passed along to the local media or not.

I wrote an apologetic email, telling her what had happened, saying that I hadn't had the chance to get back in touch because of Vanessa's funeral and all the claims on my time that sad event had involved. And then, just to forestall any requests to get together the following day, which was a Sunday and therefore a time when she might actually be available, I said that I would be spending the day at Jackson's house. Not a complete lie, although by necessity I had to make it sound as though I would be there a lot longer than currently planned.

That done, I responded to my on-and-off-again client, and told him I would be available this week. Nothing else in my inbox seemed terribly urgent, which meant I could turn my attention to the really pressing matter…getting Silas back.

Were there still Watchers in the area? Did they know that I'd returned to my condo? Silas had never provided many specifics about how the *gula* organization worked, so I really had no idea how they were set up. He'd been assigned to me, obviously, but once I'd been captured, had they withdrawn their surveillance altogether?

Somehow I doubted that. They had to know Silas was missing, had disappeared while looking for me. So they must still be keeping a close eye on the Pasadena area, just because Silas had known that Lucius was holed up somewhere around here, even if he hadn't been able to provide an exact address.

What that meant for me, I didn't know. With not-Brian next door and watching my every movement, it wasn't as though I could start wandering the neighborhood, pretending to take walks on the off chance I might encounter one of Silas' compatriots. That sort of behavior would have been out of character even before I met Silas or Lucius Montfort, and would be doubly so now. And I doubted any of the *gula* would take the risk of approaching me...or would they? How did a Watcher know someone had been turned into a semivive? Silas had been able to tell, or at least it seemed that way. Then again, that first semivive's attack on me had made it pretty obvious he wasn't exactly a good guy.

Possibly the semivives smelled different, just as Lucius had pointed out that my niece Addison smelled strange because of the insidious disease attacking her blood cells. Once again, I just didn't know. I hated that, hated this feeling of blundering in the dark.

I'd bought some time for Silas, though. He would be safe tomorrow, because I was taking Lucius to meet with my brother. If the meeting went well, then Lucius would be happy, and Silas would be granted a reprieve. Good for Silas, but not so great for humanity, if my visions were to be believed.

One step at a time. I would figure out a way to stop Lucius. I had to. But not until Silas was safe. After all, setting up laboratories and researchers took time, even for someone with my brother's resources. It wasn't as if Lucius and Jackson would shake hands and the next day they'd be handing out immortality pills or something. But....

My hands were shaking. Resolutely, I closed my laptop and got up from the desk where I sat, then went into the bedroom. By that time it was nearly ten. Early to go to sleep, but right then I just wanted this horrible day to be over. The next morning, I would regroup, try to figure out my best course of action. I had to seem enthusiastic about whatever Jackson and Lucius cooked up together, if only for a little while. In the background, though, I'd have to be doing whatever I could to make sure Silas got away before Lucius' plans were too advanced.

Maybe Detective Ortiz, my contact at the Pasadena P.D.? He believed in me, knew my visions were true. If I told him exactly where Silas was being held captive....

Assuming he even wants to listen to you, I

thought in some disgust. *You had the police department trying to track you down because of a possible kidnapping, only to learn that apparently you were shacked up the whole time with a millionaire investor. That's not exactly the sort of behavior that's going to endear you to Raoul Ortiz.*

Still, I could handle the detective's contempt, if he would at least listen to me. That was a pretty big "if," though. And I didn't even know whether I could safely reach out to him. Maybe my phone was bugged. Maybe Lucius had some way of tracking every email I sent.

No, that was ridiculous. He might be L.A.'s master vampire, but he wasn't the goddamn NSA or something. And really, beyond the surveillance system at his mansion, I hadn't seen any indication that Lucius was at all familiar or comfortable with modern technology. Come to think of it, I'd never even seen him use a cell phone.

All right, even following the assumption that I could safely get a message out without Lucius knowing anything about it, I'd have to analyze very carefully how that scenario would play out. I'd have to convince Raoul Ortiz to take a large contingent of officers with him, because this wasn't the sort of situation where it would be safe to show up at the mansion with only a partner. The semivives alone would overpower two regular mortal men. And if the police made their visit after dark, in the hopes of meeting Lucius himself, that would be even worse. You'd need an army of cops to go up against the four vampires and their semivive slaves.

No, it would be so much better to have the *gula* handle the situation. They'd know what to do, wouldn't underestimate their opponents.

Problem was, I had absolutely no idea how to contact them. I'd have to hope they'd reach out to me, and manage to avoid Lucius Montfort's notice at the same time.

Good luck with that.

CHAPTER THREE

SIX-THIRTY HAD NEVER TAKEN SO LONG TO roll around. Despite my flimsy excuse of being at Jackson's house, Candace called me before ten o'clock, demanding to know exactly what the hell was going on. As I'd feared, my story of a mountain tryst with Lucius wasn't sitting very well with her.

"You don't do things like that," she said in answer to my feeble explanation that he'd basically swept me off my feet. "You are not the type to get 'swept,' whatever that's supposed to mean. I don't care how much of a blowout you had with your sister." My friend stopped there, as though realizing that Vanessa and her terrible death must be a very delicate topic of conversation for me, especially since it was easy enough to read between the lines and realize that the two of us had probably parted on bad terms. A sigh, and Candace continued, "Doesn't a guy with that kind of money have a satellite phone or something?"

"I don't know," I said. "Maybe he does, for emergencies. The thing is, I didn't ask. I didn't *want* to call anyone."

"Not even me," Candace put in, sounded wounded.

Oh, hell. "I knew you were buried at work," I told her. "I didn't want to bug you. And honestly, I'd only planned to go away for a day or so. But we were having such a nice time—and it felt so good to be away from everything—that I just sort of let the week pass a lot faster than I'd intended."

A long pause, and then Candace said, "I'm sorry, Serena—that still doesn't sound like you at all."

Of course it didn't, because, as I'd tried to explain to Lucius, I had never been the sort of person to run off with someone I barely knew, or to basically drop off the face of the planet so I could avoid my problems. I shrugged, even though I knew my friend couldn't see me. "I guess it all just got to me. Haven't you ever done anything crazy?"

"Yeah, I stayed with Tyler about three months longer than I should have."

"That's not what I meant."

She huffed out a breath. "Okay, there was that one-night stand in Cabo. About which you are still sworn to secrecy."

"Of course," I said. She'd gone on the trip to Cabo San Lucas with several mutual friends from college, but I'd stayed home. Not because I couldn't afford it, but because at the time I was just twenty and didn't have full control of my money yet...and my parents absolutely put their collective feet down about me going to Mexico with a group of unchaperoned college sopho-mores. After I'd heard about what went down on that trip, I was glad that my parents had been so strict. One of the girls had her money and jewelry stolen out of the hotel room, and two of the others almost ended up with alcohol poison-ing. Candace had gotten off lucky—all she'd had to do was the walk of shame back to her hotel after spending the night with a guy whose name she couldn't even remember.

So anyway, my friend wasn't exactly in a position to give me a lot of grief about losing my head and shacking up with Lucius Montfort for a few days.

"I'm surprised your mother didn't disown you," she remarked.

"Oh, she's still angry with me. But I intro-duced her to Lucius yesterday at the reception, and I think she likes him." All right, "like" was probably a strong word. However, since he was handsome, wealthy, and successful, he ticked off all the line items for the type of person my mother considered a good match for her daughter, and that meant she most likely wouldn't give me too much grief over the disappearing act I'd pulled.

Once again Candace went quiet. Then she asked, "What about Silas?"

Oh, shit. I'd been so preoccupied with making sure everyone believed my relationship with Lucius, I'd completely forgotten that my best friend knew all about Silas. Or rather, she knew I liked him a lot, had kissed him. Things had moved so quickly after the one night he and I spent together, I'd never had the opportunity to tell her that we'd become intimate, but she still knew I had strong feelings for him. And since she knew me, she also knew I wasn't the fickle type.

"Um, well…that didn't really work out."

"Excuse me?" Her voice fairly vibrated with disbelief. "One day you're telling me he's the best thing since sliced bread, and the next you're dropping him for this Lucius guy? That's also not like you. I mean, it took you months to get over Travis walking out on you."

"That was different," I protested. "I'd been

seeing Travis for years. We were engaged. I'd only gone out with Silas for dinner and lunch, kissed him a couple of times. We both realized our relationship was…inappropriate…and so he backed off."

"Was that before or after Lucius Montfort came on the scene?"

"After, of course. I mean…." I broke off there, because she truly had caught me off guard. My family hadn't known about Silas, and so I hadn't been forced to explain myself on that issue with them. But Candace? She'd obviously flipped over into full-on lawyer mode. Desperately, I said, "You don't know what it was like. I realized that Silas wasn't right for me, and then Lucius came along and…."

"And you got swept off your feet. Yes, you told me that already." She stopped, and I heard her let out another breath. "There's something very strange about this, Serena."

Talk about the understatement of the century. It was almost physically painful not to tell her the truth, but I didn't dare. Not yet. Knowing Candace, she'd go charging off on a crusade to bring every law enforcement official she knew right down on Lucius Montfort's head, and I couldn't let that happen. Not while Silas was his prisoner. Not before I had a concrete plan for getting him safely away.

"I know it sounds crazy. Believe me. But, last time I checked, starting to get involved with someone and then realizing they're not the person for you isn't a federal crime. Weren't you warning me about Silas anyway? Weren't you worried he was after me for my family's money or something?"

"Yes, I was," she replied, sounding defensive. "And I don't think I was out of line for having those worries. This thing with Lucius, though… something about it doesn't pass the sniff test."

Sometimes Candace was just too damn perceptive. I couldn't tell her she was right, though. I had to pretend I was besotted with the master vampire, although of course she didn't know anything about his true nature. And she needed to stay blissfully ignorant on that subject.

"Well, I'm sorry that I'm not following some predetermined timeline for how these things are supposed to work," I said. "Jesus, Candace, I've had enough to deal with this week without you taking a dump on me for trying to find a little happiness."

This time she took so long to reply, I almost thought she'd hung up on me. I even pulled the phone away from my ear to make sure the call was still active. But there was the little green phone icon, though, so I knew she was still there.

Then she said, "I'm sorry, Serena. I know…I

know you're going through a lot. Just...be careful, okay? I don't want to see you get hurt."

She sounded so contrite that I wanted to burst into tears. I hated myself for having to carry on this charade with her, but I had no choice. Maybe someday I'd come out on the other side of this mess and would be able to tell her the truth. Until then, though, I could only keep up the act.

"It's all right," I told her. "I know you're just trying to look out for me, and I appreciate it. But I do need to get going. I have to leave for my brother's place in a little bit, and I still haven't even put my face on."

A total lie, of course—Lucius wouldn't be picking me up for hours and hours. I knew I needed to end the phone call, though. If I kept talking to Candace, I worried that I'd really slip up, would make some kind of unrecoverable mistake. I couldn't take that risk right now, not with Silas' life on the line.

"Okay," she said. "Take care. I'll call you in a few days."

"Talk to you soon."

I ended the call then, and set my phone down on the dining room table. For some reason, my heart was beating fast, and my hands shook. Lies upon lies upon lies.

Where would it all end?

~

As he'd promised, Lucius arrived promptly at six-thirty. He wouldn't be able to be out and about this early in the very near future—the switch over to Daylight Savings Time was less than a week away. We'd have to adjust our schedule. Then I told myself that I couldn't let this drag out for longer than a week. One way or another, I'd have to get Silas free of him.

For now, though, I smiled at the vampire master, let him kiss me on the cheek before I locked up the house and followed him out to where the Mercedes with its semivive driver waited in one of the guest parking spaces at my complex. I'd noticed an odd blurry movement behind the blinds in the condo next door as we passed by. Not-Brian, watching his master take me away? Maybe. I hadn't seen hide nor hair of my neighbor all day, but that wasn't too surprising. I'd spent the time cleaning my place, getting rid of the dust that had accumulated in my absence. Good thing Lucius had stolen me away on my housekeeper's off week, or I would have had to explain to Teresa why I hadn't been there to let her in. Since I was always home, I'd never given her a key.

Lucius asked for my brother's address, so he might let the driver know where we were going.

I provided it, knowing that by doing so I was giving the vampire access to my brother and his home, but I rationalized that particular worry by trying to convince myself Lucius probably could have dug up that information himself if he really wanted to. And yes, Lucius would now be able to freely come and go in my brother's home because he would have been invited in, but I told myself Lucius had no reason to harm Jackson or his family. Quite the opposite, in fact. The vampire needed my brother's resources to get the cure for vampirism he so desperately desired.

We headed up to the 210 Freeway and drove east. Lucius laid his hand on mine where it rested on the leather-upholstered seat. His fingers were cold, but by now I was used to that; I didn't flinch.

"How was your day?" he asked, his tone pleasant.

Was he hoping I would say that I'd spent the entire time pining for him? I wouldn't go that far, because I knew he probably wouldn't believe it. "Fine," I replied. "I did some housework."

He frowned. "Don't you have someone who takes care of that for you?"

"Yes, but this wasn't her week to come in. Things were dusty. It was fine."

After lifting my hand to his mouth, he kissed my fingers. I made myself smile, even though I wished with all my being that I could pull away. "I don't want you to work too hard. I would hate to see these lovely fingers roughened with menial tasks."

"Housework never killed anyone," I told him. "I didn't mind doing it. Really, I just dusted and vacuumed and wiped down the countertops. It's not as if I was on my hands and knees, scrubbing floors or something." I tilted my head at him and asked, "Who keeps that enormous mansion of yours clean?"

"The semivives, of course," he replied as he released my hand. "I would not trust any outsiders to do the work. Those who are not on duty guarding the grounds take care of the house. It is an arrangement that works well enough."

Apparently, because even though the mansion was gloomy and gothic enough for a Hammer horror film, it did seem to be spotlessly clean. "That makes sense."

He nodded, but I could tell other matters occupied his thoughts, because his gaze moved from me to the lights of the cars we passed on the freeway, and his brows drew together in an abstracted little pucker. "Tell me of your brother, Serena. How best should I present my case to him?"

Was Lucius Montfort actually asking me for

advice? From the serious expression he wore, it would seem so. I paused for a moment, trying to think of the best way to answer him. While the last thing I wanted was to give him any information that would help his cause, I also needed this interview to go well. Lucius had to think that he had me and my brother on his side. Anything less, and Silas' life could be in danger.

"Well, he's a politician, obviously," I said. "He's used to reading people. He has good instincts. But, unlike a lot of politicians, he's a fairly straight shooter. He doesn't like lies."

"I should tell him exactly what I am?"

From the skeptical expression Lucius wore, I could tell he wasn't thrilled by that angle of approach. I actually did understand why he might feel that way, but I didn't see how we could get around it. "What else can you do? Your whole 'pitch' is about using the special antibodies in your blood, isn't it?"

"True." He was quiet for a moment, rubbing abstractedly at his chin. Right then, with the dimness inside the car helping to conceal the pallor of his skin, he looked far more human than usual. Or maybe it was something about his aspect, about how he suddenly didn't seem nearly as sure of himself as he usually was.

"It's hard, isn't it?" I asked. "To have to reveal what you are, I mean."

"You are very perceptive." Once again his hand sought my hand, but this time he only laid his fingers on top of mine, let them rest there gently. "Yes, it is one thing to speak openly of my condition with someone who's already aware of it, as you were. I have lived this long because I've been careful. A reckless vampire is one who won't see his first century, and I have been on this earth much longer than that. I know I must speak to your brother, because you have seen it is his resources that will end this curse and allow me to once more walk in the light, but...."

"You'll be fine," I said, my tone perhaps a little too hearty. "Jackson is an open-minded person."

"Open-minded enough to believe that I'm a vampire?"

This question was delivered with a curl of the lip, and I couldn't help smiling slightly. "Well, it is rather a leap of faith. But I'll be there to back you up."

"Ah, Serena." His fingers curled around mine, cool, strong. For some reason, though, I didn't feel like pulling my hand away. Was it only because he'd just shown me a rare moment of vulnerability? "I do consider you to be a great gift. I am so glad that you were wise enough to abandon your foolish infatuation with Silas Drake."

What could I do except smile? Of course I hadn't abandoned Silas—I loved him now more than ever. He had tried to save me. Now I would have to do my best to save him. Lucius didn't seem to notice my diffidence, thank God.

"We—wouldn't have worked out in the long run," I said. "You were right about that. I don't think I could have handled that kind of life. We didn't have much in common."

"But you and I…?"

I leaned my head against his shoulder. The gesture served a dual purpose—it would help to make Lucius think I wanted to be close to him, while at the same time it allowed me to look forward, so he couldn't see my face.

"All right, on the surface most people would say that a woman in her late twenties from Southern California doesn't have a lot in common with a centuries-old vampire from…?" I paused there. "Where are you from, anyway?"

I could feel his body shift beneath my cheek, but he answered quickly enough. "I have lived so many places that it doesn't seem as if I'm from anywhere in particular anymore."

It figured that he wouldn't give me a straight answer. He could call me his precious gift and offer me the world…but clearly the world he was offering didn't include the truth. I knew better than to press him, though. He still wouldn't give me the answers I wanted, and my insistence would only anger him and probably arouse suspicions I'd done my best to quell.

Letting it alone, I said, "Well, I'm sure that most people would think you and I didn't have anything in common, either, but we seem to appreciate a lot of the same things. Art, and beautiful antiques, and books. Your library is amazing."

He passed a hand over my hair. "I am glad you see it that way. I had hoped…." The words trailed off, and he didn't complete the thought. "At any rate, if we can convince your brother to lend his assistance, then you and I will have a great deal to look forward to."

"Walks in the sun."

"And so many other things." His arm tightened around me, and we rode the rest of the way to my brother's house in silence, all our thoughts focused on the future.

I had a feeling the future I imagined looked very different from his.

CHAPTER FOUR

My brother's California home was located in the foothills above Claremont. If you kept following the road which passed the upscale development that was his second residence, then eventually you'd make it all the way up to the Mount Baldy ski village, but at this time of year, the snow was nearly gone, except on the tallest peaks.

We had to stop and give our name to the guard at the gated entrance, and when we pulled up into the sweeping driveway, two Secret Service agents approached the car. Lucius rolled down the window. "We're here to see Senator Quinn. My name is Lucius Montfort, and this is the senator's sister, Serena Quinn."

The taller of the two agents nodded. "I.D., please."

Lucius pulled a slim wallet from his breast pocket and handed it to the agent. The man inspected it closely before giving it back. His gaze moved toward me, but he didn't ask for my identification, since he knew what I looked like. "He's expecting you. Go on in."

A pleasant nod, and Lucius pushed the button to roll the window back up. "He's well protected, I see."

"Because he's officially running for President. I think he always had protection in D.C. because of some of the committees he's on, but he never had Secret Service protection here in California before."

"Ah."

We both got out of the Mercedes. "My driver will wait with the car," Lucius told the agents as we passed them by. Neither of them seemed to find this behavior at all out of the ordinary, because they only nodded and resumed their original positions near the walkway that led to the front door.

As we approached that door—doors, really, a pair of them set with beveled glass and nearly ten feet high—I could feel my stomach start to clench. Yes, I'd sounded confident and ready for this conversation when I spoke to Lucius, but as the reality of the situation began to become more clear, I realized that I was going to have to walk in there and convince my brother, my pragmatic, practical brother, that the man who'd come here with me wasn't truly a man at all, but an undead creature who'd been born centuries earlier.

I'd barely rung the bell before Jackson was opening the door. He smiled pleasantly at Lucius and me, but I knew that didn't mean much. His whole life was spent in letting people see only what he wanted them to see. Inside, he might very well be eaten up with curiosity as to the purpose for our visit, but he'd never allow us to see it.

Instead, he said, "Lucius, good to see you again. Serena, come on inside. I thought we could talk in the study—it's a little friendlier in there."

Having been to this house several times before, I knew exactly what he meant. It was a large place—six bedrooms and a corresponding number of bathrooms, if I recalled correctly—with high ceilings, a sweeping staircase off the foyer, and a whole lot of high-end art and furniture. Some might call it extravagant, when he had an equally large home in Alexandria, Virginia, but this had been his first house, the place where he'd been living when he married Bethany, where he'd brought his children home from the hospital. Since I'd been raised in an equally impressive residence, it wasn't until I'd seen our family through Bethany's eyes that I'd actually thought about how intimidating it would be to a small child to live someplace where you perpetually had to worry about mussing the shining travertine floors or getting sticky fingers on an expensive faux-finished wall. It was just part of being a Quinn, I supposed.

The study, however, was built on a smaller scale than the rest of the rooms on the home's main floor, although it was still larger than the living room at my condo. Bookshelves lined the walls, and there was a fireplace with an oak mantel and granite surround, although the day had been mild enough that a fire would have been pure affectation. Since this was Jackson we were dealing with, of course no fire had been lit.

"Go ahead, sit down," he said, gesturing toward one of the two leather couches that faced each other across a coffee table of carved oak. "There's water, but if you want anything else—"

"Water is fine," I said hastily, then shot a quick glance over at Lucius, hoping I hadn't overstepped. "Is it fine for you?"

"Yes, thank you," he replied as he seated himself on the sofa.

Since it would have looked suspicious for me to continue hovering next to the couch, I sat down next to him and reached for one of the Waterford tumblers on the coffee table. A matching pitcher filled with water waited nearby, so I lifted it and filled the glass, then offered it to Lucius. "Here you are, Lucius."

He murmured a thank-you as I poured myself some water, and settled back on the couch next to him. During all this, Jackson sat across from us, a faintly quizzical expression on his face, as though he was still trying to figure out what the two of us were doing together.

Good question.

Unfortunately, I wouldn't be able to tell him the truth. Not yet, anyway. With any luck, I could end this entire farce sooner rather than later. So much depended on the *gula*, and whether they would be able to devise a way to safely approach me.

I couldn't let myself get distracted by those logistics now, however. I had to focus on convincing my brother that Lucius wasn't what he seemed. And I'd have to continue pretending that I was crazy about him until the charade was no longer necessary. That day couldn't come soon enough.

"So...." Jackson began. He didn't bother with the water, but sat slightly forward in his chair, hands resting on one knee. "If this is about clearing the air with Mom—"

"Oh, no," I cut in. "We've made our peace. Or at least, she seems to have backed off for now, so I'm going to let it alone. No, Lucius and I wanted to speak to you about something entirely different."

"Serena told me about your daughter Addison," Lucius said. His expression was appropriately grave, silvery eyes fixed on my brother.

Jackson didn't seem very pleased by that revelation. "I would prefer that information not become public knowledge," he said, the words cold, clipped.

"No worries," Lucius told him. "I respect your need for privacy during this trying time. However, I may possibly be able to offer some assistance."

"'Assistance'?" My brother glanced over at me, a faint frown touching his features. Not much, just a deepening of the lines between his brows, but enough to tell me he couldn't figure out where this was all going. "I was unaware that you were an oncologist, Lucius. I thought you were a businessman."

"I've played many roles during my life," Lucius replied. "Doctor was never one of them, though. No, what I am proposing is not precisely a medical solution."

This comment only seemed to further mystify Jackson. He pushed himself farther back into the leather armchair where he sat and crossed his arms. "I'm not really one for holistic treatments or alternative medicine. I think it's probably better if I wait to hear what the specialists at UCLA have to say."

"You misunderstand me," Lucius said calmly. "I am not offering some quack treatment of herbs or a macrobiotic diet. Rather, it is because of who I am that I might be able to help you."

This time Jackson didn't bother to reply, but only sent a quick glance in my direction, as if asking where the hell I'd dug up this guy, and why was I wasting his time?

"This is going to sound kind of crazy," I said quickly. "So please, Jackson, just bear with us for a moment. What Lucius is saying is that because of his...condition...he might be able to help Addie."

"What condition?" my brother demanded. "Do you have leukemia, too?" From the way his eyes narrowed as he looked at Lucius' pale face, I could tell that Jackson was trying to determine whether the other man's pallor was due to sickness rather than a distinct lack of melanin.

"Oh, no," Lucius said. "I am quite well. No, what Serena refers to is my vampirism."

Dead silence. Jackson looked from Lucius to me and then back again, face completely expressionless. Not because he wasn't feeling anything, but rather because he was feeling too much. Going deadpan was his way of sorting through his emotions before he had to decide on the best way to react.

"Is this a joke?" he asked finally. "Because if it is, I think it's in very poor taste."

"It's not a joke," I told him. I looked him straight in the eyes. My own expression was probably pleading, urging him to listen before he passed judgment. "I told you it was going to sound crazy. But Lucius really is a vampire. The antibodies in his blood might—if processed correctly—be used to cure Addie's leukemia... and maybe a great many other things. We just don't know for sure, because his kind generally try to avoid notice, to stay away from anyone in authority, and that includes doctors and medical researchers. But he wants to help you, Jackson."

My brother straightened in his chair, his hands clamping down on his knees. When he spoke, he directed the words at Lucius, not at me. "I don't know what you've told my sister, or what mind games you're playing with her, but I'm going to tell you now that we Quinns are not people you want trifle with. I'm going to ask you to leave. Serena will stay here. Clearly, she needs some kind of help if you've actually convinced her to believe these crazy stories."

Through all this, Lucius sat quietly, a half-smile playing on his thin lips. "I admire your desire to protect your sister. Believe me, though

—I have convinced her of nothing that isn't the truth. It is a tribute to her strength and her purity of heart that she did not flee from me when I revealed to her what I actually was. But perhaps you need a demonstration."

"Of what?" Jackson asked. He didn't move, but I could see how tense he was, as though ready to launch himself from the chair and block whatever this madman—in his eyes, at any rate —intended to do next. "Drinking blood?"

"I would never do anything so gauche. Not to my host, the brother of the woman I love. Besides, as Serena could tell you, we latter-day vampires tend to get our blood from hospitals and blood banks, not by committing murders in back alleys. You don't truly think she would be with me if I were capable of committing such crimes on a daily basis?"

"I don't know what to think, except that you've somehow managed to convince her of this crazy story. But I—"

Jackson didn't have a chance to complete the sentence, because in the next instant, Lucius had launched himself from the couch, moving with such speed that I could barely tell it was him. The dark suit and the pale hair helped, but still, I had barely blinked before he left the room and returned, holding in his hand a silver-framed picture of Jackson and Bethany on their wedding day. Since I didn't recall seeing it in the living room or elsewhere on the ground floor of the house, I guessed Lucius must have fetched it from the master bedroom upstairs. No human being could have gotten up there and back down to this ground-floor study in the amount of time that he had been gone.

From the way Jackson's eyes widened as Lucius set the portrait down on the coffee table, I figured he must have done the same mental math. "How...? What...?"

"It is one of our gifts," Lucius said. "A vampire's gift, that is. Extreme speed comes with long life. I don't know precisely why. Something about the way vampirism enhances our normal physical processes, I suppose."

My brother didn't respond, only sat in his chair, staring at Lucius. I was fairly certain that I'd never seen Jackson so shocked, so at a loss for words. Since I'd gone through a similar process of realigning my world view after I realized my visions were real, weren't crazy fever dreams born of the trauma I'd suffered in my accident, I could understand why it was taking him a little time to process everything.

At last he swallowed, hard, and looked over at me. "How long have you known?"

"Almost from the first time I met him," I replied, which was nearly true. After all, Silas had already identified the man in one of my visions as a vampire, so I knew who Lucius was as soon as our eyes first met. But since I couldn't really tell Jackson that, I went on to add, "He didn't want to lie to me."

My brother nodded, but then something about his mouth went grim. Turning his attention to Lucius, he asked, "Did Vanessa know?"

"No," Lucius said. "We had not progressed to a point in our professional relationship where I felt comfortable telling her such a thing. You see, Serena, because of her psychic powers, is already far more open to such concepts than Vanessa was. In time, yes, I would have told her, because I do not like the idea of working closely with someone and keeping such a secret. It would have come out, most likely when she requested a daytime meeting. Alas, her tragic death prevented me from confiding in her."

Jackson listened to all this carefully, his hazel eyes taking on a laser-beam focus I knew all too well. When he was ready to explore an idea, learn something new, nothing got in his way. That he looked like that now...well, I couldn't decide whether it was a good or a bad thing.

"So that much is true about vampires? You can't go out in daylight?"

"The touch of the sun's rays is harmful to us,

and ultimately fatal if the exposure continues long enough. We do what we must to avoid it."

A small pause as Jackson appeared to digest that information. "I can imagine that might hamper your activities."

"Not as much as you might think. Although it does help to live in a large city, where it is less likely that one's neighbors will notice anything strange about your patterns of behavior."

"I can imagine," my brother said, his tone dry. This time, he looked over at me. "And you don't have a problem with any of this?"

Well, of course I did…I had multiple problems with it…but I couldn't tell Jackson that. "It took a little getting used to. But I suppose in a way it was a relief. After all, a vampire isn't going to find anything all that strange about a psychic, right?"

I actually hadn't meant the comment as a judgment on my parents' treatment of me—or Jackson's, for that matter. However, I could tell from the way my brother winced slightly that he thought I was casting some shade, even if the sub-context hadn't been intended.

"I suppose I can see that," my brother said. "But…."

"Neither of us expects you to accept every aspect of our relationship," Lucius said. "Then again, having family members who oppose a connection for one reason or another is hardly something new. Our reason for being here is not to ask for your blessing, Jackson, but to offer assistance. It has long been rumored that vampire blood can provide its own set of beneficial qualities, apart from the obvious, but no one of our kind has had access to the sorts of specialists and facilities that could prove such a hypothesis once and for all."

Jackson's eyes narrowed. "But you think I can provide those things."

"You are a man of great wealth," Lucius said, almost carelessly. "I myself am far from poor, but my holdings can't compare to yours. Above that, your position gives you the power to reach out to those who can help. I wouldn't begin to know who to ask to set up such a laboratory...but I have a feeling you do."

A heavy silence fell. I could practically hear the wheels and gears turning in Jackson's head, how he was trying to decide whether Lucius was only offering empty promises, or whether there might be something to his statement that the peculiar qualities of his blood might provide a cure for a beloved child.

"What do you get out of it?" he asked abruptly. "You can say whatever you like about blood banks and such, but I'm having a hard time seeing a vampire as a pure altruist."

"Oh, that I am not," Lucius said, the corners of his mouth lifting in one of his almost-smiles. "Yes, it would please me to help you, because that will please Serena. However, just as a more detailed analysis of my blood—and the blood of my compatriots—should yield results when it comes to diseases of the blood, and the more general ailments associated with aging, I am hoping that a little quid pro quo will allow you to provide me with the benefits I want."

"What would this 'quid pro quo' involve?" Jackson said. His voice was almost expressionless, but I saw how his jaw hardened when Lucius made it clear that Addie's cure wouldn't come without strings.

"Nothing too terrible, I assure you. It is human blood that keeps vampires alive, but precisely what is it in their blood that allows such a thing to occur in the first place? I am looking for scientists and technicians who can isolate that vital element, and distill it."

"To what purpose? It sounds as if you're able to get by with purchased blood, so why do you need human blood analyzed?"

"Why, to become more human again," Lucius said, eyes widening slightly, as if such a thing should be completely obvious. "Believe me, the novelty of an existence spent entirely in the dark wears off after the first few decades. I want to walk in the sun again, to not fear the light. And," he continued, his eyes moving to me briefly before he returned his gaze to Jackson, "to perhaps one day have a family. Such a thing is not possible now, but with the right cure...."

He trailed off there, as I held myself very still and tried not to let any of the sudden spasm of panic that had taken hold reveal itself in my face. No, Lucius and I hadn't been intimate yet, thank God. He hadn't even hinted at trying to make our relationship more physical, and I sure as hell wasn't going to bring up the subject, not when we were experiencing a fragile but effective détente at the moment. However, the mere idea that he'd thought of such a thing, had contemplated having children with me, if the more negative aspects of his vampirism could be cured... that scared the living crap out of me.

Or it could all be an act. He could have brought up the notion of having a family with me because quite possibly that was something Jackson would want to hear. My brother had never been happy about Vanessa's revolving door of lovers, had always hoped that one day she'd settle down. When my accident had sent me to near-death and then returned me to this world with the very unwelcome gift of seeing the future, he'd probably thought I was a lost cause when it came to ever having children of my own.

Now, though, with Lucius mentioning that he hoped for a cure because he could then be able to father children...it put an entirely different spin on things.

"I see," Jackson said, which didn't tell me very much. His tone had been completely neutral. "That is, I see how this could be a mutually beneficial project. But...."

"You have misgivings. I understand that. See the specialists at UCLA tomorrow. Hear what they have to say. It's entirely possible that they will be able to help you, in which case you won't need my assistance." Lucius shrugged then; to somehow who didn't know him very well, he looked entirely unconcerned as to whether or not Jackson would decide to go ahead with the project they'd just discussed, but I could see the tension in his neck and jaw. Despite believing that a future where he would be nearly human again was a foregone conclusion, thanks to my visions, he still wanted to hear from my brother that it would really happen.

"You think they won't, though. Be able to help Addison."

"I am not a doctor. I assume your daughter has already seen doctors on the East Coast."

"Yes," Jackson said, the syllable short and clipped, as though he didn't want to dwell on those futile doctor visits any longer than he absolutely had to. "A great many, at some of the world's best hospitals. They all said they couldn't help us. The people at UCLA...." He paused there to run a hand through his hair, mussing the perfect razor cut. "Well, we'll see."

"Of course. All I'm asking is that you consider my proposal, should the interview not go as you hope."

"I'll think about it. That's all I'm willing to commit to at the moment."

"I can't ask for anything more than that." Lucius took my hand, and went on, "I assume you didn't tell your wife that we would be visiting this evening."

"No. I didn't know why you were coming over, so I didn't see the point. She has enough on her mind already."

"Of course she does. We will go now, so there's no chance of our being here when she returns."

"I appreciate it," Jackson said, and I couldn't even tell whether he was being sarcastic or not.

Still holding my hand, Lucius got up from the couch, which meant I had to rise with him. I'd remained silent during most of the conversation, since it was really the vampire who'd had to sell the idea of research into his blood. Now, though, I said, "Thank you for seeing us, Jackson. And really—think about what Lucius had to say. He only wants to help."

"I know. And I appreciate it."

Did he, though? He was back to wearing the blandly pleasant expression I always thought of as his politician face, so I couldn't tell what he might be thinking. On the surface, Lucius' "quid pro quo" didn't sound so terrible. Just a little blood to analyze, so the researchers could isolate the element in human plasma that allowed the vampires to have such extended life, and then turn it toward making that life more normal. Since I'd seen such a thing in my vision, that surely meant it would come to pass.

But then I thought of the warehouse I'd seen in my first vision while being held in Lucius' home, of the lines of people going inside while men in strange, plain uniforms kept watch. All those young, healthy people. No one under twenty, or over thirty-five, from the looks of them. Clearly they weren't there of their own volition, or the guards wouldn't have been necessary. Maybe they were all being compelled to donate blood...or possibly something far, far worse. I just didn't know.

As Jackson and Lucius exchanged their goodbyes, I couldn't prevent a chill from running over me. No matter that my visions tended to come true the majority of the time. I had to make sure this particular one never came to pass, or I knew I would have the weight of many lives on my conscience.

For now, though, I had to summon a smile and thank my brother, let Lucius curve his arm around my waist as he guided me to the car. The two Secret Service agents, who'd apparently been keeping watch on the front porch the entire time, regarded us with flat, wary gazes. I didn't acknowledge them, only climbed into the back seat of the Mercedes and waited for Lucius to join me there.

He was quiet as the semivive driver backed us out of the driveway. Once we were headed south on Baldy Village Road, however, he turned toward me, his smile one of triumph.

"That was splendid, Serena," he said. His cold hand grasped mine, and he leaned toward me. "Now I am certain the future you saw will come true. We are so very close."

I nodded, and shut my eyes as he kissed me. I told myself I had done this thing to make sure Silas remained alive.

But was that reason enough?

CHAPTER FIVE

"You ever find yourself questioning your life choices?"

Silas had been half-dozing—sleep was a welcome respite from the hell his life had become —but he jerked awake as soon as he heard Michael St. John's voice. After sending an ironic glance around the cellar where he was being held captive, Silas replied, "Sometimes."

The vampire came farther into the cellar. He had on a black leather jacket over a dark shirt and faded jeans, but that didn't tell Silas much about what was going on outside. Like *gula*, vampires didn't feel heat and cold quite the same way as ordinary humans did, and so the clothing they wore was mostly affectation, rather than a response to the world's changing temperatures. Of course it must be nighttime, or else St. John wouldn't be up and about, but that was all Silas could know for sure.

"Lucius not home again?" he asked. The reason why Michael St. John continued to come visit him in his cell eluded Silas. Boredom? A perverse desire to engage in an activity that would surely annoy his master, should Lucius ever find out? Impossible to say.

"No, he left a while ago to pick up Serena. I don't know where they were going, though."

It took a few seconds for those words to penetrate Silas' brain. Then he frowned. "Lucius went to pick up Serena? She wasn't already here?"

"No, apparently he sent her home last night. I don't know why."

St. John's expression was guileless enough. As far as Silas could tell, the vampire wasn't lying. But what could this development mean? Clearly, she hadn't entirely escaped from Lucius' web, because he was going to fetch her. She wasn't a prisoner, though.

Not a prisoner here, Silas thought then. *It's not as if her condo is neutral territory, not with her neighbor turned into a semivive. That arrangement would allow Lucius to still keep an eye on her, even if she isn't in his house.*

And that meant it would be much easier to get her away from him, take her north where she would be safe. Of course, the problem with that particular scenario was that Silas happened to still be locked up here. But perhaps one of the other *gula* would see that she had returned home, would realize the safest thing to do was remove her from her condo.

Whether they would risk such a thing while he himself was held captive by the vampire... that was more difficult to guess. They had already lost two of their own because of Lucius Montfort. It could very well be that the members of the Conclave wouldn't make that call, not when they couldn't be certain of the outcome. And they would not want to endanger Serena. That realization offered some comfort. Not much, but a little.

"Surprised?" Michael St. John said, correctly interpreting Silas' silence. "Yeah, me too. But I've given up trying to ferret out all of Lucius' motivations."

"And yet you remain," Silas remarked.

"Well, of course I do. You ever hear of a vampire's fledgling just taking off into the great unknown?"

"No. But then, I would also have to admit that I've never met a fledgling quite like you."

St. John shrugged. "Is that a compliment?"

"No. Just an observation." Silas shifted his weight slightly; he tried to change his position every so often so that his limbs wouldn't get too accustomed to being in a particular orientation. Since the vampire seemed to be open to conversation, Silas decided he might as well try to see whether he would answer any more questions. "Do you remember when Lucius made you?"

That question elicited a lift of an eyebrow. "I wasn't aware that I was granting an interview."

"You're not. You don't have to tell me. I was just curious."

Michael St. John came a little farther into the room, and took a seat on a stack of empty pallets. He glanced toward the door, and then back over at Silas. "Yes, I remember. I was playing at a club in Los Feliz."

"You're a musician?"

"Classically trained guitarist, actually." The vampire ran a hand through his hair, then shrugged. "Anyway, I provided background music at a Mexican place. Good gig—five nights a week. Steady work, which is more than a lot of musicians in L.A. can say."

That might have sounded like boasting, but even though he'd only lived in Los Angeles for a few years, Silas knew that what Michael St. John had just told him was nothing more than the truth. He inclined his head, and the vampire continued.

"So one night this guy comes up to me and

says he senses a real passion in my music, tells me that he thinks I have a real future." Another lift of the shoulders. "To tell the truth, at first I thought he was gay, was trying to pick up on me. That's kind of the vibe Lucius gives at first, with those perfectly tailored suits and that not-quite British accent of his."

"I assume that wasn't his intention," Silas said, his tone dry. In truth, it would have been much easier if Lucius Montfort's predilections lay elsewhere. Then he wouldn't have to worry so much about the vampire master's intentions when it came to Serena. Unfortunately, if Michael St. John's comments on the topics were even halfway accurate, then Lucius definitely had an interest in the psychic that was far from the merely cerebral.

"No. He said he had a business proposition for me, that he was opening a restaurant of his own and was scouting talent. He asked me to meet him at his house the next evening. It was a Monday—my night off—so I figured it couldn't hurt to talk to him, see what he wanted. If he tried to get physical, well, I thought I should be able to take him."

If they had both been human men, and the odds at all even, then Michael probably would have been correct. He was slightly taller than Lucius Montfort, and a little more heavily muscled. No doubt he'd thought he would come out ahead in a physical confrontation, should matters progress to that level. What he couldn't have known was that Lucius was not an ordinary man, but a vampire possessed of unnatural strength and centuries of cunning.

"I assume it didn't turn out well."

"No." Michael St. John drummed his fingers on his knee, a nervous gesture. Silas wondered then whether the vampire still played the guitar, or whether he'd abandoned that pursuit as the long, weary years of unwanted immortality began to stretch before him. "He—well, he talked about the club he was setting up, a tapas kind of place, and how he wanted to have background music there. We had a glass of wine, something Spanish. He said it was something he wanted to serve at his club. Then he gave me a strange look and asked me if I'd like to live forever. I told him that usually I didn't think much beyond the next week. He smiled, and then he lunged and sank his teeth into my neck. I could feel myself dying—literally. Everything was going black. But there was this one pinpoint of light...this one thing I could hang on to. I realized later that was Lucius, being my lifeline. I didn't want everything to end there. It felt like when I was a kid and my parents took me to Santa Monica to swim in the ocean. Lucius was my buoy. I swam to him, and he pulled me out of the water. Problem was, when I dried off—to continue the metaphor—I realized I was a vampire."

It was the first time Silas had ever heard a vampire describe the process of being made into one of the undead. Although the *gula* had contact with vampires, in general it was only to face off before one or other of them ended up dead—permanently dead, that is. Most vampires were not exactly in a confessional mood when they had dealings with one of the Watchers.

"What did you do?"

"Well, I was pissed off at first. I didn't ask for any of this." St. John looked away, his gaze fixed somewhere beyond the racks of wine that filled the cellar, far away from this dark, windowless chamber. "But you know, there are worse things than being forever young, than not ever having to worry about making the rent or any of the other thousand pieces of piddly shit that made up life before. Even so...." His words trailed off there, and in the gloomy illumination given off by the emergency light over the door, Silas could see the way the vampire's mouth twisted.

"Even so?"

"Even so, I wish he hadn't done it. I couldn't lie to my parents. I mean, how the hell do you tell your mother and father that there's been a sudden change in your circumstances, and you can't go out in daylight anymore? They're going to think you're crazy, you know?"

To be honest, Silas hadn't given a lot of thought to what happened to fledglings once they'd crossed over into the land of the undead. For one thing, a master vampire generally sought out those who were open to that sort of lifestyle, who didn't have a great deal to cling to. Orphans often made very good vampires. "I suppose that would be difficult," he allowed. "So what did you do?"

A thin smile. "Lucius helped me fake my death. What other options did I have? I was close with my family. They were proud of me for being a full-time musician, even though I wasn't exactly drowning in fame and glory. So...I decided that Lucius was right, that it would be better for everyone involved if they just thought I was dead. With his resources, it was easy enough. He had my car totaled, and one of Leticia and Tristan's victims placed inside the burning wreck. The guy matched my general physical description, was wearing jewelry my parents would know was mine, so no one asked too many questions. No autopsy. No matching dental records or anything like that."

That made sense. Silas had sometimes wondered how he managed to get a recent fledgling like Michael "off the grid," so to speak. Both Leticia and Tristan had died at a time when records were far more haphazard than they were today, so covering up their deaths wouldn't be nearly as difficult. "So no one ever knew?"

"No." Michael pushed himself up off the stack of pallets where he'd been sitting and took a few steps toward the door, every movement filled with nervous energy. Truly, he was the most "human" vampire Silas had ever met, but that made sense. He hadn't been living this undead existence for much more than a decade. "And I never told anyone. I wish I could say that I got used to it, but...." A negligent shrug, but Silas could see the nonchalance was feigned.

"You don't enjoy it."

"No." St. John grinned, although the expression was more of a grimace. "I can admit that to you because Lucius knows it all too well. Tristan and Leticia—they're good vampires. They like the hunt, the kill. Me, not so much. Most of the time I live off the bottled stuff. It tastes like ass, but that's better than killing people."

Truly, Michael St. John did seem to be rather an extraordinary vampire. Silas experienced another flare of anger at Lucius Montfort, but this time the rage was not for what he'd done to Serena or her family, but the victim he'd made of the young man who stood before Silas now.

Usually, a vampire master would choose those who were ruthless and cunning—like Leticia Carver and Tristan McVey—because those qualities were necessary to the vampire life. However, although he could be capricious and bitter and sarcastic, St. John was neither cruel nor sly.

Whether Silas could use the vampire's better nature to his own advantage, however, remained to be seen.

He settled against the wall, the chains of his manacles clanking slightly. "So why the allegiance to him, when you clearly have no desire to live this life?"

Michael St. John raised an ironic eyebrow. "You know the answer to that as well as I do, *gula*. A fledgling can't betray his master. Loyalty flows in our blood, because it's his blood that flows there as well. I'd like to help you...I really would. But I can't. Although I do appreciate these little chats. For obvious reasons, these aren't the sorts of things I can discuss with Leticia or Tristan, let alone Lucius."

Of course not. Silas gave a weary shrug. "I thought so. But I must continue to ask. Serena's life may depend on it."

At that remark, St. John shook his head. "Oh, I don't think so. As far as I can tell, he thinks the moon rises and sets with her. I still don't know what he's up to, but he seemed unusually excited about something this evening. Not that he told me where he was going, only that he would be fetching her."

And thank God the master vampire had allowed Serena that small piece of freedom. She was smart enough that she would use it to her advantage as soon as she thought it was safe. What she planned, he couldn't be sure, and it was better that way. Complete ignorance would prevent Lucius from getting any useful answers out of him.

"Well," Michael St. John said, "I should probably leave you to it. Lucius didn't really say when he would be back, and better that he not catch me down here. Sweet dreams."

Those two words were the vampire's parting shot, since he let himself out and locked the door immediately afterward. Silas didn't bother to protest; St. John came and went as he willed. This captivity was onerous, true, but sooner or later it must end. In the meantime, his cell had been made somewhat more comfortable by the addition of a chemical toilet, a basin of water, and a few extra blankets. He had no idea whether Serena had requested those items for him, or whether Lucius had made sure they were put in place so she would have no reason to complain of his treatment. It didn't really matter. He would survive this, and be with her again.

And in the moment he truly knew Serena was safe, he would be sure to drive a stake right through Lucius Montfort's shriveled heart.

~

Lucius walked me to my front door. I didn't bother to protest, to tell him he didn't need to follow the little protocols a normal couple might abide by, because lord only knew we were anything but a normal couple. I had to keep pretending, had to make him think I welcomed every extra moment we spent together.

Once we were there, however, my heart began to beat a little faster. What if he wanted to celebrate by forcing his way in, by making me his physically? I had told myself I would make that sacrifice if I had to, because keeping Silas alive was more important than anything else, but….

I honestly didn't know if I could go through with it, should Lucius press me.

But although he kissed me, thanked me again for the meeting with my brother, he didn't try to come inside once I'd unlocked the door and disabled the alarm. No, he stood inside the doorway and said, "How soon do you think you might hear from Jackson?"

"I don't know," I replied. "He likes to think things over. He's deliberate. So it could be a while. Or...." I stopped there, because the thought which passed through my mind right then was dreadful enough that I really didn't want to voice it aloud.

"Or...?"

His expression was neutral, but I could tell he expected me to answer. I swallowed, then said, "Or it could be that the news he gets from the doctors at UCLA is bad enough that he can't afford to wait. I just don't know. Obviously, Addie is sick enough that she couldn't get any help from the doctors back at John Hopkins or Walter Reed. But I know people who were told they were dying who got treatment at UCLA and lived, so it could be that they have the cure Jackson and Bethany are looking for." I reached out and took Lucius' hand, squeezed it slightly. "And I also know that I'll call you as soon as I hear anything. Or rather," I amended, since I remembered that communications with a vampire would by necessity be hampered by his sleeping habits, "I'll contact you as soon as you're able to take the call. Okay?"

"Yes, of course." He raised my hand and

pressed it to his lips. "Sleep well, Serena. I will speak with you tomorrow evening."

Then he let go, and turned and went down the hallway toward the staircase. I stood there, smiling, until he was out of eyeshot, then locked the door and reengaged the alarm. Not because I thought a locked door would keep him out—he'd already been invited into my condo, and therefore could come and go as he pleased—but because I needed the psychological reassurance that a Schlage lock and the burglar alarm provided.

I glanced at the clock on the stove. It was 10:17. Early, and once again I had to murmur a thanks to the universe that Lucius hadn't tried to stay longer. Why, I wasn't sure, except that I'd just done him a huge favor, and so he possibly sought to reward me with a decent night's sleep.

Ha. Sleep was the last thing on my mind right then.

I went to the kitchen and fetched myself a glass of water, then went upstairs to my little loft office space. My laptop sat on the desk. I opened it up and logged in, then turned off the wireless. After that I got out the adapter which would allow me to plug directly into the cable modem. I still wasn't sure that Lucius really could hack into my computer or the wireless in my house, but I figured I might as well take as many precautions as possible.

Next I opened up the VPN software that would allow me to go out onto the internet without anyone being able to track which sites I was viewing. The first thing I wanted to do was try to satisfy my curiosity, although I didn't know how successful I would be.

I pulled up Humboldt County on Google Maps and started cruising around, just trying to see what I could find. The *gula* compound had to be there somewhere, but a county was a pretty big place to explore, and Silas had never mentioned whether the place where he'd grown up was near any of the towns I saw now—Eureka, Arcata, Ridgewood—or whether it was located out in what appeared to be vast expanses of heavily wooded lands. To preserve their privacy, the Watchers were probably out in the middle of nowhere, which meant I was basically looking for a needle in a haystack.

But then….

There was a road that led out of a place called Fortuna. It wound away into the forest, moving roughly northeast. I followed it along until it turned into not much more than a dirt track. That dirt track moved even deeper into the forest, this time due north. One might expect such a trail to peter out to nothing eventually...

but it didn't. It went to an area that looked like a large clearing in the forest, with apparently acres and acres of green grass. And in that clearing was a series of buildings, mostly houses, although there appeared to be a few structures larger than single-family dwellings. The school? The *gula* offices? I knew so little about how their compound was organized that I really couldn't begin to guess.

For all I knew, I'd just found the private getaway of a Hollywood star or producer, but I didn't think so. Somehow I knew in my gut that this was where the *gula* were located. What I was supposed to do with that information, I had no idea. It wasn't as if I could get in my SUV and drive the five-hundred-plus miles to that flyspeck on the map, not with Lucius Montfort's semivive lackey living next door and watching every single move I made. Still, it somehow comforted me to see those tiny indistinct shapes, to let myself think that was where Silas had grown up, that somewhere in all that green, so different from Southern California's golden-brown hills, he and I might be able to make a future together.

Out of nowhere, the window for my Messages app popped up. *Serena Quinn, perhaps you should have been a private detective.*

I startled and nearly knocked over my glass of water. What the hell? No one should have been able to see what I was up to.

Who is this? I typed back.

My name is Felix. Perhaps Silas mentioned me.

The name wasn't familiar. Then again, Silas and I hadn't been given much of an opportunity to really talk about the *gula* before not-Brian kidnapped me and took me to his master. *No, sorry,* I wrote. *He didn't give me a lot of detail.*

Understandable. We know that Lucius Montfort has allowed you back in your home. Are you well?

I'm fine, I typed. *So you have been watching my house?*

Of course. We're Watchers. It's what we do.

Even though I couldn't see the expression on this Felix's face, somehow I got the impression he was teasing me. *Then come and get me,* I wrote. *I know where Lucius lives. I can take you there. We need to rescue Silas.*

A pause. Then the message came back, *We can't do that. Not yet. We need to know what he's up to, why he finds you so valuable.*

What, other than my visions? Or maybe having a brother who's running for President?

What does your brother have to do with it?

I hesitated. After all, I'd taken for granted

that this person was who he said he was, but what if he wasn't? What if he was one of Lucius' vampires—not that any of them had seemed particularly tech-savvy, either—or someone he had working for him?

How do I know you're really a friend of Silas?

You don't, came the reply. *Except that I know he was called to Paris by the Conclave, only to cancel his trip when he discovered you had been taken by Montfort. Just as I know that one of our own, Emanuel, was supposed to watch over you but instead was murdered by a gang of Lucius Montfort's semivives. Again, this is all knowledge the vampire master might also possess. So you will have to make a decision, Serena Quinn. You will need to decide whether to trust me, or to go blindly on your own.*

Damn it. More than anything I wanted to know I wasn't alone in this, but saying the wrong thing to someone who might be an agent of Lucius Montfort's would only expose me to him, would show I wasn't quite as on board with his plans for world domination as he thought.

Then again...a few of the things Silas had mentioned made it sound as if the *gula* had their own computer experts and hackers. It would take someone like that to know their location was being explored. Maybe they had an alarm that went off when anyone surfed too close on Google Maps. I had absolutely no idea how that would work, but the notion sounded at least halfway plausible to me. Someone with that kind of technical skill would also be able to pierce my VPN, to talk to my computer even though I'd done my damnedest to mask my identity. So far I'd seen absolutely nothing from Lucius or any of his cohorts to show they had the technical skills to accomplish such a feat. And it couldn't be any of the semivives, because most of them didn't have the functional brain cells to do much more than carry out orders and possibly tie their shoes...on a good day.

I took a breath, then typed, *Lucius is plotting to use the antibodies in vampire blood as a sort of cure for my niece Addison's leukemia. That will get my brother Jackson—and all his resources—on board to fund the project. In exchange, those same researchers will be able to isolate the factors in human blood that keep vampires alive and immortal, and to alter those factors so they allow vampires a chance at a normal existence.*

At first, I didn't get a response. That last message showed it had been received at 10:38 p.m., so I know Felix had seen it.

Then he replied, *Ah. Now I understand. And your visions?*

My visions told him this thing was a possibility. More than a possibility, because I'd say they come true at least 90% of the time. I don't think Lucius would have approached my brother if he hadn't seen this as basically a sure thing.

Another pause, followed by, *And you're certain Silas is still alive.*

Yes. I've seen him. Lucius is holding him captive in his wine cellar. As long as I continue to cooperate and give Lucius what he wants, Silas will be safe. Or at least, that's what Lucius has told me. I don't trust him, but I can't risk anything happening to Silas. That's why you have to go rescue him.

We will. Or rather, we will wait for the proper opportunity. These matters need to be handled with care and precision.

Just about the last thing I wanted to hear. I didn't want care and precision—I wanted the *gula* to go storming in there like a bunch of commandos and get Silas out. Because if he was freed, then I was free, too. I could tell Jackson that Lucius was only using him to get what he wanted, namely, immortality without the nasty side effects of vampirism, and then we could all go on with our lives.

But then I thought of my niece's pale face, of her listlessness, when she had always been a lively child, bright and curious. Could I deprive her of a chance at a cure? I knew that vampire blood clearly had benefits for humans, or else I wouldn't have seen Lucius and Jackson talking about selling immortality in that one terrible vision.

Damn it.

So what is the "proper opportunity"? I typed.

I don't know yet. We will have to wait and see. It is good news that Silas is alive, for we had feared the worst, after what happened to Emanuel and David.

I didn't know who David was. Apparently, yet another body in Lucius Montfort's long list of victims.

I will contact you again, Felix went on. *For now, be careful. Be watchful. You are playing a dangerous game, Serena Quinn.*

Didn't I know it. Not that I had much choice. My heart had been given to Silas Drake, and now I could only continue down this path and pray that its end would see the two of us together, and not the dreadful future of my vision.

I'll be careful.

Good.

Nothing after that. I wasn't expecting more, and yet I sat there for a few more minutes, staring at the screen. I didn't know this Felix person at all, and yet I'd been reassured by our conversation, by having the chance to talk to someone who knew the truth, who wasn't part of this whole elaborate charade. There was no one I could confide in, not even my closest friend. But this stranger had offered me a lifeline.

Smiling slightly, I closed the laptop and went to get ready for bed.

CHAPTER SIX

I slept well that night. And it was heaven to wake up in my own bed, to follow my own routine in the morning, surrounded by my own house, my own belongings. No fresh bread to make toast, of course, but I had some frozen English muffins on hand, and I put those in the toaster oven as I savored my morning coffee, secure in the knowledge that I wouldn't have to deal with Lucius Montfort for a good nine hours.

And although I couldn't do much with the information, I also felt heartened that I'd been able to locate the *gula* compound. Did Lucius know where it was? Probably; their home base really hadn't been all that difficult to find online. However, I guessed that none of the vampires would go near the place, simply because they would be greatly outnumbered. I still didn't quite understand the uneasy détente that seemed to exist between the Watchers and the vampires, but it seemed that both groups did what they could to stay away from confrontations, and avoided attracting notice as much as possible. Lucius had only reached out to me because of my abilities. Somehow I doubted I would have ever been a victim of his, or of any of the other vampires in his coven, for the simple reason that my family was a prominent one, and my mysterious death would have attracted too much attention. That was the main part of the reason why Lucius continued to be irritated with Tristan and Leticia—the vampire master might not have harbored any particular feelings for Vanessa, but her murder would continue to be investigated long after the killing of someone without her connections might have slipped into the background.

The thought made an odd little twinge go through me. I hadn't been all that close with Vanessa, due to the difference in our ages and the simple fact that we really didn't have very much in common, but it still hurt...a lot. Just the thought that I wouldn't ever see her again, wouldn't get to vicariously experience her triumphs and her continuing success, pained me more than I wanted to admit. Luckily, so far I'd managed to avoid seeing either of her murderers —or rather, Lucius appeared to have arranged things so I wouldn't have to cross paths with Tristan or Leticia. I supposed managing such a task wasn't terribly difficult in a house that big, especially when, despite his coaxing me to adopt more of a night owl's schedule, I simply wasn't awake during the hours when the vampires were most active.

For now, though, I found it soothing to take a shower in my own bathroom, to prepare myself in a leisurely fashion for the rest of my day. Yes, I knew this calm would end, that Lucius would summon me to his home as soon as the sun set, but in the meantime I could pretend everything was back to normal.

Or mostly back to normal. In the back of my mind, I kept fretting about what the doctors would say to Jackson and Bethany. I prayed— probably harder than I'd ever prayed for anything before—that the specialists at UCLA would turn out to be true miracle workers, and that they'd tell my brother and my sister-in-law that they had an effective cure for Addison's leukemia. Because if that turned out to be the case, then there was no way Jackson would go along with Lucius' schemes. There wouldn't be any point. And then I could tell my brother the truth, and he would help me free Silas. Or maybe that would be the signal the Watchers had been waiting for, and they'd rescue their captive compatriot. I really didn't care who stepped in and saved the world, as long as *someone* did.

After my cleaning frenzy of the day before, the kitchen trash was full. I figured that taking the garbage to one of the dumpsters down by the garages shouldn't cause too much trouble—even not-Brian couldn't give me too much grief over performing such a simple chore, since I wouldn't have to leave the condo complex. As I was coming back up the stairs, however, I saw him waiting for me on the landing. A frown creased his sandy brows.

"Just taking out the trash," I told him, figuring I might as well be proactive.

"Oh." He glanced past me, as though he expected someone to be there. Who, I had no idea. Did he think I was using taking out the trash as an excuse for an assignation down by the dumpster? Who would I even be meeting with?

I noticed his front door was ajar. Inside, I could see Brian's big 17-inch MacBook Pro sitting open on the dining room table. From this distance, it was hard to see exactly what he was working on, but, judging by the combination of pictures and text, I guessed it must be a product brochure for one of his clients.

"Back to the grind, huh?" I said, pointing toward the laptop.

His frown deepened. "Yes. Brian—that is, I had some projects due this week. But...."

"But?"

He shrugged then, but I could tell something was bothering him. His speech and mannerisms were close enough to those of the old Brian that I didn't feel completely in the dark when it came to interpreting his moods. "But...that part of me, the design part...it's not working. I open projects I was working on, and I feel like I should know what to do, but I don't."

Despite everything, I couldn't help but feel sorry for him. It wasn't his fault that Lucius had turned him into a semivive. I remembered what Silas had said about semivives losing any creative spark they might have had, which was why Lucius wouldn't have dared turned my sister into one of his half-living slaves. Her talent would have been gone, and such a loss would have been immediately apparent to anyone who knew her.

"Do you want me to take a look?" I asked. "I took a couple of design courses in college."

The gratitude in his expression would have

been almost comical if the situation hadn't been so sad. "Would you?"

"Sure."

I followed him into his condo, and he shut the door behind me. Nothing about the place looked any different from the times I'd been over there previously, but why should it? Brian was newly made a semivive, and so retained far more of himself than those who'd been Lucius' slaves for years. He wouldn't have made any material changes in the place where he lived; doing so would have only drawn his partner Lewis' attention to a personality shift Brian had to try to keep secret for as long as possible.

As I'd guessed, the project on the laptop's screen was a brochure—for a new golf resort in Palos Verdes. Even though I wasn't an expert, I could tell that the layout looked clunky and pedestrian, with none of Brian's flair for combining fonts, or the little decorative motifs he used to make a project truly his. I also knew that I was out of my depth here. I was no designer. I knew just barely enough to tell his current project wasn't working, but there was no way I could figure out how to fix it.

That assessment must have been obvious enough in my expression, because the corners of Brian's mouth turned down. "That bad?"

"I'm afraid so." I looked away from him back to the computer screen, but I had no words of wisdom to offer. "When do you need to turn in your first comp?"

"Friday."

Well, that was better than having it due the very next day. It still didn't give us that much time. And I knew there was no way in hell I could possibly fix the layout for him. However, a sudden notion struck me. "Why not subcontract it?"

"What do you mean?"

"I mean…put an ad on Craigslist, or post the project on Outbrain or something like that. With that kind of arrangement, you can specify that the work will be anonymous, and so you can turn it in to your client as something you did yourself."

Brian frowned again, but this time his expression was considering, rather than annoyed. "Maybe…."

"I'll even pay for it," I offered. "That way, you won't have to justify the expenditure to Lewis."

"You'd do that for me? Why?"

Well, there was a good question. The simple answer was that I hoped something of the real Brian survived inside the semivive. Brian was my friend. It seemed second nature to help him out, even though he really wasn't the person he'd once been. Unfortunately, I didn't know if that kind of simple altruism was something a semivive could comprehend. So I said, "If I help you, that helps Lucius, right?"

The frown erased itself from Brian's brow. "I hadn't thought of it that way, but…yes."

"Well, then. Do you have the original bid you put in for the job? It would help to have that on hand while we're putting the ad together."

"I do…it's in the file cabinet upstairs. Just a minute."

He left, and I had to force myself to stand there and act like I wasn't dying to go digging around on his laptop, just to see if he had any incriminating emails from Lucius. But no, the vampire master was a lot of things, but careless wasn't one of them. I still wasn't sure exactly how he communicated with his semivives, but I was fairly certain it didn't involve emails or texts. Telepathy?

Brian came back downstairs with a manila file folder in one hand. "Everything is in here," he said, handing it over to me. Clearly, he wasn't worried about me seeing what technically was privileged information.

Luckily, the contract was very specific. I made some notes, and allowed myself a mental whistle at the amount he was supposed to be paid for the project. I'd known that Brian was very successful, and highly in demand, but if he got commissions like this every month—or more than one every month—he'd be well into six-figure territory without breaking a sweat.

I wasn't going to offer that much in the ads I was putting together, but I thought I could put a price on the project that would make it worth many designers' time, even if they weren't yet at a point in their careers where they could command the kind of prices Brian did. As for where I'd get the money, well, I had an extremely healthy chunk sitting in my bank account. My allowance from my parents was sent via electronic transfer on the first of every month, and I didn't need even half of it to live very comfortably, since the condo was paid for. Anyway, I could afford to help out Brian. No one would even notice the money was missing.

Together we drafted an ad, and I helped him set up an account on Outbrain so he could post the project. We also put the ad on Craigslist, just in case.

"I'm sure you'll get lots of bids," I told him as I got up from the chair where I'd been sitting. "Even with such a short turnaround."

"Thank you, Serena. I know Lucius will be

very pleased when he hears of how you've helped me."

I smiled, even though I did so only for Brian's benefit. I didn't dare tell him that I couldn't care less whether Lucius was pleased or not. "Well, we're all in this together, aren't we?"

"Yes…I suppose we are."

Brian let me out, and I went next door to my place. By then it was almost lunchtime, but I found I wasn't all that hungry. Instead, I went and retrieved my cell phone from my purse, but there were no new messages. I didn't know for sure when Addison's appointment at UCLA was supposed to be, since Jackson hadn't been very specific about that. They might even be driving out to Westwood now. I'd hear when I heard, and not a moment sooner.

If I went back online and started rooting around on Google Maps, would Felix pounce on me again? Or would he think our conversation of the night before had been sufficient, at least until one of us had new information to act upon?

Even though I'd literally walked into my condo not five minutes earlier, I already felt restless, stir-crazy. Maybe it was simply that even my limited time outside had told me it was a beautiful spring day, the kind of day meant for strolling around Old Town Pasadena and doing some leisurely shopping. Ironic, considering I'd lived like such a hermit before Silas entered my world and changed it forever. Back then, I generally wouldn't venture out unless I absolutely had to.

I hadn't had a vision for several days now. In the past, I wouldn't have thought such a gap particularly noteworthy—I often went two or three days, or sometimes as much as a week, without having my thoughts invaded in such a way. While I was living in Lucius' mansion, however, the visions had come fast and furious. His influence? I didn't know. Right then I would have almost welcomed a vision, just because it would have given me something new to obsess over.

Visions didn't appear to be in my immediate future, though. Eventually I got hungry enough to fetch some frozen Trader Joe's samosas and stick them in the toaster oven. I had nothing fresh in the house, so at some point I'd really need to go to the store. Not on my own, of course; I'd have to get not-Brian to drive me.

I was just about to head next door and ask if he could take me to TJ's, and then to Whole Foods, when my cell phone rang. Immediately I turned around and ran to pick up the phone. I looked down at the screen.

Jackson's number.

Fingers shaking a little, I pushed the green

button to accept the call. *Please let it be good news…please let it be good news….*

"Hi, Jackson."

"Hi, Serena."

He sounded tired. That couldn't be good. "Did you talk to the doctors?"

"Yes." A long pause. "They don't think they can do anything, either. They ran a few more tests, just to be sure, but, based on what they've seen so far, it doesn't look good."

My heart seemed to plummet somewhere to the depths of my stomach, lying there like a stone. I swallowed. "But don't you have to wait for the results of those tests to come back before you can know for sure?"

"Technically, yes, but they've seen enough from her charts that they don't think those tests are going to change much of anything. We're — well, Bethany's pretty upset."

"So you haven't told her."

"About our little 'meeting' last night? No. I wasn't going to say anything until I had a definitive 'no' from the doctors here. Besides, every time I try to think of how I'll broach the subject to her, I mentally rewind that conversation and think about how crazy all of it sounds. I mean, I was there…I saw what Lucius could do…but I won't exactly have visual aids when I talk to Bethany."

No, I supposed he wouldn't. I hesitated, trying to think of what I could possibly say to make this all better, but the truth was, I didn't possibly see how it could be all better. Either Jackson fell in with Lucius and gave him the backing he needed for his "vampire serum," and therefore locked in place the terrible future I'd seen in my visions, or my brother refused that request, and stood by and watched his daughter die.

"Well, you don't have to tell her right away," I said, trying to sound reassuring. "I mean, you'll want to think it over."

A long pause, one that made a nervous tremor go through my body. Then Jackson replied, "What's to think over? If I don't work with Lucius, give him the resources he needs to effect a cure, then we lose Addie."

Shit. Never mind that I'd been thinking basically the same thing just a few moments earlier. Did I dare protest, tell my brother something of what I'd seen in my vision of the future? Could he go through with this, knowing that, even if he saved Addison and extended the lives of many other people—people who could afford it, of course—he'd also be committed to giving Lucius as much healthy blood as he required to create the serum that would make his vampire existence much more tolerable?

I honestly didn't know. I wanted to believe he would do the right thing, but judgment often went right out the window when it came to dealing with a child's illness. Anyway, the question was moot, because I couldn't have him hold off on working with Lucius while Silas was still a prisoner. How long did it take to set up laboratories, hire researchers? If you were going through normal channels, probably months or even years. But Jackson knew the clock was ticking, that a cure had to be found sooner rather than later. There was always plenty of empty office and tech space in Southern California, especially out in the Inland Empire. Using his money and his clout, Jackson could probably have a working team up to speed within ten days or less.

Maybe much less, if I knew anything about my brother.

"I know," I said. "Did they—" I broke off then, because how could I possibly ask my brother if the doctors had told him how long his daughter had to live?

He seemed to guess, however, because he said, "We might have six months. Maybe. More like three or four. I don't have time to wait. I just don't. Addie doesn't have that much time. You'll see Lucius tonight?"

"Yes," I replied. "He's sending a car for me,

probably a little after six. So I—I can talk to him when I see him."

"Good. Tell him I'm ready to go on this. Tell him I'll get him whatever he needs. Tell him—" Jackson stopped himself there. I'd heard the tremor in his voice, knew how close he must be to losing it altogether. "Just tell him I'm ready to go ahead."

"Okay, Jackson. I'll let him know."

"Thanks." Another one of those pauses. What he wanted to say, I didn't know, because when he continued, the words were innocuous enough. "Anyway, I need to get going. Bethany took the kids down to the cafeteria for ice cream, but we need to get on the road back to Claremont."

"Are you going to stay here in California? I know your spring recess isn't for a month—"

"Probably. I don't know. Nothing's been decided yet. I may do a lot of flying back and forth. I know the climate here would be better for Addie, and she's missed so much school already that it won't matter. We'll get a tutor for her, and for Griffin and Taylor, if I have to. I've got to go, Serena. We can hash out the details later. Just let Lucius know that we need to proceed."

"I will, Jackson. Take care."

"You, too, Serena."

He ended the call, and I was left to stand there in the dining room as I stared down at the cell phone in my hand. Just like that. Now the events leading to my vision had been set in motion.

And I had no idea whether I could stop them.

CHAPTER SEVEN

THE CHARCOAL-GRAY MERCEDES CAME FOR ME
at six-fifteen. Brian had sent me a text letting me
know when the car would arrive. Had the semivive driver contacted him so he could contact
me? It looked that way. Apparently Lucius
didn't want to give my number out to just
anyone, even if that person happened to be one
of his slaves.

A warm glow lingered on the horizon, but
the sun was gone. I sat in the back seat of the car
and knotted my cold fingers together, wishing
there was some way I could lie to Lucius, could
tell him that I hadn't heard anything from my
brother. Doing so would only delay the
inevitable, however; the master vampire would
find out soon enough that Jackson wanted to go

ahead with the research, and then he would want to know why I had deliberately misled him.

I really didn't see a way out.

The mansion seemed nearly dark as we approached, although once we drove up to the porte cochère, I saw a few lights gleaming on the ground floor. Maybe the house always looked like that; after all, I was usually already inside when night fell.

The semivive driver helped me out of the car. This time, even though I generally avoided touching any of Lucius' half-living servants, I was glad of the assistance, of the man's steadying hand. Although I'd taken care in getting ready, had put on one of my favorite skirts and a ballet-neck top, done my hair and makeup, I realized all those preparations had only been part of a vain attempt to give me confidence, to make me think I was prepared for this meeting.

I wanted to turn and run. Instead, I walked calmly through the porte cochère and entered the house. Waiting just inside was Lucius, who offered me his arm. As I took it, he looked down at me and raised an eyebrow.

"My dear, you seem somewhat agitated."

"We need to talk."

Without missing a beat, he said, "You have spoken with your brother?"

"Yes."

"Ah. Then it appears it's a good thing I decanted that '73 Bordeaux I had been saving. This way."

He guided me into the dining room, where the aforementioned Bordeaux sat on the table, along with a covered tureen that turned out to contain *coq au vin*. After he'd pulled out a chair for me and had seated himself, he poured some of the wine into the wine glasses that had been waiting at each place setting. Although he lifted his glass, he didn't drink.

"Tell me."

"They're still waiting on some tests, but the prognosis isn't good. Jackson said to let you know that he's ready to proceed." I sounded so calm, as though all this was happening to someone else's family. But that was the only way I knew to keep myself together.

No response at first. Lucius held his glass up toward the candles in the candelabra at the center of the table, as though inspecting the liquid it contained. The reflected light glowed within the dark wine, glinting in shades of bloody garnet.

Then he said, "That is unfortunate."

"'Unfortunate'?" I repeated, thinking that was the understatement of the century. "I thought this was what you were hoping for."

"Contrary to what you might think of me, I

certainly am not one to wish a fatal disease upon an innocent child. While I am glad of the opportunity to have this research finally undertaken, I would have preferred not to do so because a young girl has been stricken with such a malady."

I watched Lucius carefully, but I couldn't see anything in his expression except a certain regret. If he was experiencing any triumph at the prospect of getting his own much-desired cure, he didn't show it.

"So, Serena," he went on, "let us drink to your brother's people finding a cure quickly."

I couldn't really refuse, and so I raised my own glass and clinked it gently against Lucius', then sipped. So heavy and dark, almost port-like in its intensity, but with a dryness one would never find in that after-dinner liquor. The previous week, I wouldn't have trusted the wine, decanted as it had been rather than being poured safely out of a sealed bottle. Now, however, I knew that Lucius had no need to resort to such tricks. He trusted me. After all, hadn't I just given him the keys to the kingdom, so to speak?

"That is something worth drinking to," I said. "Jackson said to let him know what you think you will need."

"As to that, I am not a scientist." Lucius drank some more of the Bordeaux, then set down his glass and reached for the heavy spoon cradled in the tureen so he might dish us both some of the *coq au vin.* "He would know better —or at least, he has the means to hire consultants who can tell him what kind of researchers we need. But surely hematologists, and virologists, and a number of technicians."

And project managers, and QA people, and...well, at that point my imagination ran out, because of course I'd never worked in a lab of any kind. Jackson probably had only a hazy idea as well, but he would be able to hire managers to handle all those logistics for him. As to how long it might take before they found a cure...who knew? The scene in my vision seemed to have taken place in the near future, but even a few years from now was too long, if the timeline Jackson had given me was at all accurate.

"He'll get people on it right away," I said. "He actually has a staff that works for him full-time here in California, managing his own trust. They're completely separate from the staff in Washington, D.C., so I assume he'll have someone from the California group go scouting for a building to lease, that sort of thing."

Lucius' lip curled slightly. "Yes, I suppose he would want to keep these activities as separate from his 'official' duties as possible. But he still plans to continue his run for President?"

"As far as I know, yes. The family already discussed it. Addison doesn't want her illness to prevent him from running, or at least that's what Bethany told me. Of course, that was before the meeting with the doctors at UCLA. Jackson said his schedule was going to be up in the air, because he still has almost a month before Congress has its spring recess, but I think he's going to try to keep things appearing as normal as possible. If any of his possible opponents get a whiff of any of this, there's going to be blood in the water."

The half-ironic twist remained on Lucius' mouth. "Yes, politics is rather a blood sport, isn't it?"

I didn't exactly shudder, but a tremor went through my body. Yes, that was a good phrase for it. Always having to watch everything you said and did, keeping the trash locked down so no one could go rooting through it, making sure there wasn't a single word or interaction that could be held against you. I honestly had never understood how Jackson could live like that, but he seemed to thrive on the intrigue.

"For some, I suppose," I admitted as I sipped at my Bordeaux. "I think Jackson looks on it more as a calling. I'm not sure how he's going to explain his family staying here in California when he'll be heading back to Washington, but I'm sure he'll think of something."

"A change of schools, perhaps?"

"Maybe. Although almost everyone in Congress who has school-age children sends them to private schools in D.C. There are a few who have tutors, and a couple whose families have stayed in their home states to avoid disruption. That's a lot easier to pull off when you live in Maryland or even Connecticut or Rhode Island, though. Flying back and forth to California eats up a lot of time."

"Well, as you said, I'm sure he'll come up with a plausible explanation. Now eat your *coq au vin* before it gets cold."

This last was delivered so gently that it was barely an admonishment, but I went ahead and picked up my fork. Despite my jumpy nerves, I was hungry—there wasn't a lot for me to eat back home. I really would have to set up a shopping trip with Brian in the very near future. As I cut off a piece of the rich, wine-braised chicken, Lucius said,

"That was a very kind thing you did for Brian this afternoon."

I paused mid-bite, then remembered to finish chewing. "It's nothing."

"I don't think so. You saw that he was suffering, and proposed an clever solution." Lucius stopped there for a moment, elegant fingers playing with the handle of his fork, although he didn't raise it to his mouth. "It is one thing I do regret about making my semivives…this loss of self, of the creative spark within a person. Unfortunately, there doesn't seem to be any way around it. For them to follow my command, they must give up a good deal of their individuality."

"How many of them do you have?" I had to hope the question sounded innocent enough to him. What precisely I would do with that information, I didn't know, but it always helped to know how many enemies you might be facing.

A shrug. "A dozen. They perform an assortment of duties for me, but that is a good number to have on hand. Enough so they are not spread too thin, but not so many that they become difficult to keep track of."

Lucius seemed very mellow this evening. I thought I understood why—he could relax about getting his serum, because Jackson had agreed to fund and staff the project. In the vampire master's mind, he was probably already looking ahead to those walks in the sunshine.

Walks he would want to take with me. I told myself that nothing had been set in stone yet, that the future was fluid and therefore could be changed, but I still could feel a tremor of disquiet move through me. This would have been a lot easier if I'd known the *gula* were going to arrive on scene at any moment and take Silas away. Felix had advised patience. Unfortunately, I was feeling anything but patient right then.

But because Lucius appeared so relaxed, I thought it safe enough to ask my next question. "How do you communicate with them, anyway? I've never seen them use a cell phone, or a walkie-talkie."

A thin smile. "I have no need of such things. They are bonded to me, bonded because of the inoculation of my blood they've been given. I speak to their minds, tell them what I need them to do. It's in the same way that they report to me. This comes to me more as impressions than discrete thoughts, but our communication works very well. After all, vampires have been making semivives for centuries, long before cell phones existed."

I supposed I should have thought of that. Lucius' explanation told me why the semivives never seemed to speak very much, why they appeared to come and go by instinct, even when following orders I had never heard. Everything transmitted through thought—efficient, quiet, and very difficult to subvert.

I'd been very careful in what I said and how I acted around not-Brian, and apparently that had been a wise decision. That didn't mean I wouldn't be doubly careful going forward.

"That makes sense," I said, my tone neutral, and then took another bite of *coq au vin*.

"You disapprove."

"Of course I do," I told him, setting down my fork. "Taking people's lives away, just so you can make them your servants? I care for you, Lucius, but do you honestly believe I would ever be okay with that sort of thing?"

There. I had to hope my remark provided just the right mixture of the old self-righteous Serena, blended with the woman who claimed to love him. If I wanted to be perfectly honest with myself, I still didn't know for sure that he'd actually fallen for my act. He could be meeting my lies with more of his own, and laughing to himself the whole time, laughing at the silly mortal woman who actually thought she could fool an immortal being who'd lived for centuries.

In which case, he was only using me for as long as he found me and my connections worthwhile. After he had what he wanted—his serum —quite possibly he'd dispose of me the way Leticia and Tristan had disposed of Vanessa.

But if I believed that, then I'd also have to believe that my visions weren't true, and the serum would never come to be. After all, the future I'd been shown seemed to indicate that

Lucius and I had an intimate relationship. That was the problem with trying to predict the future, even when you were given guideposts. You just didn't know. Not for sure. Not one hundred percent.

"No, I didn't think you would agree with the practice." Lucius reached over to where my hand rested on the tabletop, and ran his long index finger across my skin, down to my wrist. By that point I was used enough to him touching me that I didn't even shiver, and instead summoned a smile for him. "That is one thing I admire about you. Your soul is still pure. I appreciate that quality, because innocence generally gets trampled with the passage of time. We are all quite a group of jaded souls here."

"Even Michael?" I asked. "I got the impression that he...hadn't been around quite as long as the rest of you."

"Yes, Michael is a young vampire," Lucius said. "But I certainly would not call him an innocent."

I couldn't argue with that statement, mostly because I didn't know Michael St. John well enough to comment. We hadn't exchanged many words, although something about his brittle sarcasm made me think he'd resorted to such outward displays of irony in order to hide a deeper hurt. "I suppose no vampire can be inno-cent," I said. "After all, you do kill people."

"None lately."

"Except my sister."

Lucius withdrew his hand from mine, a frown touching his brows. "I've already told you that I don't agree with Tristan's and Leticia's actions. But they have touched no one since, and I...." The words drifted away as his frown increased. He reached for his glass of Bordeaux, took a large swallow. "Would you believe me if I told you I hadn't claimed a life in more than a year?"

My first instinct was to say no, I didn't believe him. Such a response probably wouldn't elicit a positive response, and so I only lifted my shoulders. "Do I have any reason *not* to believe you?"

"No. This is the truth, Serena. As I told you before, bottled blood has little savor, but it does keep us alive. I grew weary of the killing, weary of the hunt. When I learned of your existence, however...." The silvery eyes brightened, and I had to force myself not to look away. "That gave me something to look forward to. Meeting you, that is."

Which is why you sent one of your semivives to manhandle me on the street and try to kidnap me, I thought sourly. I wouldn't bring up that ancient history, though. Throwing it in his face would only show that I really wasn't on his side after all. A woman who was truly in love with him would have let it go.

"Well, I hope I was everything you expected," I said lightly as I picked up my fork once again.

"Everything and more. When I first saw you at the reception following your sister's fashion show, you took my breath away." He continued to watch me, and I felt the blood rise to my cheeks.

I also couldn't help the sensation of unease that began to fill me. No, he hadn't said or done anything remotely threatening, and yet once again I wondered how long he was going to play this game, of being passionate and romantic, but never requiring anything more of me than a kiss and the occasional caress. I also couldn't help wondering whether this was yet another one of his ploys, that toying with me in such a way satisfied him more than actually taking me to bed.

Well, if that was the case, he could continue to play cat and mouse for as long as he wished. The uncertainty was still far preferable to the alternative, of having to be intimate with him just to keep Silas alive.

I made myself look at the vampire, and

prayed I was a good enough actress that he wouldn't see anything except admiration and love in my eyes. "I'm glad you found me, then."

"Oh, yes. I knew I must have such a prize." He smiled, and I forced myself to smile in return, even though inwardly I writhed. A prize. Yes, something to be captured, and owned. Even if I had never met Silas, had never loved him, I knew that sort of comment would have prevented me from ever caring for Lucius Montfort. "You need someone who will appreciate you, not turn away from you because your gifts were something he couldn't accept."

Obviously, he was talking about Travis, the boyfriend—well, fiancé—who'd dumped me after my accident, once he realized my brain wasn't ever going to be exactly the same again. Yes, Travis was a jerk, but I'd gotten over it. Anyway, Silas did appreciate me, accepted my psychic talent as just another part of me, like my brown hair or hazel eyes. Moreover, my *gula* didn't expect me to be anything more than what I was. He didn't want anything from me, only wanted *me*. Maybe that was part of why I loved him, because of that acceptance. Talk about pure souls—his truly was.

But I couldn't talk about Silas. I had to pretend that he'd been relegated to a neglected corner of my brain, just as he'd been relegated to captivity in the wine cellar somewhere below my feet. When I was alone, then I could think of him, of the depths of his dark eyes, the way his heavy hair fell against his cheeks, of how strong he was, of how safe I'd felt in his arms. Around Lucius, I needed to act like Silas didn't exist, or I might betray how much I truly did care for him.

"Well, it seems I've found him—or he's found me," I said, and reached for my glass of Bordeaux.

"Yes," Lucius said firmly. "You have. Never forget that, Serena. We are meant to be together. The universe wants us to be together. Never doubt that."

"Oh, I don't," I told him, and smiled before taking a sip of wine. So the universe wanted us to be together? Considering everything I'd gone through because of the accident that had almost killed me and its aftermath, I had a few bones to pick with the universe, thank you very much. Anyway, Silas had been assigned to watch over me, had come to love me first, so if I really wanted to believe in the universe's wishes, I'd say that my Watcher had the original claim on my heart.

We were both quiet for a few moments after that, as I went back to my neglected *coq au vin* and Lucius poured himself more Bordeaux. The food really was excellent, and I wondered where he'd gotten it.

"I need to go to the store tomorrow," I said abruptly, and he raised an eyebrow.

"Indeed?"

"Well, I just thought I should tell you," I continued, knowing I must sound like an idiot. "So you can let Brian know. After the week I spent here, I don't have much left to eat at my place."

"Of course. It's a reasonable request."

His inflection was so neutral that I couldn't really tell what he might be thinking. I also worried that he might use my empty cupboards as an excuse to get me to return here. After all, why waste time and energy shopping when I could stay here at the mansion and have gourmet takeout brought to me every night?

Apparently the need to make my family think that his and my relationship was a perfectly normal one was more important than having me here at his side every waking moment, because Lucius seemed content to leave it at that. He went on to ask me where he thought my brother might set up his lab, and whether it would be a good idea to be introduced to the project manager as an investor in the project, so he might come visit when he wished.

I pointed out that he would have to time his

visits for after work hours, considering how he couldn't expose himself to the sun, and for a moment he looked almost disappointed. Then he brightened, however, and said, "I will request that your brother hire enough staff to have two shifts. That way, someone will always be working during the times that are more convenient for me to make an inspection."

In a way, that made more sense. Time was of the essence here. Having double shifts would allow the work to continue at a much faster pace. Cost wasn't a factor, so I doubted Jackson would raise any objections. For all I knew, he'd already thought of that kind of setup.

"I'm sure that won't be a problem," I said.

"Of course not," Lucius replied, and smiled. For some reason, his canine teeth looked very sharp in the glow of the candlelight. "Now that we have your brother on our side, nothing can stop us."

CHAPTER EIGHT

No sign of Michael St. John this evening. Which meant...what? That Lucius was staying in tonight, and therefore the younger vampire wouldn't have the opportunity to come down to the cellar and speak with his captive?

Most likely. That also meant Serena must be here as well, because Silas couldn't imagine that the vampire master would stay home alone, not when he had his prize to share his meal with him. What a counterfeit that was. Yes, to pass in regular company, vampires could eat and drink —and use the bathroom, to eliminate the waste their bodies couldn't really process—but the whole thing was a sham. Only one thing sustained them. Just one.

To occupy himself, Silas had experimented with pulling on the manacles that bound him to the wall. As he'd feared, they wouldn't budge at all—or rather, the steel bolts had been driven so deeply into the concrete that he couldn't get them loose, no matter how hard he tried. However, he'd felt the heavy cuffs on his wrists begin to slip up his hands. Maybe it was only that the air down here was so very cold, and so his hands and fingers were slightly shrunken compared to the state they'd been in when he was first brought to the cellar. Whatever the reason, he thought he might be able to pull his hands free, if he was given enough time to accomplish the task. He had to be careful, though, because if he yanked too roughly, the manacles would abrade his skin, and he would begin to bleed. The vampires would smell the blood.

And he really didn't want to think about what would happen after that.

Now, though, with the realization that Serena might be somewhere right over his head, Silas couldn't help yanking on the manacles once again. They bit into the widest part of his hands, just below his thumbs, but it did seem as if they'd moved a fraction of an inch. Or maybe that was only wishful thinking.

He liked to believe that they'd shifted. He imagined himself pulling free, slipping into *gula* form so he would be at his full strength, then roaring into Montfort's mansion. The vampire would be at his table, most likely, pretending to play the gracious host. And then Silas would burst on the scene, break off one of the legs from the dining room table, and plunge it into the vampire's heart. Serena would be free of her captor. Silas would take her and run, take her far away from here, all the way to the *gula* sanctuary in Northern California. They would be safe, free to live their lives.

A pretty fantasy. Maybe someday it would even come true. For the moment, however, he was still trapped here.

Shooting a baleful glance up at the ceiling — and by extension, at the house and its owner — Silas sat back down and began working on the manacles once again.

Lucius hadn't even accompanied me on the return trip to my condo. Seeming somewhat distracted, he'd kissed me good night, then had the brown-haired semivive drive me home. This behavior should have been a relief — after all, if Lucius didn't say goodbye at my door, then there wasn't much chance of his trying to push his way inside for a "nightcap" — but at the same time, I couldn't help being somewhat puzzled.

Well, I wouldn't brood on the situation. I'd survived another evening with him, and that was the important thing. When I checked my phone right before I began to get ready for bed, I saw a text from not-Brian.

Shopping at 2 o'clock?

Okay, I typed back. *Thanks.*

That at least was settled. I wondered whether I should have asked if he'd gotten any nibbles on his ad for a graphic designer, but I figured I could ask him when I saw him the next day.

Nothing from my brother. But he had a full plate, and I knew he'd get started on setting up the research facility soon enough. Even for someone with my brother's impressive resources, these sorts of things didn't happen overnight.

In my bed again, alone in my room. I was glad of the chance to be still, to be in the one place that was truly my own. I closed my eyes and breathed in.

And then….

The room couldn't grow hazy, because my eyes were already shut. However, from the rainbow shimmers that appeared against my closed eyelids, I realized I was about to have a vision, the first one in several days. Although some part of me was glad that I was lying down and not walking up the stairs or standing at the sink with an electric toothbrush stuck in my mouth, I still couldn't help tensing, worried that this new vision would only be a continuation of the horrible ones that had haunted me while I was being held captive at Lucius Montfort's mansion.

But the shimmers behind my eyelids turned bright and green, and I realized I was looking at a large grassy field dotted with white and pale purple wildflowers, the clearing ringed with tall pines. Overhead was a sky of the sort of deep, deep sapphire blue that you never saw in the L.A. basin. Against that sky waved an elaborate kite, all red and gold, in the shape of a Chinese dragon, with long red streamers that fluttered in the breeze.

I glanced down, and saw that the kite was held by a little dark-haired boy, maybe four or five. Really, the kite seemed too big for him, and yet he managed it well enough as he trotted along, giving the kite string a tug now and then to keep it on course.

"Maybe let out the string a little bit," came a female voice, and I turned to see a man and a woman sitting on a blanket, a large picnic basket resting between them.

Not just any man and woman.

Silas and me.

I was wearing a loose white sleeveless blouse and jeans, and Silas had on one of his ubiquitous

T-shirts, although this one was in a sky-blue shade, a color far lighter than anything else I'd ever seen him wear. The fresh breeze blew a strand of his overlong hair in his face, and he pushed it away. He was smiling, though, and looked more relaxed than the intense man I knew.

Although I'd never seen this place before, I knew where it must be. Up in Humboldt County, outside a little town named Fortuna. The *gula* compound, or someplace very close by. Silas and me together.

Watching our son.

I hadn't heard my vision-self call his name. Maybe that was for the best, so we wouldn't be influenced when the time came. But oh, he was such a beautiful child, with Silas' night-dark hair and my hazel eyes, tall and sturdy, happy and healthy. And he was with us, which meant the *gula* blood had bred true. We'd been allowed to keep him. He hadn't been sent away to be raised by strangers.

"Watch me, Mommy!" the little boy cried, and began running with the kite, dragging it along behind him. As I watched, I worried he might stumble on the uneven ground, might trip and fall, since all his attention was fixed on the kite and not where his feet were going. But he charged ahead steady and sure, strong little legs moving in a blur.

In the vision, I laughed and praised him, and Silas leaned in to pull me close, to give me a fierce hug. Shimmers danced behind my eyelids, and the vision faded. When I opened my eyes, I realized I'd been weeping, tears trailing down from the corners of my eyes to dampen the hair at my temples.

I wanted it to be true. God, how did I want it to be true.

And yet....

Which was my future? The nightmare of the visions where I'd been with Lucius, or this seemingly picture-perfect family trio, in a future where clearly both Silas and I had survived, and been lucky enough to have a *gula* son.

I sat up in bed and rubbed at my eyes, wiping away most of the tears. The room wasn't completely dark, because some faint illumination from the little salt lamp nightlight in the bathroom made its way in here. My hand went out and rested on the empty part of the bed to the right of me, as though searching for the man who should be sleeping there. Crazy, I knew, because Silas had never actually been in this bed with me. Still, right then I wanted him more than ever. Needed him.

After clenching the sheets in my hand, I let go and brought my knees to my chest, hugged them against me. Even though the room was warm, a shiver went through my body. Never before had I experienced a set of visions that showed me two different versions of the same future. I didn't know what to make of it, except to think that perhaps everything hinged on whether or not Silas was freed. No, that didn't make sense; I didn't want to believe the abandoned woman I'd seen at the party with Lucius in one of my visions would have forgotten herself so entirely that she would allow her protector and former lover to be killed. But what would have made that alternate Serena go with the vampire, rather than the *gula* she loved?

As with everything else in my life, I had far too many questions and not enough answers. I pulled in a breath, recalling the fresh green of the meadow, the way the sunlight had danced on my son's dark hair, the strength of Silas' embrace. For now, I'd have to let that be enough. I could cling to that image, pray for that moment of togetherness to be my future.

Maybe it would be enough to give me the strength to get through whatever else might come next.

〜

As promised, not-Brian came over to get me at promptly two o'clock the next day. I was ready, wearing one of my favorite embroidered tops and a pair of faded jeans and some flats. No matter what, I had to look normal, just in case I ran into anyone I knew. A remote possibility, since most of the people still in my circle of acquaintances would be at work at the time of day, or—in the case of my mother's friends— probably weren't the type you'd bump into at Trader Joe's. Not that they didn't like the store's offerings, only that they had people to take care of that sort of thing for them.

"Any luck with your ad?" I asked as we pulled out of the garage beneath the condo Brian and Lewis shared.

"Yes," not-Brian replied. "I had three good candidates. Funny—I can't do the work myself, but I can look at someone else's work and determine whether it would be a good fit."

"I'm glad to hear that." Had he hung on to that ability because he hadn't been a semivive long enough to completely lose sight of who he'd been, or did certain parts of the brain survive, even under the influence of a vampire's foreign antibodies? It would be something else interesting to research, although I doubted the lab my brother planned to establish would focus on anything along those lines. No, the first order of the day would be seeing if vampire blood could cure my niece.

Well, that's the story Lucius wants Jackson to believe, I thought as we cruised west on Cordova Avenue. *But I'm pretty sure the research on how human blood affects vampires is going to be given just as much weight.*

Humans made immortal by vampire blood. Vampires given the ability to walk in the sunlight, to procreate, thanks to a concentrated serum of the necessary factors in human blood.

Maybe it was an echo of the vision I'd had the night before, but I couldn't help wondering what a child of mine with Lucius would look like. Had he always had that pale hair, or had it turned white as the years and decades rolled by? Leticia's hair was fair as well, but it was an ordinary light blonde, not Lucius' albino white. Tristan and Michael both had dark hair, true. Neither of them was as old as Lucius, though.

You'll never find out what such a child would look like, I told myself, *because you're not going to have one. You'll have a son with Silas, a boy with his father's dark hair and your eyes.*

If I kept telling myself that, would it someday come true?

Not-Brian pulled into the parking lot at Trader Joe's. Although it was a little early for people to be off work, or for moms to swing by after they'd picked up their children from school, the place was still fairly crowded, and we had to take a space at the far end of the lot. Not that I minded; it was a beautiful, mild spring day, so spending a little extra time outdoors was fine by me.

As we began to get out of the car, not-Brian put a hand on the hip pocket of his jeans and grimaced. "I can't believe it—I forgot my wallet. And I told Lewis I would pick up a few things for us."

"I can get them for you," I offered, but he shook his head.

"No, then I'd have to explain why they weren't purchased using our debit card. I—" He broke off there, looking vaguely embarrassed. In fact, he appeared so much like the old Brian for a few seconds that I wanted to put my arms around him and give him a hug. I didn't, of course; that wasn't really my old friend standing in front of me, no matter how much the semivive might look like him. He went on, "Sometimes I forget things. I try to hide it from Lewis, but I can tell he's starting to wonder what's going on."

Gently, I put a hand on not-Brian's arm. "Then why don't you run back and get your wallet? It's going to take me longer than that to get everything I need." Which was only the truth. Going roundtrip from TJ's to our condo complex would take roughly fifteen minutes at the most.

"I'm not sure…."

"It's fine, Brian. I'm just going to shop. My cupboard is bare." I offered him what I hoped was a reassuring smile, and he glanced at the store, then back at the car.

"If you're sure…."

"I am. I think the only thing you really need to worry about is getting a parking place when you come back."

That remark made him smile as well, although there was something lopsided about the expression, as if he didn't have quite as good a grip on his facial muscles as he used to. "All right. Just—just make sure you don't go anywhere."

"I won't go any farther than the liquor section. I swear."

He appeared to wrestle with himself for a moment more, then nodded. "Okay. I'll be back in ten minutes."

"Don't speed until you have your driver's license with you."

No reply, just a little hitch of his shoulders before he headed back to his car. I'd already retrieved my reusable shopping bags from the trunk of Brian's Audi, so I went on toward the store's entrance.

Most rational people would have thought that was my cue to bolt...but how could I, when I knew doing anything so obvious would only prove to Lucius that I'd been stringing him along, that I didn't care about him at all?

Maybe one day I'd have the opportunity to tell Lucius Montfort exactly what I thought of him, but this wasn't that day.

Instead, I started to make my way through the store, gathering up all the items I needed — berries and yogurt for breakfast, salad fixings, a few frozen meals in case I didn't end up going to the mansion for dinner every night. As I headed toward the dairy section, thinking I could use some cheese for snacking, a large blond individual got in my way.

"Excuse me," I said, angling my shopping cart so I could maneuver around him. Tripping over people was sort of an occupational hazard at Trader Joe's.

"Serena Quinn."

Startled, I looked up at him. Bright blue eyes bored down into my face. He was handsome, with almost model-perfect looks. Certainly someone I'd remember meeting, even if he wasn't really my type. I'd always gone for the darker guys. "Do I know you?"

He smiled. "We met online the other night. My name is Felix."

That revelation made me want to gasp out loud, but I knew better than to do anything that might attract attention. Right now, we just looked like a couple of acquaintances who'd bumped into each other at the store. Keeping my voice down, I asked, "What are you doing here?"

"I was sent. We're getting ready."

I glanced around, but luckily, no one seemed to be making a beeline for the dairy section right then. Still in an undertone, I said, "To bust out Silas?"

"Yes."

"So you know where he is."

"Yes."

"How?"

"I'm not at liberty to go into that."

He might have been a *gula,* but he talked more like a Navy SEAL. Looked like one, too, with his short-cropped fair hair and the muscles that bulged out from under his T-shirt. "When are you going to rescue him?"

"Soon. I can't tell you more than that. My superiors wanted me to see for myself that you're all right." Those shocking blue eyes scanned me up and down, but there was nothing prurient about his regard, more like he was checking for any obvious signs of abuse. "I'm surprised to see you here by yourself. I wasn't expecting to be able to approach you."

"My semivive babysitter forgot his wallet. I told him to go get it, that all I'd be doing is shopping anyway."

"He trusts you that much?"

"Apparently, everyone thinks I'm madly in love with Lucius Montfort."

"But you're not."

"No. I'm just doing what I have to in order to keep Silas alive. The sooner you can free him, the sooner I can stop playing kissy-face with that ghoul."

To my surprise, Felix chuckled. "I can see why Silas likes you. Well, we'll do our best, Serena. Now, though, I think I had better disappear before your semivive comes back. Try to act as if nothing untoward has occurred."

"No problem." And it wouldn't be. My heart might be racing at the prospect of Silas regaining his freedom in the very near future, but lately I'd become the queen of pretense. Not-Brian would never notice anything.

Felix inclined his head toward me, then walked on by, headed in the opposite direction from where I'd just come. I gathered my breath and went over to the liquor section, thinking that it couldn't hurt to have a couple of bottles of wine on hand. Or maybe more like five or six.

That was where Brian found me a few minutes later, apparently weighing the merits of two different bottles of pinot grigio. He glanced down at my nearly full shopping cart and nodded, as though reassuring himself that all I could have been doing for the past ten minutes was grocery shopping.

"Hey," I said. "I'm almost done. Do you want me to just hang out here while you get the things you need?"

"Sure. It won't take me very long."

"Sounds good."

I smiled, and he went off toward the frozen foods section. Then I let out a breath, and clutched the handles of my shopping cart.

Help was coming. I only had to hang on for a little while longer...and pray that Silas would be all right.

CHAPTER NINE

AFTER I RETURNED HOME AND PUT AWAY MY groceries, I got out my phone to check for any messages. For some reason, I was halfway expecting to hear from Felix. He'd been able to message me on my computer, so I didn't see why he couldn't send a text to my phone.

Nothing from him, though. There was, however, a voicemail from Jackson.

A fairly lengthy one, actually, letting me know that a combo office/lab space had been rented out in Rancho Cucamonga, and that a project manager was already on board and taking care of the rest of the hires. They should be up and running within the next few days. He'd need a sample of Lucius' blood, and, ideally, the blood of all the vampires, so that their similarities and differences could begin to be logged and tracked.

That was moving fast, even for Jackson. But I thought then of my niece's pale face and listless behavior, and a chill went through me. We didn't have a lot of time.

My brother ended the call by saying, "I have to go back to Washington tomorrow. However, I've told the project manager—Shelby Gutierrez—that you'll be my point person here in Southern California. Go ahead and get in touch with her when you have the samples. I figured you'd want to handle that part of it, since I can't really see Mr. Montfort allowing outsiders to come to his house and collect blood samples." A pause, and then Jackson added, "If you could, I'd really appreciate it if you could stop by and spend some time with Bethany. She's having a hard time with this, but there's a vote on Thursday in Washington that I can't miss. Take care."

I set down the phone, taking note of the time. Three-thirty. A while yet before Lucius would send the car to pick me up. I didn't like the idea of having to collect the vampires' blood, but I knew Jackson had been right about that. No way would Lucius allow an LVN or other medical personnel inside his house to handle the task. All right…how hard could it be? I could always look up the technique on YouTube.

We'd need supplies, though. Needles and syringes…rubber straps to increase the blood flow to the areas where I'd be collecting the samples…alcohol swabs…culture bottles. I really didn't feel like going to a medical supply store; after my accident and extended hospital stay, I'd had enough of that sort of thing to last me a lifetime.

I could ask Brian to go, however. It wasn't as if he could refuse me, not if I told him the supplies were specifically intended for a project of Lucius'. And his leaving me alone in Trader Joe's proved that I wasn't about to bolt, even if my babysitter went out of range for a while.

A text seemed easier. I composed a list of the necessary items, then sent it over to not-Brian, with the addendum that I was feeling a little tired but knew I'd be up late at Lucius' place, and would he mind terribly if he ran the errand without me?

I got a "no problem" text only a minute later. Good. One other thing taken care of.

After that, I didn't have much to do except wait. I checked my email, only to find that my flaky client had postponed yet again. Thank God. In the back of my mind I'd been trying to come up with excuses for blowing him off until all this was settled, but now I didn't have to worry about it. Yes, maybe I should have cut him loose anyway—it wasn't like I needed the money—and yet I couldn't quite bring myself to do that. Pretending that I had clients and work to do made me feel as though I was still somewhat connected to the real world, even if tenuously at best. If I admitted to myself that, one way or another, I probably wouldn't be taking on another freelance project ever again, then I'd commit myself to a life separate from everyone else, whether as Lucius' captive lover, or Silas' partner in the world of the *gula*.

About forty-five minutes later, Brian dropped by with the supplies. I could tell he was curious, but, like a good little semivive, he wasn't going to ask questions about his master's private projects. A pang went through me as I contrasted his current behavior with the old Brian, the real Brian, who always had what seemed like a hundred questions about everything.

"And now I have to get back and pretend I was working all day," he said. "Luckily, my subcontractor sent me some comps just before you texted me, so I have something to put on the screen and pretend is mine."

His tone was almost rueful, and I could tell

on some level the subterfuge bothered him, even if the semivive part of his brain knew it was necessary in order to keep fooling Lewis for as long as possible.

"I hope it all looks good."

"I think it does," he said. "But I want to take another look at everything before I submit any feedback. Good afternoon."

He let himself out then, and I locked the door behind him. Was it that I had simply gotten used to the differences in not-Brian's personality, or had he somehow become more like his old self? I guessed it must be the former, since Silas had made it sound as though the semivives would continue to deteriorate a little more each week and month as time wore on. Lord knows the ones working for Lucius around his property didn't seem to have much personality at all.

It wasn't the sort of question I could ask the vampire. I also didn't know if there was any chance of a semivive returning to himself once the vampire who'd made him was killed. Maybe a stake to Lucius Montfort's heart wouldn't just solve my problems, but Brian's as well. I prayed that would be the case. The last thing I wanted was for the semivives to perish at the same time as their master. They didn't deserve that.

Since the time when I'd be in his company

was quickly approaching, I pushed those thoughts about Lucius out of my mind. I couldn't be anything except helpful and sweet and encouraging around him, and that sort of façade was a lot more difficult to maintain when you were secretly contemplating different ways to drive a sharpened stick into someone's heart.

I also couldn't let myself dwell for too long on the imminent attack by the *gula* in order to rescue Silas. How many of them were even in the area? Clearly, the higher-ups in the Watchers organization had decided that they needed reinforcements, or I doubted Felix would have been sent down here to Southern California.

Enough of that. I couldn't seem nervous or fidgety or preoccupied. I still had an hour, so I spent it watching YouTube videos of people drawing blood. Good thing I wasn't the squeamish sort. The sight of blood had never really bothered me, although I'd seen enough of my own spilled during the accident that I was okay with never repeating the experience.

Then came the knock at the door, and the brown-haired semivive waiting to drive me to the mansion. I took my bag of supplies with me, and once again followed him down to the Mercedes. Fifteen minutes later, I was at the mansion.

This time it wasn't Lucius waiting for me, but Michael St. John. He offered me a smile I didn't believe for a second, then said, "Good evening, Serena. You're looking very lovely tonight."

Which was a pile of crap, and, from the ironic smile Michael wore, he knew that as well as I did. I'd gotten so caught up in watching the YouTube videos that I hadn't refreshed my lip gloss or even brushed my hair, and I still had on the same jeans and embroidered Mexican blouse I'd worn to Trader Joe's. Oh, well. Lucius would have to learn that I wasn't going to "dress for dinner" every damn night.

So I only smiled sweetly in return and said, "Thank you, Michael. But where's Lucius?"

"He's in the library. Come along."

I followed him, even though I knew the way well enough. As we walked, I wondered what had Lucius so preoccupied that he hadn't been there to greet me. Or maybe this was another one of his subtle little mind games, his way of showing me that I wasn't quite as important to him as I might think.

Whatever. I'd share Jackson's news with him, and explain about the blood samples. Lucius should be pleased with how quickly things were progressing, and I wouldn't worry about the rest.

"I haven't seen Tristan or Leticia lately," I remarked to Michael.

He shot me a sardonic glance. "Lucius told

them to stay out of the way. He didn't want them upsetting you."

"That was very thoughtful of him."

"I suppose. Not that they need much of a reason to make themselves scarce. They always did prefer hunting to hanging around the house."

So I'd heard. I wouldn't comment on Michael St. John's remark, mostly because talking about the two other vampires only made my suppressed rage come welling up again. I hid it as best as I could around Lucius, and of course I couldn't say anything about the two vampires to Jackson, since he and the rest of my family still believed that a would-be robber had killed Vanessa. And as much as my brother wanted to find a cure for his daughter, I kind of doubted he'd be okay with being in bed with the person connected to her real murderers.

We stopped at the open door to the library. "Here she is," said Michael, quite unnecessarily, since Lucius had looked up as soon as we approached.

"Thank you, Michael. Good evening, Serena. And what is that in the bag? A present?"

"Sort of," I replied, then cast a sideways glance at the younger vampire, who still stood next to me.

Of course Lucius immediately picked up on

the hint. "That will be all, Michael. Thank you again."

From the way his brows drew together, I could tell that Michael St. John wasn't exactly thrilled about being dismissed like one of the help. He didn't protest, however, but only nodded and said, "Sure," then took off down the hallway.

Even so, I closed the library doors behind me before I approached Lucius and set the bag down on the table at the center of the room. "I heard from my brother."

"Yes?"

Nothing in Lucius' expression indicated anything except mild curiosity. And standing there, being that close to him—it was strange, because only a few hours earlier I'd been thinking murderous thoughts about him, and now he seemed all too real, the silvery eyes focused on my face, his pale hair falling loose onto his shoulders. It was so much easier to contemplate killing him in the abstract than to do the same thing when he stood right next to me.

Did I really want him dead? Or did I simply want him to leave Silas and me alone?

"Jackson already has the research facility leased," I said quickly, directing my attention to the bag so I could pull out the items within and set them on the table. "He also has a project manager. She's overseeing the rest of the hiring process. Because all that's getting set up this week, he said we should go ahead and get blood samples. Yours, and the rest of your vampires."

Judging by the way Lucius frowned slightly, I could tell he wasn't thrilled by that request. "All of us? Why?"

"I assume because the researchers will want as large a sample pool as possible," I told him. "Or at least, that's my best guess, based on a couple of years of college biology. I'm no expert. But it makes sense to have samples from all of you so the technicians can see if human blood interacts with all of you in the same way. Conversely, it may be there's enough variance in your blood samples that the antibodies from one of you might make a more effective serum for curing cancer...or making someone immortal."

He smiled then, and seemed to relax slightly. "Of course. I am not one who is well versed in the sciences, but it does make sense that there might be minor variations among us." A pause, and the silver-bright eyes glinted down into mine. "You will be the one to draw our blood?"

"Yes," I said. "I mean, Jackson didn't think you'd want an outsider coming here. I've read up on it, and watched some videos."

"And you don't mind?"

Well, of course I minded. If I wanted to

spend my day drawing blood, then I would've studied to be an RN...if my science and math courses had been up to snuff. But I'd already agreed to this, so I didn't see any point in delaying. "I told him I'd do it. It's all right. Just don't hate me if I hit the wrong vein or something."

"I'm sure you'll do fine." Another of those hesitations. "No, I wasn't thinking so much of the actual act of drawing the blood, but that you'll be forced to have close contact with Leticia and Tristan while doing so."

I'd already confronted that unpleasant reality, so I merely shrugged. "I can't say I'm happy about it, but it needs to be done. I know you've told them to stay away from me, and I appreciate that. But I also can't let my anger get in the way of trying to find a cure for Addie."

"No, I suppose you wouldn't. You do tend to put everyone else first."

His tone had softened, and the way his eyes held mine made me want to look away. I couldn't, though. I had to gaze back at him and pretend I wanted nothing more than to be there in that moment, standing close and basking in his praise.

"I'm not sure my mother would agree with that statement," I said, summoning a smile that I hoped looked more or less natural. "But anyway,

I suppose I can start with you, and then Michael, since he's here."

"I will summon Tristan and Leticia."

"Like you do the semivives?"

"It's not exactly the same thing, but yes, I can reach out to them, mind to mind, and tell them to come home." His eyes closed briefly, and his head tilted to one side, as if he listened to voices only he could hear. "They are far away—in Hollywood, to be precise—but they should be back within the hour."

"That's fine. That'll give me time to do you and Michael." Lucius' eyebrows lifted, and I added hastily, "Get your blood drawn, I mean."

"I assumed that was what you meant. Well, let us get started."

He pulled off the dark jacket he wore and tossed it onto a nearby armchair. Deftly and quickly, he removed the cufflink from his shirt cuff and then rolled up the sleeve. Watching him, I couldn't help but be uncomfortably reminded of when he'd done the same thing in my vision of that future party, even though now I'd be taking his blood rather than adding something to it.

His arm was very pale. I could see the blue veins standing out in the crook of his elbow, although they weren't as prominent as they'd been in my vision.

Well, give it time, I told myself as I got out

the rubber strap and tied it off just above his elbow. *A few years of administering serum shots, and I'm sure he'll end up looking like an extra from* Trainspotting.

It was good that I could spot his veins so easily, though, as it made the task at hand a little less fraught. I tapped my finger against his skin, feeling how cool it was under my fingertip. It seemed strange and somehow intimate to touch him there. We'd kissed, and once he'd lain on top of me while he forced his mouth on mine, but we'd always been fully clothed. The only places we'd touched one another's skin had been on our hands, or our faces.

But I didn't want to think about that. Instead, I worried my bottom lip with my teeth as I cleaned his arm with an alcohol pad, then took one of the hypodermics and pressed it against his skin. Just the slightest bit of resistance, and then the fine needle sank into his vein. Immediately the syringe began to fill with deep garnet-colored liquid.

It looked like normal blood to me. I didn't know why I'd expected it to shimmer, or maybe be purple, or green.

He's not Mr. Spock, I thought wryly as I pulled out the needle and immediately put a cotton pad on Lucius' arm. *Vampires don't bleed green.*

"Can you hold that while I put this down and get some first aid tape?" I asked.

"Certainly." Lucius pressed several fingers against the cotton pad. I honestly hadn't been sure how vampire blood would react to this sort of procedure, whether it would continue to flow even when pressure was applied to the site of the wound, but I didn't see any signs of it soaking the cotton.

I plunged the hypodermic into the sample bottle and pushed down on the syringe to empty it. Then I picked up the tape and pulled off a few pieces so I could secure the cotton pad to Lucius' arm. After I was done with that, I got out one of the labels not-Brian had bought for me, wrote "Lucius Montfort, 3/9/2017" on it, and affixed it to the bottle.

"Very efficient," he remarked as he watched me put the sample of blood into a little padded plastic case. "One would think you'd done this many times before."

"Thank YouTube. God knows I've given blood enough times, but it's a whole different deal when you're not on the receiving end."

"Still. You impress me, Serena."

An unwelcome flush touched my cheeks, but I busied myself with getting out a fresh hypodermic and syringe so I could take Michael's blood next. "Well, thank you. Maybe I have a backup calling in case the whole copyediting thing doesn't work out."

Lucius began to roll his sleeve back down. "My dear, you didn't need those copyediting jobs before, and you certainly don't need them now."

Something about those words rankled. "Maybe 'need' isn't the right word. I never wanted to be a lady who lunches, like my mother. I don't want to be some idle rich girl."

A pause as he reinserted the white gold and diamond cufflink into the sleeve of his dark shirt. Then he said. "You are certainly not idle. Your visions have helped people. And now—now you are assisting with a project that could change the world."

Too bad there was the very distinct possibility I could change it for the worse. Yes, I wanted a cure for Addison, but I didn't want to think about all the people who might be forced to contribute blood to give vampires a chance to live a normal life, nor the way the one percent might buy their way into immortality. To be honest, the older I got, the less comfortable I felt with my family's wealth. Jackson spoke like a man of the people when he was running for office, but he still hadn't hesitated when it came to using his own considerable resources to get this research project up and running. It wasn't as if Joe Blow down the street could have managed the same thing.

"You're quiet," Lucius said.

"Am I? I guess I was just thinking about the research facility," I lied. "Tomorrow I'll need to meet with the project manager, get these samples over to her."

"Speaking of which, here's your next patient."

I glanced over at the door to see Michael St. John leaning up against the jamb, looking as if he hadn't a care in the world. Maybe he didn't. Lucius hadn't given any sign that he'd summoned the younger vampire, but I supposed he didn't need to. Just a little thought bat signal sent out, and all of the vampire master's fledglings would come running.

Michael's gaze moved toward the table, to all the supplies I had laid out. "Playing doctor?"

"Serena has need of a sample of your blood," Lucius said. "Please roll up your sleeve, Michael."

One dark eyebrow lifted, but the vampire did as instructed and came toward the table where we stood. As he walked, he unbuttoned his cuff and pushed up his sleeve. His skin was pale, too, although nowhere near as white as Lucius'.

"I didn't know you were a nurse," Michael remarked as he held out his arm to me.

"I'm not," I said shortly. Something about Michael St. John always seemed to rub me the wrong way, like he was trying desperately to find something to mock about everyone and everything he encountered. Maybe it was just a coping mechanism, but I found it tiring.

His veins weren't as easy to locate as Lucius' had been. I tapped here and there on the inner crook of his elbow, trying to ignore the smirk he wore. Finally, I was able to find a vein that looked viable, so I tapped it again for good measure before poking the hypodermic through his skin.

He winced slightly. I noticed how he didn't watch as the syringe filled with blood. A vampire, squeamish at the sight of blood? Or maybe it was just his blood in particular, rather than blood in general.

At any rate, Michael didn't speak as I finished taking the sample, then handed off the syringe to Lucius so I could place a cotton pad on his arm and tape it down. I noticed that Lucius went ahead and emptied the sample into another bottle, then placed a label on it and wrote down Michael's information in block caps as precise as an architect's. Good. One less thing for me to do.

"Anything else?" Michael asked as he rolled

his sleeve down. "Urine or stool samples?" A sly smile. "Semen?"

I tilted my head in annoyance, even as Lucius said smoothly, "No, Michael, that's all for now."

"Good. Because losing that blood's made me a little hungry."

"Not tonight, Michael." Although Lucius' tone was mild enough, I could see the way his silver eyes narrowed at his fledgling.

Michael put a hand to his chest. "You wound me, Lucius. I know we're still on lockdown. I was thinking more of a double-double and some animal fries."

A curl of the lip, and Lucius said to me, "Michael has never quite gotten over his addiction to In N Out."

"Well, I can't really blame him for that," I said. "Have you ever had a double-double?"

"Of course not. I may eat regular food from time to time, but that diet certainly doesn't include fast food."

"You don't know what you're missing," I said with a grin.

"I've tried to tell him that, too, but he never listens."

"Enough, Michael. That will be all."

With a negligent lift of his shoulders, Michael turned and left the room. Lucius shook his head.

"Sometimes it is very difficult to tell when he is being serious and when he is simply trying to bait me."

"I can imagine," I remarked. "But I wasn't joking about the In N Out burgers."

"You don't like the food I have brought here?"

He looked slightly wounded, so I decided that was a good time to move closer to him, to take his hand. "I like it very much. You have excellent taste, and obviously know all the good restaurants in town. No, it's just that some-times...sometimes it's fun to go slumming, you know?"

"You would like to do this sometime? Go out in the car and get a burger?"

The thought of Lucius Montfort, with his aristocratic features and elegant dark suits, sitting in an In N Out burger while surrounded by college students and families with kids running around, made me chuckle slightly. "If you don't mind eating in the car. I suppose you could have one of your semivives vacuum it out afterward."

This suggestion didn't seem to sit well with him, because he frowned. "I am not sure about that. Why don't I have one of my servants go to get these burgers and bring them back to the house?"

"Because the closest In N Out is way up on Foothill Boulevard. The food would be cold by the time it got back here." He seemed discomfited by that explanation, so I went on, "It's fine. We don't have to have a burger."

"Good, because I sent one of my semivives for Thai this evening. I thought it would be a good change of pace."

I couldn't argue with that...especially if sticky mango rice was on the menu.

"That sounds fine," I told him. "And probably much healthier. When is —"

I'd been about to ask, *When is it going to get here?*, but stopped because I heard footsteps at the door. Looking away from Lucius, I saw Tristan McVey and Leticia Carver standing there, arms crossed, both of them wearing the kind of scowls I wouldn't want to meet in a dark alley.

"Well, we're here," Leticia said ungraciously. "What do you want?"

If it weren't that I knew going up against a vampire was a very bad idea for a mortal, I would have charged across the room and tried to slap that frown right off her perfect face. I clenched my hands into fists at my sides, even as Lucius said,

"I want you here to do *my* bidding, Leticia. My apologies for interrupting your hunt, but since I know you are merely prospecting and not going in for the kill quite yet, I don't think I have caused you too much of an inconvenience."

Tristan, whom I'd barely heard utter ten words in my presence, put in, "It is an inconvenience. But you are the master. We do as you say."

"Yes, you do. Serena here needs samples of your blood. Tristan, you first."

The vampire looked from his master to me and back to Lucius. "Why?"

"Because I command it. Now, come here."

A corner of Tristan's lip lifted. A snarl, or his attempt at a crooked grin? Either way, I was very glad I wasn't facing him alone. He approached me, shrugging out of his leather jacket as he did so. No sleeve to roll up here; he wore a dark gray T-shirt under the jacket.

I didn't dare meet his gaze as I retrieved a third hypodermic and syringe for his sample, sure that he would see the blazing hatred in my eyes if I looked at him directly. Like Michael, Tristan was pale, but his was the pallor of someone who never saw the sun, not Lucius' near-albino complexion. Tristan's veins were a little more prominent than Michael's, however. A function of the vampire's age? I didn't know, and supposed it didn't matter much. I was simply glad that I didn't have to spend much time hunting for a likely spot to poke with the needle. The entire procedure was over and done with in less than a minute. This time Lucius also stepped in to take the syringe away from me and deposit its contents in a sample bottle so I could apply the cotton to Tristan's arm.

The dark-haired vampire moved away as soon as he could. Lucius looked up from the syringe, which he'd just placed in the box next to the vials containing his own and Michael St. John's blood. "Now you, Leticia."

Her lower lip pushed out slightly. She looked for all the world like a rebellious teenager being told to do her chores. Well, a teenager with the body of a bikini model, I supposed; just like the last time I'd seen her, she was wearing a tight-fitting dress that revealed an insane amount of leg, only this dress was a shimmery dark silver rather than red. "Do I have to?"

"Since I just told you that you did, yes, you have to. Come here."

She stepped closer. I'd never been this near her, and now I could see the utter perfection of her fair skin, the long lashes coated with mascara. Her hair hung nearly to her waist, fine and pale as cornsilk.

And how I wished I could grab one of the nearby chairs, break off a leg, and stab it through her chest. I wasn't sure why the sight of her enraged me so much more than Tristan's presence had, except that there was something about her attitude which seemed inherently hostile and yet at the same time superior, whereas Tristan appeared mostly bored.

Unfortunately, it was not the time to seek revenge for Vanessa's murder. One day…maybe. Once he was free, Silas would probably be all too happy to wipe this nest of vampires off the face of the earth. For now, though, I still had to play the role of Lucius' complicit partner.

"Let's try your left arm," I said, and she thrust it toward me, nearly striking me in the chest.

Lucius said mildly, "Play nice, Leticia."

She let out a huff and didn't reply, only stood there as she stared into the middle distance, purposely not meeting my gaze. Fine by me. I didn't want to have to look her in the eyes. And I didn't mind smacking her arm a little harder than I needed to in order to make a vein pop up. Her mouth tightened, but she didn't say anything, no doubt not wanting to risk her master's ire.

Another vial of deep red blood, and I was done. Lucius took it from me and wrote out the final label as I taped some cotton to her arm.

"How long do I have to keep this thing on?" she asked, looking down at the crook of her elbow in disgust.

"Until it stops clotting," I said. "Judging by how quickly everyone else has bounced back, no more than ten minutes. It won't get in the way of your clubbing."

"Like you'd know anything about that," Leticia retorted. Her scornful gaze took in my faded jeans and loose blouse, my almost nonexistent makeup.

"Probably not," I admitted. "I generally have better things to do with my time."

"Ladies," Lucius cut in. "Thank you, Leticia. And Tristan. That will be all. You can go back to your…clubbing."

"We will," Tristan said. "Come along, Leticia. We still have most of the night ahead of us."

They went out, Leticia with a decided flounce that would have earned her a lecture on her attitude if she'd been my mother's daughter. I had to laugh at myself. The thought of my mother getting in Leticia's face was somewhat amusing, but I knew it would never happen. Thank God. I didn't want that vicious bloodsucker going anywhere near anyone else in my family.

"What now?" Lucius asked. He held the box with its bottles of blood in both hands, as if it was some kind of royal present.

"That needs to be refrigerated. We can store it in the fridge here, and then I'll take it home with me and put it in the refrigerator there. I'll have to put it in a cooler when I transport it to the lab, since it's probably at least a half-hour drive from here." I paused, frowning slightly. "Jackson told me it was in Rancho Cucamonga, but he didn't give me the exact address. He's kind of distracted. But I'll text him and get it from him."

"Good. In the meantime, let us take care of our precious cargo."

Lucius led me out of the library and down the hall, toward the kitchen. The last time I'd been in this part of the house, I'd demanded that not-Brian take me to see Silas. Had Brian ever told his master about my request? I didn't know, and I didn't dare ask. And I made sure to not even glance at the door to the wine cellar as we headed toward the refrigerator.

In there were packs and packs of blood. I tried not to look at them as I set the little box with its own vials of blood on the top shelf. Actually, the interior of the refrigerator was strangely schizophrenic, since on one side was all that blood—clearly purchased from a blood bank—and on the other much more prosaic offerings like cartons of yogurt, a package of bagels, a six-pack of Diet Coke, and a few more odds and ends.

Semivives drank Diet Coke? Who knew?

I didn't say anything, though, as Lucius shut the refrigerator door. "Well, that's done. I hope the procedure didn't ruin your appetite, since our dinner has arrived."

"No, I'm still hungry."

His eyes met mine. "Good. As am I."

CHAPTER TEN

SHE WAS UP THERE. SILAS KNEW IT. HIS KIND had a decent internal clock, and so even though the cellar had no windows, he knew that night had fallen, and that meant Lucius would have summoned Serena to his presence.

Silas didn't know which was worse…the long hours of grinding boredom, or the knowledge that the woman he loved was so close physically, but might as well be on the dark side of the moon for all he could reach out to touch her.

The thought made him tug at the manacles again. He'd stopped earlier today because he knew he was coming dangerously close to breaking the skin, but now he couldn't seem to prevent himself from straining against the uncaring steel. He had to get out of here.

Pain was something he could ignore. What

he couldn't ignore was the blood that began to trickle down over his hands. He stopped then, swearing under his breath. There was nothing to wipe away the cursed liquid except the ragged jeans he wore, or the thin blanket he'd been given to sleep on. He decided to use the blanket, simply because if he did somehow manage to get away, his unkempt appearance would cause enough consternation without him sporting bloodstained Levi's as well.

The door opened, then closed again. Michael St. John paused at the entrance to the cellar and shook his head. "Bad move, Silas. You're lucky that Lucius is otherwise occupied—and that I just ate, or that blood might be just a little distracting."

"Lucius let you hunt?"

"Hardly." St. John came a little farther into the room, stuck his hands in his jeans pockets, and grinned. "I decided to treat myself to a double-double at In N Out. That was almost as good as having a pint of someone's O-negative."

Just the mere thought of a double-stacked cheeseburger made Silas' stomach growl. They weren't precisely starving him, but a few pieces of cheese and some bread weren't exactly enough to satisfy.

"Sounds like I should have gotten one for

you, too," the vampire said, still grinning. "How thoughtless of me."

"What do you want? You really need to get a hobby if the best thing you can think of to do with your spare time is come down here and talk to me."

A shake of the head, and Michael St. John remarked, "Well, I thought you might be interested in what Lucius is up to. I got a little more clarification this evening. But if you're not, I can head upstairs, binge-watch some *Walking Dead* or something."

Silas refrained from commenting that the vampire should know all about being one of the walking dead. If St. John really was in possession of valuable information, the last thing Silas should do was quash any attempts to divulge said information. In truth, he should be thanking God Michael hated his master so much that he was willing to give his supposed enemies the particulars of his plotting. "So what is he up to?"

"I'm still not sure what his end game is, but tonight he got blood samples from all three of us —Tristan and Leticia and me. I bumped into the other two while they were leaving, and they were *not* happy."

Blood samples? What was Lucius doing with samples of vampire blood? "Was Serena with Lucius while this was going on?"

"Yes. She was actually the one who drew the blood."

Silas frowned. If asked, he would never have thought that taking blood samples was in Serena Quinn's skill set, but she was a surprising woman. "Did Lucius give blood as well?"

"I think so. When he put away the vial with my blood in a little plastic case, I saw there was another vial in there already. I have a feeling it was his, although I can't know for sure."

"Did he say what he was doing with it?"

"No. He and Serena didn't talk much during the procedure. But surely if he's taking samples, he must intend to have it analyzed. What else would Lucius be doing with it?"

Good question. Silas thought that Michael's instincts were probably correct. Why, though, would Lucius be ordering an analysis of vampire blood at this stage of the game? What purpose would it serve?

More than ever, Silas wished he'd had the chance to talk to Serena, if only for a few minutes. She would have told him what was going on. Unfortunately, he hadn't seen her since a few days earlier, when she'd stopped in on her way to her sister's funeral. She'd made sure he had water, wasn't being mistreated, but he'd been able to tell from the stiff, formal way she spoke and the way her eyes didn't quite meet his that she was only stealing a few minutes with him. Lucius had her on a very tight leash, even if he had given her the freedom to stay at her own home rather than here in the mansion.

"And Lucius has said nothing to you."

"To me?" Michael St. John chuckled. "I'm usually the last to know anything. He and Serena left the house last night and went someplace, but I don't know where. I don't dare ask the semivives, since they'd only tell Lucius that I'd been snooping."

Yes, although the semivives worked in this house and probably performed certain menial tasks on behalf of the other vampires who dwelled here, their true allegiance was to Lucius and Lucius alone. They would feel it their duty to inform their master that one of his fledglings had been asking too many questions.

"And of course you can't follow him."

"No. I'm not that stupid." St. John paused and ran a hand through his shaggy dark hair. "I don't even know why I'm telling you all this, except…."

"Except what?"

Dark eyes met his. They were slightly narrowed, as though the vampire had stopped to try to analyze his motivations and still wasn't quite sure what they might be. "Except that whatever Lucius is plotting, I'm pretty sure I won't like it."

~

The food was still very warm when the semivives set it in front of us, proof that whoever had gone on the takeout run this evening truly had gotten there just as Lucius and I were finishing up with our little blood drive in the library. It had been a while since I'd last eaten Thai food, and the savory yet delicate aromas awakened a hunger I hadn't even realized had been lurking.

We ate in the small game room, which apparently was Lucius' choice of venue for meals with me. Or rather, it appeared that he chose this space when he was feeling mellow, when he didn't have a reason to try to make me feel powerless, or insignificant.

Of course, he wouldn't have any need to do such a thing now, not when everything seemed to be going his way. Tomorrow I'd deliver the samples, and the research would begin. Maybe. I didn't know if Jackson's project manager, this Shelby Gutierrez, could actually get a team together in that short an amount of time. What I did know was that pretty much everyone my brother worked with tended to be hyper-competent and an overachiever, which meant that Ms.

Gutierrez had fairly good odds of having everything up and running by the time I made it out to Rancho Cucamonga the next day.

Lucius dished up cashew chicken and rice, and used a pair of tongs to set several egg rolls on my plate. I noticed he'd chosen a dry rosé for our meal, probably so the wine wouldn't compete with the delicate flavors of the food. As I took a sip, I tried very hard not to think of Silas, chained up in a cellar somewhere below my feet. All I wanted to do was get up from the table and run down to see him, but since I didn't have the keys to unlock his manacles and certainly wasn't strong enough to yank them out of the wall, the most I'd accomplish with such a stunt would be to let Lucius know exactly where my true loyalties lay.

"That was a good evening's work," he remarked as he drank from his own glass of rosé.

"Yes, it was. I hope that four samples will be enough."

A faint line appeared between Lucius' brows, here and gone before I could barely register it as a frown. "It will have to be. The nearest vampire coven to Los Angeles is in San Francisco, and I very much doubt they would appreciate being asked for blood samples. It would be considered a gross invasion of their privacy."

"Do you know them?" I asked, intrigued

despite myself. I knew so very little about this strange supernatural world that existed alongside the "real" world, the only world I'd known...up until a few weeks ago.

"Not really. Nicholas Fielding heads the vampire coven there, and has reigned in that city since sailing ships brought immigrants there from around the Cape of Good Hope. His coven is slightly larger than mine—I think there are ten of them altogether, unless they have lost some of their number to the *gula*." Lucius' mouth curved slightly, but it wasn't from amusement. More like...contempt. "Nicholas tends to be a careless master. That is part of the reason why I decided to come to Los Angeles. I knew that the master of San Francisco would not have the stomach to challenge me."

"Vampires are territorial?"

"They tend to be. After all, because of our... dietary requirements...it's necessary that we don't overpopulate any one area." Lucius set down his wine glass and reached for an egg roll, although he didn't immediately take a bite. "Personally, I think ten vampires in a city the size of San Francisco is far too many, even if they do range out to the East Bay or northward to do their hunting."

"That's why you only have the three fledglings?"

"Yes."

"And you've never considered making any more?"

His gaze lingered on me for a moment, and it seemed as if the temperature in the room dropped by at least ten degrees. No…he'd said on more than one occasion that he would never attempt to turn me, because the risk of me losing my psychic powers during the process was far too great. "Not really. If I lost Tristan or Leticia or Michael, then perhaps I would attempt to find someone to take their place, but that is the only reason why I would do such a thing."

"Ah." I wondered if he ever got bored being around the same three people all the time. However, I didn't have the courage to ask the question, just because I worried that he might think I was criticizing the choices he'd made in his fledglings. Instead, I picked up my fork and helped myself to a mouthful of cashew chicken and steamed rice. The food was excellent, but beginning to lose some of its heat. I needed to eat more and talk less.

Apparently Lucius wasn't bothered by such concerns, because after taking a single bite of his egg roll, he set it back down. "It's always a balancing act, deciding how many to have in one's coven. But I tend to err on the side of caution."

"Tristan and Leticia have been with you for a long time."

"Yes."

"What happened to the fledglings you had before them?"

His expression darkened, and he reached for his wine. "Murdered by the *gula*."

"But I thought—"

"That they only watched, only did what was necessary to maintain balance in the world?"

"Well—"

"It is a pretty story, Serena, the one Silas must have told you." Lucius' mouth tightened with barely suppressed rage. "Of course he would have to make it sound as if the Watchers had goodness and decency and justice on their side, that they only swoop in to attack vampires when the vampires themselves are the offenders, the ones who have gotten too greedy, have killed too many innocent humans. The actual truth is, if they have an opportunity to kill one of us, they will. They view us as being outside nature, unnatural, even though one might say the same thing for a race of beings who walk among men and appear to be them, but who have the ability to change into something monstrous."

Monstrous? I didn't see the *gula* that way at all. Oh, I'd definitely been scared out of my wits when Silas changed into his alternate form that first time, but once I saw that his gargoyle shape was only another version of him, was still Silas, then I realized he wasn't a monster at all. Far from it. I'd made love to him while he wore that form because I had to prove to him that I loved all of him, not just the handsome face he usually presented to the world.

However, I couldn't say anything about that to Lucius. The master vampire wasn't a fool; no doubt he knew I'd been intimate with Silas, although whether he guessed that I'd slept with Silas while he was in *gula* form was an entirely different matter.

Anyway, I wasn't about to go charging in with a defense of the Watchers, not when I still knew so little about them. At least I'd gotten to meet another *gula,* and, as far as I could tell, Felix had also seemed forthright and interested only in my welfare.

"As with most things, I have a feeling the truth is somewhere in the middle," I said, my tone mild. The last thing I wanted to do was get in an argument, but I also wasn't going to blindly agree that the vampires were just a bunch of victims. Anyone who could leave a trail of bodies like that throughout their existence definitely wasn't a victim.

To my surprise, Lucius didn't appear offended. "Ah, Serena, you are quite the diplomat. It is not that I expect you to defend my kind…only that I would ask you to refrain from trying to defend the *gula*."

"I think I'm going to stay out of it." I reached for my wine and sipped, then took a larger swallow. It seemed the safest thing to do right then.

A chuckle. "Then I will let the matter rest, since I can tell you don't want to talk about it."

I offered him a relieved smile. "That sounds like a plan."

He only shook his head, and picked up his neglected egg roll and finally ate it. We both consumed our food in silence for a few minutes, during which time Lucius quietly refilled my wine glass. I drank some more, then reflected what an odd situation this was. He wanted to see me every night, but he'd done nothing to advance our relationship. I couldn't help but be relieved by his forbearance, but still…I wondered.

Maybe it was the wine that made me bold. Or maybe I just wanted to have some idea of what to expect. After all, if he knew that I'd been intimate with Silas after being acquainted with him for only a week, then Lucius must realize that I didn't have any scruples about premarital sex, or sex after being with someone for a very short time. Really, if you did the math, I'd known Lucius for almost twice as long as I had Silas when we consummated our relationship.

"Lucius…." I began, then stopped. I couldn't think of a way to say it without sounding as though I was propositioning him, and that was the last impression I wanted to give.

He set down his fork and looked across the table at me. There was nothing in those silvery eyes except mild curiosity, and yet I didn't know if I should continue. "What is it, Serena?"

I bit my lip, then looked down at the napkin that covered my lap. Ivory damask, a contrast to my well-worn jeans. "I suppose I was wondering why you—that is, you've kissed me, but you haven't tried anything else. I—I appreciate the restraint. But it's something I've wondered about."

Since he was too far away to reach out and easily touch my hand, he pushed his chair out from the table, then stood and came over to me. His fingers wrapped around mine, and he had me get up from my chair as well so I could stand next to him.

"I sensed that you were…reticent." A hand brushed over my hair, then moved downward so he could twine a few strands around his finger. "Perhaps some part of you still cares for Silas, perhaps you are struggling to fully accept my vampire nature." He bent and kissed me, but briefly, just a quick touch of lips against lips. "But the real reason I have held back...."

"Yes?" I asked, glad that he hadn't forced the kiss. Yes, I was getting used to it by now...sort of...but I also would have worried that a more forceful kiss might be a prelude to deeper intimacies, that he would have thought my question signaled a desire for matters to progress further than they already had.

His hands wrapped around mine. Chilly, but I was used to how cold his touch always seemed to be. Was it warmer in the hours after he'd killed someone and drunk their blood? I didn't know, because, as far as I'd been able to tell, Lucius hadn't fed in the traditional vampire way since I'd come into his orbit.

"Because you've given me hope, Serena," he said. "Because you've shown me a future where we can be together as normal people. And because I know that future is out there, I'm willing to wait for it. As I said, I want to walk in the sun with you...and then I want to take you inside and make love to you, just as an ordinary man might. I have lived a very long time. I have the patience to wait a while longer, because I know you—and the experience—will be worth the wait."

I couldn't allow myself to sag with relief. All I could do was smile up at him and say, "I suppose that does make sense." And, because I had to keep up the charade, I added, "That makes me very glad Jackson is fast-tracking this research project. With any luck, you won't have to wait very long at all."

Those words obviously encouraged Lucius, because he bent and kissed me again, far more passionately this time. I had to admit to myself that his technique was very good. Was he equally as skilled in the bedroom? A different Serena, a Serena who'd never known Silas Drake, might have wanted to find out. As it was, I could only be glad that Lucius had set this arbitrary deadline for the consummation of our relationship.

The ticking clock that seemed to dominate my world had just gotten a little louder, though. As much as I hoped that Jackson's researchers would find a cure for Addie, that meant they'd also be searching for the magic bullet which would make vampires more human. Once they succeeded, I would have run out of excuses.

My only hope was the *gula*, waiting and watching for the perfect opportunity to free Silas. They had to succeed. Otherwise, the future I'd seen in my visions would most certainly come true.

CHAPTER ELEVEN

SOMETIME DURING MY DINNER WITH LUCIUS, Jackson had texted me the address for the research facility in Rancho Cucamonga, along with a number where I could reach Shelby Gutierrez. The next morning, I got in touch with her, and set up an appointment for one o'clock that afternoon. The blood samples had been safely stowed in my refrigerator overnight, and Lucius had already given instructions to Brian that he was to drive me wherever I asked him to.

Luckily, Lewis and Brian had an ice chest stored in their garage, so I just borrowed that to transport the blood. Since it was a warm day, I put it in the back seat of Brian's Audi rather than the trunk so it could take advantage of the air conditioning as we drove.

Neither of us spoke much on the drive. I kept quiet because I didn't have any idea how much the semivive knew, and I didn't want to let something slip that might make Lucius angry. I wasn't sure of the reason for Brian's silence, but guessed he was taking his cue from me and had decided it would be better not to talk.

Just as well. I was preoccupied, trying to think of the best way to discuss the project with Shelby without sounding too desperate. I didn't know how much Jackson had told her, and planned to let her do most of the talking. For all I knew, all I'd actually have to do was drop off the cooler of samples and then beat a hasty retreat back to Pasadena.

Still, because I was there representing Jackson, I'd dug out one of the few professional-looking ensembles I owned, a charcoal gray pencil skirt and fitted pale blue silk blouse, and the gunmetal-gray sling-back pumps that went with the outfit. I hated those shoes because they killed my feet, but I figured a couple of hours in them wasn't the end of the world. I needed to look like the sister of a senator and a presidential hopeful, and not someone who worked in a New Age shop or something.

The research facility was located in an office park, one of those ubiquitous multi-story developments that had been built in the boom times of the early 2000s, before the stock market crashed and the real estate market collapsed with it. Ever since then, property managers had had a devil of a time keeping them even partly occupied. No wonder Jackson had found a site for the research project so quickly...and probably at a bargain rate.

I told Brian to stay in the car. The old Brian, my friend, would have asked me why he couldn't come along. The semivive Brian, however, only nodded and turned down the A/C somewhat so it wouldn't tax the engine too much as he sat there and idled.

There was no lettering on the door to show what the office suite was being used for. Just the number, the one Jackson had given me. Still, I knew this was the place, because as soon as I stepped inside, a slim woman in her late thirties, wearing a lab coat and with her dark hair pulled back in a ponytail, approached me.

"Serena Quinn?"

I set down the ice chest I'd been carrying and extended a hand. "Yes. You must be Dr. Gutierrez."

"Shelby, please."

"Of course." I stole a quick look around. A receptionist's desk had been set up in that front room, and there were even potted palm trees standing guard in the corners, but I didn't see anyone else around.

"I figured ancillary staff would be last," Shelby said. Her manner was very businesslike. She was attractive in a thin, strained sort of way, as though she never quite got enough sleep and was always focusing on the next problem to be solved. Her glance moved to the ice chest that sat on the commercial-weave carpet next to me. "Are those the samples?"

"Yes."

"Let me take them." She bent and grasped the cooler by its handle, and lifted it. "Come on back so you can see the rest of the operation."

That sounded good. I'd take mental notes, give Jackson a report. He should know what he was getting for his money.

We went down a short hallway, past what appeared to be doors to a restroom and a store-room. The corridor ended in a pair of metal doors, the glass in them half-covered by stickers with the biohazard warning.

Apparently Shelby wasn't particularly worried about biohazards, because she breezed right through the doors and led me out into a large, open laboratory with multiple worktables, numerous computers, and an assortment of scientific equipment I barely recognized—test tubes and pipettes, sure, but also larger glass beakers and autoclaves and lord knows what else. Well, that was the whole point of hiring Shelby Gutierrez, so she'd order the necessary items and hire the essential personnel so we could hit the ground running.

Not that I really wanted them to run too fast. Not after what Lucius had told me the night before.

I wondered if there was any way to ask Shelby to focus on isolating the factors in the blood I'd just brought, and worry about the analysis of human blood later. The problem was, I really had no idea how much Jackson had told her, and so I worried about making a misstep and blurting out more than I should. My brother had said he was trusting me to handle this, but he hadn't given me a whole lot of guidance.

"Here we are," she said, stopping in front of a large industrial stainless-steel refrigerator that occupied an alcove at the back of the room. She set down the cooler, then carefully drew out the plastic box with its precious cargo of blood samples. Yes, if something happened to them, I supposed I could get Lucius & Co. to provide more, but I really didn't want to go through that all over again, at least not before I absolutely had to. I assumed at some point I'd have to supply another round of vampire blood, just because of the nature of the tests that would have to be performed. That evil day could be put off for as long as possible, though.

"Um, I'm not sure how much Jackson has told you—" I began, but Shelby waved a hand.

"All that has been handled," she said smoothly. "I know that time is of the essence. The entire team will be ready to start tomorrow morning."

"But—"

She arched an eyebrow at me. "I know this research is of a delicate nature. Senator Quinn has provided me with very detailed instructions. I do appreciate you bringing the samples to me personally, but there's very little else you need to do, except wait for us to provide results. Which we plan to do as soon as is feasible, given the constraints of the scientific method."

"Oh," I said flatly. I supposed I should have been relieved that I didn't have to explain anything to her, didn't have to pick and choose when it came to deciding what to say.

Even so, I felt oddly deflated. Maybe I'd just pumped up this little errand in my mind to make me feel as though I was more important to the project than I really was. In the end, though, I was only the messenger.

A messenger in excruciating four-inch pumps, I thought wryly, looking at the stylish but much more practical kitten heels Dr. Gutierrez was wearing.

"Senator Quinn did tell me that you are to be our prime contact while he is back in Washington." Shelby paused there and gave me an inquiring look. "I don't suppose he told you when he would return to Southern California."

"Not really," I confessed. "I know he had to go back for a vote, but he didn't say if he was going to stay longer to conduct any other business, or whether he was just going to turn around and come right back after he'd voted on this particular bill. It could be that he wasn't sure, and wanted to wait and see what came up while he was in D.C."

"I suppose that makes sense." She seemed to hesitate for a moment. "You don't need to worry about a thing, Ms. Quinn. We know that we are working with extraordinary specimens. Everyone who comes to work here will be required to sign a nondisclosure agreement. Anyone who violates that agreement will have to face your brother's lawyers. I assume you know what that means."

Of course I did. The entire Quinn family had access to the very best lawyers money could buy. And, in Jackson's case, access as well to the sort of people who could quietly make you disappear, although I doubted my brother would stoop to that sort of behavior. The threat of an expensive lawsuit and the knowledge that you'd never be able to work in this town again was probably enough to keep anyone who came to work here on their best behavior.

"Yes, I do," I said. "And we all are confident that we won't need to worry about anyone you hire. I only wanted to make sure that you know to give me progress reports as well, so I might pass them on to...well, those who also have a vested interest in the outcome of your research."

"Oh, I know," Shelby said. "Senator Quinn was very specific about that. You're definitely in the loop."

"Thank you. Then I suppose I'll head home, and let you get on with it."

"Yes. Now that I have the samples, I'll have the first shift come in within the hour."

Her comment should have surprised me, but I recalled how Lucius had said he wanted to have multiple shifts working here, not only so they might arrive at a solution that much more quickly, but also in case he wanted to visit the facility and perform his own inspections during the evening hours.

"That sounds great. I'll be sure to let Lu — that is, I'll make sure to pass that information on to the interested parties."

My comment aroused a gleam of curiosity in

Shelby Gutierrez's eyes, but I knew she was far too professional to ask me the question that must be eating her up inside.

What exactly is Senator Quinn doing with these blood samples?

I couldn't answer that. She hadn't said word one about vampires, which meant that my brother probably hadn't given her any information about the actual source of the blood her team would be testing. How long he planned for this subterfuge to go on, I didn't know, but it was Jackson's place to tell her the truth, not mine.

Since clearly our business was done, I thanked Shelby for her time and headed back out to the parking lot, where Brian now waited outside his car. I supposed my errand had gone on for a little too long, and he'd decided it was better not to overtax the engine by sitting there and idling with the air conditioning on the whole time.

"We can head back now," I told him, and he nodded.

The Brian I'd known might have complained about making him wait outside in the hot sun, but semivives apparently weren't programmed to complain. He opened his door, while I did the same on the passenger side of the vehicle. After that he drove out of the office park and headed back to the freeway.

I stared at the traffic that surrounded the car, brooding over what I'd just done. Yes, I knew there wasn't any way to get around transferring those samples to Jackson's researchers, but it still felt so...final. I couldn't take back what I'd just done.

Maybe it wouldn't be so bad. Maybe they'd make far more progress in synthesizing a cure for Addie than they would in creating the serum to make Lucius human again. After all, even though I'd been lumping those two projects together in my mind—possibly because of Lucius' own concept of quid pro quo when it came to helping my brother—they really were two completely separate lines of inquiry, and possibly not equivalent at all.

About all I could do was hope they wouldn't succeed with Lucius' serum first. That would be terrible news for Addie.

And it wouldn't be all that great for me, either...or the rest of humankind, come to think of it.

～

I sent a text to Jackson letting him know the samples had been delivered. After that, I got online, once again deploying my VPN and zeroing in on the Humboldt compound by way of Google Maps. Yes, you could call it my version of the bat signal, since I desperately hoped that Felix would get the hint and message me again. But I also wanted to see if I could get close enough to locate the meadow from my vision. If I could prove that was real, then it meant the vision could become reality as well, that what I had just done hadn't irrevocably set me on the path to a future I didn't want to see come to pass.

Of course there was no street view available for a location that had no streets. All I could do was focus on the satellite imagery, and get as close in as the website would allow me. I saw vast tracts of forests that seemed to spread for miles. Crazy to think that all this unspoiled wilderness lay in my own home state, a place I tended to view as completely paved over and wall to wall with people, since that was a fairly accurate description of the greater Los Angeles area. Even on the drive out to Rancho Cucamonga, though, I'd seen the foothills and mountains rising up behind the suburban sprawl, and knew that we still had our open areas here.

Nothing like this, though.

I moved my fingers on the track pad, now heading north and east, since there were only hills to the west of the *gula* compound. All I saw was more forest, and I let out an exasperated sigh. It was possible that the clearing I'd seen was miles and miles away from the Watchers' homestead, although it seemed strange to drive that far just for a picnic.

Or maybe that green meadow only existed inside my head.

My messaging app *bing*ed, and a little window appeared in the lower left-hand part of my laptop's screen.

Snooping again?

Felix?

Of course. Although it was someone at head-quarters who alerted me to the intrusion. I'm in the field down here and don't have access to all my regular equipment.

Clearly, he had enough to penetrate the VPN I used and to contact me, so he wasn't entirely without resources. *Can I ask you something?*

You can ask.

Well, that was helpful. Pushing back my irritation, I typed, *Do you know if there's a clearing anywhere near your compound? A green meadow with wildflowers—when they're in season, I mean.*

Yes. It's due north of us, about a mile and a half away. It's a quiet place. A lot of the gula kids go to play there. Why?

Nothing. That is, I think I saw it in a vision. I just wanted to make sure it was a real place.

Oh, it's real.

The relief that swept through me was so intense, I could only be glad that I was sitting down. Otherwise, my legs might have collapsed beneath me. Foolish? Possibly. After all, merely being told the meadow existed didn't necessarily mean that my vision would come true. Even so, I felt a little better about life than I had even fifteen minutes ago.

Thanks, I typed. *Do you know when you're going to try to rescue Silas?*

Serena, it's better if I don't tell you the particulars. I'm sure you'll understand why.

While I understood the need for caution, I still experienced a stab of irritation. I needed to know. I had to know how much longer I'd have to pretend around Lucius. Yes, I'd been granted a small reprieve, because at least now I knew he wouldn't try anything until he had his own "cure," but I absolutely hated being in that house, knowing that Silas was being held prisoner there and that there wasn't a goddamn thing I could do about it.

Well, you'd better get moving, I told Felix. *My brother has the lab set up to analyze vampire blood, and I just took the samples over there this* afternoon, so now it's only a matter of time before they both get what they want.

No reply at first. Was Felix startled by that revelation, or had he paused our conversation so he could consult with one of his superiors?

Then, *What are they using the samples for?*

Lucius claims the factors in vampire blood that allow them to live forever can be synthesized and used as a cure for various diseases. I've had visions where it seems clear that those factors were also being used to manufacture a limited kind of immortality, immortality that's up for sale to the highest bidder. In return, Lucius gets research into human blood and why it's so important in keeping vampires alive. The end result is that a serum is developed that allows vampires to live more like humans, including being able to walk in sunlight.

You saw this in another vision?

I saw it in the same vision. Or rather, the same series of visions. These happened while I was being held at Lucius Montfort's home, which is why Silas didn't know anything about them.

Then time is definitely of the essence. I know I said it's important that you not know exactly what we're planning, but I see now that we don't have the luxury of caution. That means I need to ask a favor from you.

Anything, I typed, and I meant it. I'd do whatever was necessary to get Silas free.

Is there some way you can get Lucius Mont-fort away from his house for a few hours? We'll still have to contend with the semivives, and perhaps the other vampires, but it will be easier to extricate Silas if the master vampire isn't home.

He wasn't asking for much, was he? Yes, I'd seen Lucius leave his mansion on a few occasions —to attend the gathering at my parents' house after my sister Vanessa's funeral, to go to Jackson's house in Claremont so we could speak in private—but clearly he preferred to stay put.

Then it came to me. This coming Thursday was my birthday. I'd tried not to think about the day, mostly because this year I hadn't felt like there was much for me to celebrate, but what better present than to have Silas freed? Surely if I told Lucius and asked him to take me out for a special birthday dinner, he would feel compelled to say yes, if only to maintain the charade that we were a perfectly normal, happy couple who did perfectly normal, happy things together.

And while we were gone, the *gula* could swoop in and rescue Silas. Any semivives in the way would be collateral damage, although I was secretly glad that Brian spent very little time at the mansion, since he had a charade of his own to maintain, that everything was just fine and he and Lewis hadn't suffered any disruption of their lives. And if Tristan and Leticia happened to be home—which was doubtful, considering their penchant for going out on their faux hunts every damn night—well, I wouldn't weep any bitter tears over their loss if they happened to get in the way.

I think I might be able to get him away for a few hours on Thursday evening, I wrote. *But I don't know for sure. I'll bring it up when I go over there tonight. How do I contact you to let you know if it's going to happen?*

You don't contact me. Just get back on Google Maps. That's how I know to reach out to you.

In other words, get out the bat signal. It made sense, though. This way, there would be no evidence that I'd been in contact with any of the *gula*—no phone number or emails or anything that could lead me to Felix.

Okay, I typed. *Usually I get home a little before midnight. I'll let you know then whether I was able to get Lucius to go for it.*

Thank you, Serena.

That was all, but I could tell Felix had signed off. We really didn't have anything else to discuss until I knew whether I'd be able to clear the coast, so to speak, on Thursday evening.

And if Lucius was recalcitrant, wanted instead to wine and dine me at home?

Then you'll think of something else, I told myself. Because I wasn't about to give up, not when I knew the *gula* were on standby, waiting for the perfect opportunity to rescue their captured comrade.

I'd just have to make sure I didn't fail them.

CHAPTER TWELVE

I COULDN'T BEAR TO STAY IN AN OUTFIT THAT required me to wear those painful heels, but I did take care to wear something I hoped Lucius would appreciate—a low-cut, dark red wrap top, and a skirt in coordinating shades of red and black and gray. A little more care with my makeup, including a matte red lip. But was it too much?

My reflection stared back at me, hazel eyes serious. Since I'd only put on a bit of brown eyeshadow and mascara, the red lipstick didn't look too overdone. I needed a strong lip to go with the colors I was wearing. After another long look, I decided it should be okay.

Someone knocked at the door. My semivive driver, I supposed, since it was now six-thirty. The pickup time had inched forward a little each evening, no doubt accommodating the gradually lengthening days. In a few days, we'd be back on Daylight Savings Time, and I supposed then I wouldn't hear from the driver until closer to seven-thirty.

No, it wouldn't matter, because by Saturday night Silas would have been freed, and I wouldn't be forced to share these dinners with Lucius anymore. It would have been nice to have had a confirmation from a vision that the future I'd glimpsed with Silas was my true one, but no such luck. I had to cling to the image of the two of us in that sunny green meadow, and hope I wasn't believing in a future which would never come to pass.

I headed downstairs, pausing to retrieve my purse from where it sat on the dining room table, and to grab a jacket from the coat closet by the front door. Again the day had been mild, but by the time I came home, it would be much colder. I didn't want to take any risks.

As usual, the semivive really didn't say anything to me, only nodded and stepped out of the way so I could emerge from the condo and lock the door behind me. Once again I was glad that no one seemed to have noticed my comings and goings; I had a feeling that not-Brian did his best to make sure Lewis was otherwise occupied during the times I was being picked up. The drop-off wasn't as big a deal, just because at that time of night the two of them should be safely in bed.

Another drive through the dusk, another fifteen minutes where I had to mentally prepare myself for the evening ahead. At least tonight I wouldn't have to worry about drawing anyone's blood, but I'd still have to convince Lucius to take me out. Thank God Thursday really was my birthday. I had a feeling he already knew the date, and so would have known right away if I was attempting to pass off another day as my special day.

Through the porte cochère, and into the house. Unlike the day before, Lucius was waiting for me immediately inside. His silvery eyes lit up as he caught sight of me, and he reached out to take my hands.

"You are looking lovelier than ever, my dear," he said, then pulled me toward him so he could kiss me. Lightly, though, as if he didn't want to disturb my lipstick.

"Thank you, Lucius," I replied. "I thought it was sort of a special occasion, since I dropped off the samples today."

"And it all went smoothly?"

"Oh, yes. The facility looked very impressive. And Ms. Gutierrez made it sound as if she had a team standing by, so they're probably working on it as we speak."

"Splendid. That does sound like a celebration. I have food and wine waiting for us, so let us go lift a glass."

I nodded, and followed him to the game room. As he'd promised, a meal already appeared to be ready to go, although I couldn't tell what it was, since all the dishes were protected by silver covers to keep in the heat. Lucius went immediately to the bottle that sat in the center of the table, and poured a good measure into each of the glasses that had been set out. He handed one to me, and then took the other for himself.

"Shall we drink to the success of our research project?"

"Absolutely," I said, and sipped at the glass of wine he'd given me. Bold, but not too heavy, with a hint of spice at the finish. "Tempranillo?"

"Yes," he replied. "You have a well-trained palate."

"My father is really into wine," I explained. "So I started drinking it when I was still in high school. He thought the European way was better —letting us kids have a taste and learn to appreciate it, instead of turning it into forbidden fruit. It was probably wise, because none of us got too hung up on the whole drinking thing when we were in college."

"Yes, you Americans do tend to be rather puritanical when it comes to alcohol. I always thought a measured approach was better. But please—do sit down."

I did as he asked, taking the chair nearest me. He put down his glass of wine and sat as well, then lifted the covers from the food. I couldn't quite identify what it was, but it smelled divine.

"Chile verde," he said. "I hope it isn't too spicy for you."

"I can handle it."

A hint of a smile, just a lift at the corner of his mouth. Then he picked up the silver ladle and put a portion of the chile verde—which appeared to be some kind of Mexican pork stew, something I'd never had before—on my plate, along with a helping of rice. After getting some for himself, he said, "I suppose it's far too early to ask if we have any kind of timeline for the project."

"Yes, it is far too early." I took a bit of the chile verde. Wow. Tasty, but he was right about it being hot. Luckily, there was enough rice on my plate to temper the sting somewhat. "But Shelby Gutierrez did say that Jackson had hired two shifts of people to do the work, so with any luck, it'll go quickly enough."

"That is good news."

For a moment we were both silent as we ate. Not for the first time, I noticed how Lucius didn't seem to have any real reticence about eating regular food, unlike his fledglings, all three of whom had appeared about as picky as a three-year-old when it came to consuming everything that was put before them. Maybe dealing with human food was a skill that came with age, or maybe Lucius forced himself to eat what he normally wouldn't, simply because he was trying to make me feel more at ease around him.

I decided I might as well broach the subject of my birthday. Delaying wouldn't make discussing the topic any easier. "Speaking of special occasions…."

He put down his fork. "Yes?"

"Well, Thursday is my birthday."

"Yes, I know. I was wondering whether you were going to bring it up."

I had to repress a flicker of irritation at his comment. All right, I'd already guessed that he knew exactly when my birthday was, but it was still annoying to think that he had access to all kinds of information about me. *Bet he knows my blood type, too,* I thought sourly, although I had to admit there were particular reasons why that sort of information would be of value to a vampire.

"Would you have, if I hadn't?"

"I'm not sure. In general, if a woman doesn't want to mention her birthday, there are often very good reasons why she wishes to keep it secret."

"Maybe, but I'm not trying to hide my age or anything. It's more that...well, with everything that's been going on, it sort of slipped my mind. This one isn't a milestone or anything."

"But it is still your birthday, and therefore should be celebrated." Lucius tapped one finger against the side of his wine glass. "What would you like to do?"

Here it came. I supposed I should be glad he had asked first. That put some of the responsibility on him. "Can we go out for dinner?"

The request clearly surprised him; his eyebrows lifted, and his head tilted as he gazed across the table at me. "I can have anything you like brought here, you know."

I'd been afraid he'd say something like that. Pushing aside my worry, since I really didn't want to get into an argument and blow the whole thing, I said, "Yes, I know that. And everything you've provided has been wonderful. But... there's just something about going out. It makes an event more festive. There are a couple of places here in Pasadena that would be wonderful —Cafe Santorini, or Bistro 45. Or the Raymond. You can choose, because any of them would be fine. But I would like to go out with you."

"In public. With me."

I summoned a smile. "Well, yes. Do you think it's that strange? I mean, we're going to be together. My visions have shown that. Doesn't it make sense for us to be seen together?"

His expression, which had been almost blank but at the same time oddly tense, seemed to relax somewhat. "Yes, Serena, it makes perfect sense. I'm honored that you would want to go to dinner with me, to a place where we might meet people you know."

The odds for such a thing weren't particularly high, considering how narrow the world of my friends and acquaintances had been lately, but I supposed there always was the risk of running into some of my parents' friends. It was a chance I'd have to take. Besides, I had no doubt my mother had already mentioned to a few of her fellow ladies who lunch that her daughter was seeing a handsome, wealthy investor who lived in Linda Vista. Such a pronouncement could only raise me in their estimation.

"Of course I want to," I lied. "I'm proud to be seen with you."

He smiled then, such a genuine smile that I experienced a pang of remorse. I hated lying to people...even to a vampire.

But I thought of Silas, chained in the cellar, and of all the deaths that could be attributed to Lucius Montfort over all the years of his unnatural life. Lying to him was a very small sin compared to his transgressions.

"And your family?" he asked then. "They won't expect to see you on your birthday?"

"No," I said, glad that at least here I could be truthful. "The last few years, I didn't want them to make a fuss. Actually, I insisted on it. So my parents are used to not doing much, although I'm sure they'll send flowers, like they always do."

"That is thoughtful of them. Well, if I'm not taking you away from your family, then I'd be honored to take you to dinner. I'll be sure to make reservations."

"Where?"

His silvery eyes almost twinkled. "You gave me some suggestions. I'll decide which one, however. That way, it can be a surprise."

"All right. That sounds like fun."

A smile. I could tell he was pleased that I wouldn't argue with him about the venue, that I'd let him make that decision. Fine by me. I really didn't care where we went, as long as it wasn't here. We'd go out for dinner and then...

...and then, Silas would be free, hopefully before Lucius and I even got to dessert.

Yes, I was definitely looking forward to this birthday.

The next day was a quiet one. I thought about going to shop for a dress for my birthday dinner, but realized the black cocktail dress Vanessa had given me to wear at her fashion show's reception was nicer than probably anything else I could find locally. And I still had some Dermablend to cover up the scars on my leg, so the short skirt shouldn't present a problem. Some part of me hated the idea of wearing the dress, just because I'd forever associate it with my sister's death, but I told myself to be practical. The dress fit me like a glove, a quality I hoped I could use to my advantage.

Anything to keep Lucius distracted.

I didn't hear from Shelby Gutierrez at the lab, but then, I really hadn't expected to. As impatient as Lucius might be, that sort of research wasn't the sort of thing where you could expect to see significant findings within the space of a day, or a week. Probably not even a month, although I hoped they would be able to come up with something to help Addison. No matter what a mess the rest of the situation was, she didn't deserve the cards the universe had dealt her. We needed to find her a cure.

And I'd already contacted Felix the night before, just as soon as I got home. Or rather, I went to Google Maps and zeroed in on Humboldt, and within the minute a message box popped up on my screen. I let him know that we were a go for Thursday night, and to plan accordingly. The only thing I didn't know for sure was the time of our reservations, but I figured eight o'clock should be safe. Besides, Felix assured me that they would be surveilling Lucius' mansion and wouldn't do anything until they saw him drive away, so that particular detail should be handled.

The hardest part was going to the mansion that Wednesday evening and pretending everything was fine, was normal, that I wasn't praying with every ounce of my being that my birthday dinner with Lucius the following night would be the last I'd ever have to share with the vampire. If he noticed anything off, he didn't give any sign of it. He didn't even look all that disappointed when I told him I hadn't heard anything from the lab. He only shrugged and said he would have been shocked to learn that they'd discovered anything so early on. Well, Lucius was used to playing the long game. Inwardly, he might be experiencing some impatience, but he knew how these things worked.

Problem was, my niece Addison didn't have the time to play a long game.

I didn't betray anything of my worry, however. Since the day had been unseasonably warm for early March, Lucius and I walked in the gardens after dinner, and spoke of what we would be able to do once a serum had been developed for him. He wanted to take me to Italy, to Greece. I'd visited when I was in high school, but hadn't been back since. I told him that sounded lovely, and that I was looking forward to sharing all those sights with him.

At the end of the evening, he kissed me, and I closed my eyes and prayed that this, too, would be one of the last times I ever had to let his lips touch mine.

Before I left, he let me know that he would pick me up at seven o'clock the next evening, and once again I was in the back seat of the Mercedes, having the brown-haired semivive drive me home.

The morning of my birthday, a delivery man showed up with a bouquet of lilies and peonies, some of my favorites. From my parents, of course. Tucked into the arrangement was a card wishing me a very happy day. I'd told my parents that Lucius was taking me out that night, and so they didn't press very hard about getting me to spend the day with them. My mother added a postscript saying that she hoped I might bring Lucius over for cocktails sometime, but that was all. Very subdued for her, and I couldn't help but be grateful.

Getting ready took a good deal of time. I washed my hair and set it with hot rollers so it would fall in heavy waves down my back, and then I spent at least a half hour on my makeup, doing my best to get it perfect. No, not as expert a job as the makeup artists at Vanessa's fashion show might have done, but I still thought I looked pretty good by the time I was finished with everything. I *needed* to look good. I wanted to make sure that all of Lucius' attention was on me, so focused that he would want to have the dinner last for as long as possible.

Then the dress and the shoes. Dead simple jewelry—my white gold Longines watch, the diamond studs my mother had given me, a thin silver rope chain around the same wrist as the watch, and on the middle finger of my right hand, the white gold and diamond band that my grandmother had left me.

When I was done, I nodded at my reflection

in approval. I did look very San Marino old money. My mother would be proud.

I had to hope that Lucius would be proud to be seen with me as well, that he'd be distracted enough by my appearance and the novelty of an evening out that he wouldn't be paying any attention to what might be happening back at the mansion.

I checked my watch. Six fifty-two. I drew in a breath, took one last look at myself in the mirror to make sure everything was still in place. My feet were already beginning to hurt from the strappy high-heeled sandals I wore, but I ignored the discomfort. I'd only have to walk from my place to the car, and from the car to the restaurant. Some wine would help me ignore the fact that heels tended to be torture devices for me now, because of the injuries I'd suffered during the accident. Anyway, I was ready to endure screaming agony, if it meant that Silas would be free soon.

Then came the knock at the door. I drew in a breath, ran my hands down the silk dress I wore, and went to answer that knock. Outside stood Lucius, looking impeccable in a black suit with a pale gray shirt and black and red tie. I realized then that I'd never seen him wear anything other than variations on that combination of colors. Didn't he ever get tired of them? Or maybe he preferred to keep things simple, because that way everything in his closet would go with everything else.

I didn't have time to ponder the question further, because he smiled at me and said, "Serena, you are simply stunning. Happy birthday."

"Um—thank you," I replied.

"Shall we?" He offered his arm.

I didn't have much choice but to take it. Locking up was a little awkward because I only had one free hand, and I didn't even bother with turning on the alarm. My parents probably wouldn't have been pleased by that lapse, but really, the security system was there more to protect me rather than the items inside my condo. Anyway, with not-Brian performing guard duty next door, I knew I didn't have much to worry about.

Lucius' arm steadied me as we went down the stairs and headed toward the area set aside for visitor parking. I was surprised to realize that the semivive driver was nowhere in sight; I'd just assumed he would be playing chauffeur this evening.

"You're driving?" I asked as Lucius opened the passenger door for me.

"Yes," he said. "I thought it would be more intimate. I can drive, you know—I just choose not to most of the time."

"Considering SoCal traffic, I don't blame you," I told him, and he flashed me a quick smile before he closed the car door and came around to take his place in the driver's seat.

We pulled out of the parking lot and headed west on Cordova. Lucius did seem to know what he was doing behind the wheel, because he appeared calm and in control the whole time, even when he had to quickly change lanes to avoid getting sideswiped by some idiot in a delivery truck who was a little too aggressive about pulling out of a driveway at the last minute. The near-miss set my heart pounding, but, as far as I could tell, Lucius didn't even blink.

Since he didn't comment on the incident, I remained silent, noting how we turned south on Fair Oaks, heading away from old town Pasadena. That seemed to nix several of my dinner suggestions, and imply that Lucius had decided to take me to the Raymond Restaurant, probably the most intimate and—possibly—the most expensive of all of them.

Not that he couldn't afford to buy us dinner there, of course. But the choice seemed to indicate that he did want this evening to be extra-special. Well, he could assign any meaning to it he wanted to, as long as by doing so we were able to stay away from the mansion for a decent chunk of time.

He aimed the Mercedes into the narrow driveway, and came to a stop at the valet station. Immediately a man in a white shirt and black tie approached the car and said, "Welcome to the Raymond, sir."

"Thank you," Lucius replied. He accepted a ticket from the valet, who then came around to my side and opened the door for me.

I got out, doing my best not to wobble on my high heels. Almost at once Lucius was there, again offering his arm, this time so he could guide me into the restaurant.

"A cocktail first?" he asked, after he'd checked in with the girl at the hostess station. "Our reservation isn't until seven forty-five."

"Sure," I replied. The bar at the restaurant was legendary, even though I really wasn't much of a mixed-drink girl. One drink shouldn't do too much to mess me up, however.

He guided me into the bar, where we were lucky enough to snag a table in the corner that one of the busboys had just finished wiping down. A waiter came to ask what we'd like, and I ordered a pomegranate martini, while Lucius got a Pimms cup, whatever that was.

The drinks came quickly. As I lifted my glass, I

took a quick glance at my watch. Seven thirty-two. Would the *gula* be converging yet, or did they still plan to wait until after eight o'clock, just to be safe?

I had no way of knowing. The one thing I did know was that I didn't dare reveal my anxiety, couldn't give the slightest hint to Lucius that this evening was anything other than the birthday celebration I'd told him it was. I had to smile, and laugh, and pray that he couldn't see the anxiety behind my eyes.

We chatted, saying nothing of much consequence because there were too many listening ears close by. Or rather, it certainly seemed as though everyone around us was absorbed in their own conversations, but you couldn't be too careful. Just as we were finishing our drinks, the hostess came into the bar to fetch us, saying our table was ready.

She led us outside to the patio, where strings of lights hung overhead and a fire crackled away in the large stone hearth off to one side. Although the day had been warm enough, the air had cooled as soon as the sun set. That didn't seem to matter out here, though, because gas-powered portable heaters had been set out at judicious intervals around the space, providing plenty of warmth. It also helped that we got a prime seat very close to the fireplace, and I was able to sit with my back to it. Even so, I was glad of the lightweight black wool shawl I'd brought with me.

A minute or so after that, the waiter came by to tell us the specials. Lucius hadn't even glanced at the wine list, but he seemed to know exactly what he wanted, as he ordered an '03 Cotes du Rhone.

"Did you have something particular in mind?" I inquired as I looked over the menu. So many things sounded interesting, but his choice was so specific that I guessed he'd already decided on our entrees.

"The rib-eye for two? That does seem like a rather special meal."

Really, as long as he wasn't ordering blowfish purée or some other abomination, I really didn't care. However, since I also didn't have an issue with red meat, I nodded and said that sounded wonderful, and maybe we could try the cedar-planked vegetables to start things off?

Lucius was amenable to that. He truly did seem to be in a very mellow mood, although I supposed he was also on his best behavior because we were out in public. For a Thursday night, the restaurant was fairly crowded, but no one seemed to be paying much attention to us.

The wine came, and Lucius pronounced it excellent, and then gave the waiter our order.

Once we were alone again, he raised his glass and said, "Happy birthday, Serena."

I lifted my glass and clinked it against his, then drank. The wine really was marvelous, complex, with rich tannins that would stand up to the steak we'd ordered, and I wished I could relax and enjoy it more. However, I knew that wasn't possible, not when I couldn't help brooding in the back of my mind over whether Felix and his team had arrived at the mansion yet. For all I knew, Silas was already free, and yet I was forced to be here with the vampire who'd imprisoned him.

Once we'd both had a few more sips of wine, Lucius went on, "I wanted to get you a birthday present, but I wasn't quite sure what you wanted."

I smiled at him. Right then, I could only be glad that he hadn't bought me anything. I knew I shouldn't feel guilty for the subterfuge I was currently engaged in, and yet I still experienced just the slightest niggle of remorse for having him take me out to this restaurant merely so the *gula* would have an opportunity to stage a commando raid. "This is enough," I said, with a tilt of my head toward the rest of the patio, toward the restaurant itself. "It's just lovely out here."

"I'm glad you like it, but I fear you misunderstood me." He paused there, and set down his wine glass so he could reach into the inside pocket of his suit jacket. "I did get you something...but in a way it's something for the both of us."

The box he produced was robin's egg blue. Tiffany blue. My heart seized up. No, he couldn't have. He didn't—

He opened the box. Inside glimmered a large square-cut diamond set in a minimalist mounting of white metal. *Platinum,* I thought faintly. *Lucius wouldn't bother with white gold.*

My stomach heaved, even as he said, "I know this may be somewhat premature, since so much depends on the outcome of your brother's research, but I found I could not wait. Serena, we will be together. I want ours to be a formal joining. Will you be my wife?"

I stared at him, mouth dry. My first instinct was to get up from the table and bolt out of there, wobbly sandals or no, but I realized that wasn't a very mature response. Worse, it would only prove to Lucius that I had no desire to be his wife...or anything else. I swallowed, just to get some moisture back in my throat. "Lucius, I —I don't know what to say."

"Well, 'yes,' is generally considered to be the appropriate answer."

He didn't sound annoyed. One eyebrow was

lifted at a rather ironic angle, but all he did was sit there, holding the box. Obviously, he was waiting to see how I would respond.

"I—" God, what to do? I realized I had to tell him yes, of course I would marry him, or the gig would be up. I didn't have any choice. Anyway, agreeing to someone's marriage proposal wasn't legally binding. I'd back out as soon as I could. For now, though….

I'd given Lucius a lot of fake smiles over the past few weeks. However, this one was the hardest to force. He had to believe that I wanted nothing more than to be his wife. So I smiled at him and said, "Yes, Lucius. Yes. Of course I'll marry you."

CHAPTER THIRTEEN

SILAS KNEW AT ONCE THAT LUCIUS MONTFORT had left the house, because Michael St. John made an appearance again that evening, about an hour or so after the same silent semivive brought Silas his meager dinner of water, an apple, and some bread and sausage. He'd eaten all of it, not because it tasted good in any way, except for the apple, but because he knew he needed to keep his strength up.

When St. John appeared, though, Silas could only smile and shake his head. "Maybe you should bring a deck of cards or something. It would help to pass the time."

"Hadn't thought of that." The vampire came farther into the cellar and leaned against one of the racks of wine. "You know what day it is?"

Silas did some quick mental math. "Thursday?"

"Well, true, but I was thinking of something a little more specific."

If it was Thursday, that meant the date was March 11th. Silas tried to think of anything significant that had happened that particular day, but only drew a blank. "Sorry. I don't know what you're talking about."

"It's your girl's birthday. Serena's birthday. And Lucius went to take her out to a fancy dinner."

Rage boiled up within Silas. He should have remembered that date—it wasn't as though he didn't have access to that information via Serena's file—but it had slipped his mind, subsumed by far more pressing matters. And knowing that Lucius sought to exploit his connection to her by taking her out to dinner...well, Silas had to keep quiet, since he knew that whatever came out of his mouth would only betray how angry he truly was.

Correctly interpreting Silas' silence, Michael St. John continued, "Don't like that idea very much, do you?"

"Not really," Silas growled.

"Well, look at it this way—you have a great excuse for not buying her a birthday present."

"Not funny."

St. John grinned and gave a careless shrug. "I wasn't really trying to be funny. I just wanted to point out a helpful fact."

"It wasn't helpful, either. If you really wanted to be helpful, you'd take these goddamn manacles off me while your master is away."

The vampire looked almost contrite. "I wish I could. I really do. But my bond to Lucius won't let me do something so obviously subordinate."

"How about, I don't know, dropping the key someplace where I can find it?"

"No go. That won't work, either. I'm afraid—"

Michael St. John didn't have the opportunity to say what he was afraid of, because a second later, three Watchers in their *gula* forms burst into the cellar. Although a human would have a very difficult time differentiating one gargoyle from another, Silas immediately recognized the members of the strike team as Felix, Aaron, and Micah. They advanced on Michael, who was caught with them between him and the door, and therefore didn't have many options. The vampire froze where he was, hands curling into fists even though he had to know he was grossly outnumbered.

"Stop!" Silas called out, and Felix paused, orange eyes blazing.

"Stop?" he said in some incredulity. "This is a

vampire, one of your captors. He must be destroyed."

"No, he isn't."

"He's not a vampire?"

"No, I mean that he isn't one of my captors. He's — " Silas had to pause there, because he wasn't precisely sure how he should label Michael St. John. Not a friend, but not an enemy, either. "He's given me assistance. There's no need to kill him."

Michael blinked but remained silent. Even though most of the time he was quick enough with a quip, he seemed to realize that in this instance, he should let other people do the talking.

Felix glanced over at Micah and Aaron, both of whom gave the *gula* equivalent of a shrug. Since Felix was clearly in charge of this operation, they would defer to him. "You're sure?"

"Yes."

A tilt of the lead Watcher's head in Silas' direction, and both Aaron and Micah hurried over to free him from the wall. The combined strength of the two *gula* was enough to tear the manacles to pieces, and just a minute later, he was free, able to stand up completely straight for the first time in days. His muscles ached, and he knew it would take some time for the stiffness to disappear completely, but he cared little for that.

"The guards?" he asked.

"We took care of the semivives guarding the property," Felix said. "No vampires, except this one here." His nostrils flared in dislike, but to Silas' relief, he didn't seem inclined to attack Michael St. John.

"Tristan and Leticia usually go out at night," he offered, clearly trying to be helpful, but Felix ignored him and kept his attention focused on Silas.

"And Lucius is out having dinner with Serena," Felix said. Silas felt his eyes widen, wondering how in the world Felix knew about that particular detail, and the other *gula* went on, "She and I planned it together. It seemed the easiest way to get him off the property."

"You planned it? How?"

"Later," Felix responded. "We don't have time to get into all that now. Let's go."

Silas recognized the wisdom of those words. Somehow Serena had managed to set up a distraction, but even the most lavish of birthday dinners wouldn't last forever. They needed to be long gone from this place before the vampire master returned. Getting Serena away from him would be another task that needed to be handled, and soon, but her rescue could be planned elsewhere, someplace safe.

"Very well," Silas said.

The three *gula* began to head back toward the door, with Silas taking up the rear. Michael St. John's voice stopped him, however.

"That's it? You're just going to leave me here?"

Silas turned around. The vampire remained where he'd been standing, only now his arms were crossed and his dark eyes snapped with irritation.

"Yes, that was the plan," Silas replied. "You would have preferred for them to hurt you?"

"Well, not exactly, but...." St. John shook his head. "When Lucius comes back and sees you gone and me completely unscathed, he's going to be royally pissed off. You need to make it look like I at least tried to stop you, or I'm going to be in a world of pain."

Felix frowned. "So you do want us to hurt you."

"Well...yeah. Just a little. Just enough to make it seem realistic."

Aaron spoke for the first time. "What would be realistic, vampire, would be for one of us to come back here with a stake and drive it through your worthless heart. Is that what you want?"

"Erm...no." Michael St. John swallowed. "Just...beat me up a little. Maybe you should do it," he added, directing his words at Silas.

"You're still in human form. It probably won't hurt as much that way."

"You're serious."

"Dead serious. Or undead serious, as the case may be."

The vampire's expression was almost pleading. Silas could see his point—when Lucius arrived here and found his semivives dead and his prisoner gone, there would be hell to pay. The least he could do was rough Michael up a little. Whether or not that would be enough to convince the vampire master that there had been a struggle, Silas didn't know for sure.

But he'd better try.

His fist came out and caught Michael St. John across the cheek. Such a blow might have shattered the fragile bones of an ordinary man, but of course the vampire wasn't really a man at all. Even so, he staggered back a few paces, then blinked.

"That was pretty good," he said. "But I'll need more than that."

"No problem."

This time his fist landed on St. John's jaw with such force that he actually was knocked off his feet. He landed on his ass only a couple of feet away from the manacles that had held Silas chained to the wall for the past few days. He lay there, panting.

"Good enough?" Silas asked.

The vampire nodded...and then his eyes widened in fear. Silas looked over his shoulder, only to see Aaron approaching, holding a splintered piece of wood in one hand. Where he'd gotten it, Silas didn't know.

"No, don't!" he cried, but it was too late.

The piece of wood flew through the air for all the world like a javelin at an Olympic track and field event. It caught Michael St. John in the chest, and he flopped backward, eyes wide, blood beginning to stain the dark shirt he wore.

"Damn it! I told you not to kill him!"

"He's not dead," Aaron said carelessly. His amber-hued eyes flicked over toward the mortally wounded vampire. "At least not yet. Let's go."

"No—" Silas couldn't leave St. John lying there like that. Not after the kindnesses—offhand as they might be—that the vampire had shown him.

"*Now.*" That was Felix. Technically, the two of them had equal rank, but Silas knew that because Felix had been put in charge of this mission, his commands had to be obeyed.

But damn it....

Silas wasn't allowed any other protests, because Aaron and Micah flanked him and all but dragged him from the cellar. As he struggled to get one last glance over his shoulder, he saw that Michael St. John's eyes had closed.

Strangely, though, he wore a smile on his face.

～

Lucius' fork clattered from his fingers. His eyes stared straight ahead, but I could tell he didn't see me. "Oh, no…."

"What is it? Lucius!"

His gaze seemed to grow less glassy, and his eyes met mine. Bleak, worried…and yet beneath the worry was a flicker of anger that looked as if it could easily grow into a raging forest fire. "Something's wrong. Michael…."

"Is he hurt?" I still didn't entirely understand the connection between the master vampire and his fledglings, but it was clear enough to me that their bond had communicated some kind of calamity to Lucius. My body clenched. Strangely, I realized that I didn't want anything bad to happen to Michael. Yes, he rubbed me the wrong way, but there still seemed something almost wounded about him, as if he'd been forced into a life he didn't want.

"Worse. I don't…." He broke off then, and plucked the napkin from his lap. "We have to go."

I didn't argue. If Michael was gravely wounded, what did that mean? Had something gone wrong during the raid to rescue Silas? Only one way to find out, I knew, and that wasn't by sitting here.

Lucius got out his wallet and carelessly dropped three hundred-dollar bills on the table. We both rose from our chairs at the same time, and were headed for the exit as our waiter came up to us. "Is something the matter? If the food isn't to your liking—"

An impatient shake of the head from Lucius, and I said hurriedly, "No, the food was wonderful. We just got a call with some bad news and have to go. But we've left enough to take care of the bill."

The waiter's gaze flickered toward the table. Immediately his posture became far less tense. "I'm so sorry."

"It's all right," I said. "Thank you for a lovely meal."

And then I didn't have the opportunity to say anything else, because Lucius had taken my hand and was practically dragging me toward the parking lot. I stumbled along as best I could, since I knew I couldn't rely on him to give me a steadying arm this time. He practically flung the ticket at the valet, and was opening the driver-side door before the Mercedes had even come to a stop.

I got in and began wrangling with my seatbelt as he pulled out of the parking lot and headed north on Fair Oaks. Almost immediately he turned down a side street, and zigzagged through a neighborhood I didn't know very well. Apparently he knew exactly where he was going, because after jogging through a few more residential neighborhoods, he turned onto San Rafael Avenue, cutting across the arroyo on the bridge there, so we could reach his own neighborhood of Linda Vista.

After that, it was only a few minutes before we pulled into the long, curved driveway that led to the house. As soon as I got out of the car, I gasped. Lying in front of the doorway were two of Lucius' semivives, one of them the brown-haired man who always chauffeured me back and forth from my condo.

"Oh, my God," I whispered. I didn't even have to feign my shock...or my sadness. Yes, I didn't think much of the semivives most of the time, except to shake my head at their complete lack of a personality, but they hadn't deserved this. They were still people, even if their minds had been broken by Lucius' control. Tears stung in my eyes, and I reached up to wipe them away, not caring what destruction that might cause to the makeup I'd applied so carefully only a few hours earlier. "What happened?"

"*Gula* happened," Lucius said grimly. His face might as well have been carved from marble, it was so cold and pale. Then his expression softened, and he held out a hand. "Come here, my dear. This is terrible, yes, but you will feel safer if you're here next to me."

I didn't argue, but hurried around the rear of the car and went up the steps so I could let him take me by the hand. Oddly, that did feel somewhat reassuring, to have his fingers wrapped around mine. And I hated myself for feeling reassured. It wasn't as though I needed a vampire to protect me from the *gula*...more like the other way around.

"Come along," he told me, and hurried into the house.

Luckily, there were none of Lucius' servants lying in here, but I had no doubt that Felix and his team would have made sure to neutralize all the semivives on the property. The others were probably somewhere out in the gardens, or by the other entrance to the house.

Lucius headed for the kitchen, and then down into the cellar. As I'd hoped, the manacles that had bound Silas were now broken and empty, their prisoner long gone. Relief began to flood through me...and then stopped abruptly when I saw Michael St. John sprawled on the cold stone floor, dark blood pooled all around him. A bloody, splintered piece of wood lay on the ground nearby, as if he'd pulled it from his body and flung it away.

"Oh, no," I whispered, as Lucius let go of my hand and ran forward. He knelt next to his fallen fledgling, and reached out to touch Michael's throat.

"He's alive. Barely." Without hesitating, he reached into his pocket and drew out an elegant silver pocketknife, then traced a careful line against one of his wrists. Immediately, blood began to well up from the wound, and Lucius pressed it against Michael's mouth. The younger vampire spasmed briefly, then began to drink from the cut in his master's wrist, as greedy and unthinking as a newborn latched onto its mother's nipple.

There was something very intimate about the gesture. My cheeks heated, and I wanted to look away, but I forced myself to stand there and watch. After a moment, Lucius pulled his arm away from Michael, and retrieved the silk square from his pocket so he might hold it against the wound.

"That will keep him for a while," he said. "But to survive, he will need to replace the blood he's lost. He will need to feed."

Although I tried not to react, I couldn't help shuddering slightly. Lucius' mouth thinned, and he got to his feet and came toward me.

"This is who we are," he said, his tone harsh. "He cannot survive without blood."

"Can't you just give him some from your supply in the refrigerator?"

"No. He needs living blood, or he will slip into a coma and die the true death."

All I could do was nod. I hated the thought of a living person losing their life to keep Michael alive, but I also knew that any protests I made would only show Lucius that I wasn't quite as on board with the whole vampire thing as I'd tried to convince him I was. As I moved, the heavy ring he'd placed on my finger earlier glinted in the light from the emergency fixture over the door. Lucius believed I was bound to him, and I had to maintain that lie until Silas came to get me. At least he was safe, although I wished with all my being that his rescue hadn't resulted in so much mayhem.

"I will take him to his room," Lucius said. "I want you to stay with him until I come back with his...donor."

His victim, I thought. But of course Lucius couldn't quite bring himself to be that forthright.

"Of course," I murmured.

The master vampire bent and picked up his

fledgling, apparently oblivious to the blood staining his expensive suit. I waited off to one side as he went to the door, then followed him down the hall and upstairs, where we went to the wing opposite the one where Lucius' suite was located.

Michael's room was nearly as large as Lucius', and a stark contrast to the bedrooms I had seen so far in the mansion. Although all the rest of them had been furnished in a style that matched the house, this space was very modern, with furniture in pale wood and stainless steel, the bed on a raised platform. Abstract art hung on the white walls.

Lucius must have noticed the way I was looking around, because after he'd laid Michael on the bed—first moving the pale gray comforter out of the way—he said, "Michael is a child of this time. He once told me...and I quote...that he 'didn't want to live in a room that looked like something out of an old horror movie.'"

Despite everything, I couldn't help smiling slightly. "That does sound like Michael."

"Watch over him. He will sleep while I am gone, but I want someone to be here...just in case."

In case of what? What if he woke up while Lucius was gone and decided, in his ravenous and not-entirely-conscious state, that I looked like a tasty morsel?

I didn't argue, though. I had to assume that Lucius knew what he was doing. Besides, I was still his prize...and now his fiancée. He wouldn't put me in harm's way...would he?

"I'll be here," I promised.

Lucius came to me, then bent and kissed me. A swift kiss, barely more than a brush of his lips against mine. "This is not how I wanted this evening to go," he said. "But I will have him restored soon enough." He touched my cheek and then was gone from the room, moving in that frightening vampire blur, now that he didn't have to worry about me trying to keep up with him.

Since there wasn't anything else I could do, I turned back toward Michael St. John. If it weren't for the blood that stained his dark blue shirt, I could have almost said he looked asleep. While he certainly wasn't all the way back, the blood that Lucius had given him seemed to have restored him somewhat, since he didn't look quite as deathly pale.

There was a black leather and steel chair in one corner. It was too heavy to move, but I sat down on it anyway, perching myself on the edge so I could immediately be at Michael's side if he stirred or called out for someone. I didn't see much sign of life, except the occasional movement beneath his eyelids, as though his eyes twitched in dreams.

I wrapped my arms around myself. It was warm enough in here, especially with the pashmina I had draped around my shoulders, and yet I felt chilled, shivers moving through my body. Probably just a reaction to everything that had happened. Over dinner Lucius had asked me to marry him, and I'd said yes. As a delaying tactic, nothing more, and yet that delay wasn't necessary any longer. Not with Silas free.

Where had the *gula* taken him? I doubted that he'd gone back to his loft in Little Tokyo. The vampires knew where it was located, and although they couldn't enter the loft itself without an invitation, that didn't mean they couldn't still hang around in the vicinity of the building, trying to catch Silas as he went to and from his home.

All the way back to Humboldt? No, I doubted he'd allow his fellow *gula* to take him that far, not when I hadn't yet been extricated from Lucius Montfort's world. Silas would only be waiting for the right opportunity to take me away as well. I was just fine with that. More than fine, really.

Which meant that right now, I only needed

to play along, just as I had been doing already. The opportunity would present itself. It had to.

I twisted the diamond on my left hand. The band was just a little too big; if I'd had any intention of going through with this marriage to Lucius, I would have taken the ring to a jeweler to be sized. No point in doing that, though, not when I hoped I'd be able to return the diamond to Lucius in the very near future.

As to how I'd explain everything to Jackson...well, I'd figure that out when the time came. Right now, I only wanted to get through the night.

The sound of footsteps came down the hallway. A moment later, Lucius entered the room. Slung over one shoulder was the unmoving body of a man, thin, hair unkempt and lank, face obscured by at least a week's worth of beard.

I got up from the chair where I sat. To my horror, the man's eyes opened when I moved, although they were so glassy and bloodshot, I doubted he even registered that I was there.

Without looking at me, Lucius crossed over to the bed and dumped the man on the right-hand side, only a foot from where Michael lay.

"Where—" I began, then stopped myself. Did it really matter where Lucius had found this poor specimen of humanity?

"It pays to know where the addicts tend to

congregate," Lucius said. He turned away from the bed, silver-steel eyes expressionless. "They make good prey—they rarely fight back, and all too often no one really pays much attention when they go missing. Of course, Tristan and Leticia claim there's no sport in these kinds of victims, but personally, I think it's better sport not to get caught."

He spoke so casually, so callously, that I could feel the bile begin to rise in my throat. "He's still a human being."

"Barely."

All right, a different tack. I didn't know for sure why I was attempting to delay the inevitable. Sooner or later, Michael St. John would wake up enough to feed, and there wasn't a damn thing I could do to stop it. "And the drugs in his system won't harm Michael?"

"No. Nothing any human can take will affect us. Drugs, alcohol—it makes no difference."

Well, there went that excuse.

Lucius' expression softened, and he stepped away from the bed and came toward me. "I know this is difficult to accept, Serena. If I could bring Michael back from this with only the bottled blood I have on hand, I would. But he must have living blood."

"I know." I looked over at the man who would soon be Michael St. John's dinner. He stared up at the ceiling, eyes still blank and unfocused. I wondered how much heroin he had flowing in his veins right then—the track marks on his arms were visible even from a few feet away. I supposed it was something that he was so high, he probably wouldn't even realize he was dead until a few hours afterward.

From the bed, there came a moan. Not from the intended victim, but from Michael, who stirred, although his eyes hadn't yet opened. But I saw his nostrils flare, saw how his mouth opened. His teeth glinted in the illumination from the track lighting overhead.

"He is waking up," Lucius said. He reached and gently touched my arm. "It is probably better if you're not here when he fully awakes, for that is when he will feed."

My stomach lurched again, all that lovely rib-eye and wine grinding in my gut. "I understand. I'll go wait downstairs in the salon."

"I'll come down to you when…when it's over. Michael will need to sleep again afterward."

I nodded, then turned away from Lucius and went out the door and then down the hall. Maybe I was a coward, but I knew I couldn't stay there and watch Michael murder a stranger.

CHAPTER FOURTEEN

THEY TOOK HIM TO THE SAFE HOUSE IN THE Hollywood Hills. Silas had only been here once before, several years earlier. As Felix—now back in his human form—drove away from Pasadena and cut across on the 134 Freeway and then down into Hollywood, Silas knew the safe house had to be where they were headed.

As hideouts went, it was fairly spectacular. The house was built on multiple levels, and had an eye-popping view across Hollywood, all the way to downtown to the east, or out to Century City to the west. A pool shimmered blue-green in the backyard.

"I have to go after Serena," Silas told Felix. Aaron and Micah had already departed in their own vehicle. Where they were staying, Silas didn't know, and hadn't asked. The Watchers had a few properties stashed around the L.A. basin; it was entirely possible that the two *gula* were holed up in one of those houses, condos, or lofts, just as it was also possible that they had taken refuge in a hotel. Better that he remained ignorant of their whereabouts, at least until their services were needed again.

"No, you are not going after her," Felix said sternly. "At least, not yet. We didn't rescue you just so you could go off half-cocked and get yourself captured again."

"You know that wouldn't happen."

"I don't know anything."

Silas scowled and looked out the kitchen window at the pool in the backyard, like a glowing jewel in the dark. For some reason the two of them had ended up in here, propped up against the kitchen counters, rather than any of a number of more comfortable places in the house...maybe because they both realized this was not a social call.

The other *gula* crossed his arms. "Look, I'm not saying that we're not going to do our best to extract her...when the time is right, and no sooner. She seems to be handling herself pretty well. Resourceful, for a rich girl."

Anger flashed within him. Silas cocked an eyebrow at Felix and snapped, "What the hell is that supposed to mean?"

"Oh, come on. I know you think you're in love with her —"

"I *am* in love with her. There's nothing to 'think' about."

"All right. Fine." Felix shrugged and went on, "All I'm saying is that she's someone who's always had everything handed to her. She hasn't had to work hard for anything in her life. So it's kind of nice to see that she isn't being a helpless victim, that she's trying to be proactive."

"Serena is anything but helpless." Silas thought of the accident that had almost ended her life, how she'd had to endure months of physical therapy to get herself anywhere close to where she'd been before the car had struck her. How she still experienced pain because of the injuries she'd suffered, pain that would never entirely go away.

"Look, we're on the same page when it comes to that subject." After running a hand through his short-cropped fair hair, Felix said, "Anyway, we have other more important matters we need to worry about. Apparently, Lucius has Serena's brother convinced that some sort of serum derived from vampire blood will help his daughter, who has leukemia. In exchange, Jackson is supposed to have his team of researchers cook up a serum that will take away some of the less desirable parts of being a vampire, like avoiding the sun, possibly even drinking blood."

That revelation knocked any further defense of Serena right out of Silas' brain. "How the hell did Lucius manage to convince Jackson Quinn of *that?*"

"Serena. She had a series of visions that showed a future where vampires were able to walk in the daylight. Now, we know that her family isn't too keen on her visions, but they also can't deny that they're highly accurate. That seemed to be enough evidence for Quinn to throw his not-inconsiderable resources at solving the problem."

Silas had begun to regret not sitting down, because his head was spinning. At least he had the tiled countertop to prop him up. "How long has this been going on?"

"Not that long. Serena says Jackson has the research facility going already, but they've only had a day to get to work. No one's going to find a cure that fast—whether for her niece, or for vampirism. But we need to shut that thing down. Having day-walking vampires is going to shift the balance of power too far in their direction."

That was only the truth. The *gula* had powers of their own, but one thing they'd always been able to use to their advantage was their ability to function whether it was night or day. If vampires suddenly didn't need to drink blood, could function in the sunlight just like everyone else, then they might not be as careful about making more of their kind. With a sinking feeling in his stomach, Silas pictured a world where the vampires began to multiply without check, far outnumbering the *gula,* who had a difficult time reproducing to begin with.

"What about Serena's niece? I know we can't let the vampires have their cure, but to deprive a child of a chance at a normal life...."

For a long moment, Felix said nothing. He looked past Silas toward the yard beyond the kitchen window, although his gaze didn't seem to be focused on any one particular thing in the landscape. Then he let out a breath, his expression sorrowful. "I don't want to condemn a little girl to death. In cases like this, there are no acceptable losses. But...." Again he paused, hands jammed in the pockets of his jeans. "If we have to weigh the death of one child against the possibility of a world dominated by vampires, then you know what we must do."

Unfortunately, Silas did know. He just wasn't sure whether he was ready to accept that reality. Besides, how could he ever tell Serena that he'd allowed her niece to die so the entire world might be saved?

~

Because I still had my watch strapped to my wrist, I knew exactly how many minutes passed before Lucius came to meet me in the salon. Seventeen. It felt far longer than that, however.

As he came into the room where I'd been sitting, I got up from my chair. "How is he?"

"He will be all right. He's sleeping again now...or at least what passes for sleep in our kind."

"Did he say anything about what happened?"

Lucius nodded, and then moved past me to go to the table where the decanter of Armagnac was located. "Drink?"

I wished I had the strength to protest, but I was feeling too shaken right then. "Yes, please."

He poured a decent measure of Armagnac into two of the brandy snifters that sat on the tabletop. Silently, he handed one to me, waited for me to take a sip. That first sip was soon followed by another. I needed something to steady my nerves, something to help me get past the realization that a man had just died in Michael's room upstairs. Even though I knew Lucius would have stopped me if I'd run up there and tried to rescue the intended victim, I couldn't help being racked by guilt. Since I'd done nothing, even though I'd known what was about to happen, wasn't I now complicit in his death?

I cleared my throat. "So...what did happen?"

"Three *gula* came here to free Silas. He must have given them the address much earlier, but was too impatient about coming to rescue you and so didn't wait for them to assist him." Those words were accompanied by a faint curl of his lip. I supposed Lucius found something amusing about Silas charging in here to save me, only to be captured himself, but I didn't find anything remotely funny about the situation. "At any rate, if they were watching the property, then they would have known when I left for dinner and seized the opening. All of my semivives are gone."

"I'm sorry," I murmured, although to be honest, I wasn't sure whether I should be mourning their deaths or glad that their souls were now freed from their bondage. "You didn't feel that, though? I mean, at dinner you seemed to know exactly when Michael—"

"The bond between a master and a semivive is different from the bond between a vampire and his fledglings. I could direct the semivives, give them orders to follow, but we did not have the same soul-deep connection that I do with Michael, or with Tristan and Leticia. So until we came here, I did not know that I'd lost them all."

What could I say? Merely repeating "I'm sorry" didn't seem like the correct response. Instead, I went over and put a hand on Lucius' arm, hoping he'd see the gesture as a sign that I truly was sympathetic to his situation. Of course I wasn't, but it seemed I still had to play the game for a while longer, at least until Silas was able to do some rescuing of his own. About all I could do was pray that rescue would come in the very near future. "What happened then?"

"They went to the cellar, where Michael was speaking with Silas." Lucius' mouth twisted again, although this time it seemed to be more from annoyance than amusement. He sipped some of his Armagnac before continuing, "I should have known that it would be difficult to keep Michael away from my captured *gula*. In a way, it was an interesting experiment."

"'Experiment'?" I repeated. "What do you mean?"

"I guessed that Michael would be automatically drawn to Silas."

I raised an eyebrow. "Do you mean Michael is gay?"

That question elicited a chuckle. "No, not at all. Michael felt a connection to Silas because he's Silas' older brother."

If Lucius had reached out and punched me in the gut, I couldn't have felt more gobsmacked. I clenched my fingers around the snifter I held, afraid that otherwise it would slip from my trembling fingers. "He's *what?*"

"A little joke of mine." Lucius drank some more of his Armagnac, silvery eyes glinting with amusement. "You know how the *gula* send away all their female offspring, and the boys in whom the gargoyle blood hasn't bred true?"

"Yes," I said cautiously. "Silas told me about that."

"Charming practice, isn't it? Ruthlessly practical, so I suppose I should admire them for their purity of purpose. At any rate, Michael was Silas' elder by some four years. He was sent away and adopted by a family here in Southern California—in Glendora, I believe. When I relocated here, I thought it would be interesting to find one of these castoffs, see if he or she had the correct temperament to become one of my fledglings. As it turned out, Michael St. John was the perfect candidate. That's not his real name, of course—it was the name he took after he entered his new life. But that doesn't change the reality of the blood in his veins, or his connection to Silas Drake."

It was all too much. I staggered over to one of the chairs by the fireplace and dropped into it. Michael and Silas were brothers. Now that I thought about it, their coloring was the same, although otherwise they didn't look terribly alike. Not that it mattered—I had plenty of friends whose siblings barely resembled one another. In my own family, the connection was more obvious, but that also didn't mean much. I drank some Armagnac, hoping it would steady me. "Do either of them know?"

"No. I have no idea whether Silas even knows he has an older brother. Oftentimes, the *gula* never mention those who were born first and discarded." Lucius finished the remaining liquor in his glass, and went over to the table with the decanter and poured himself some more. He sent an inquiring glance in my direction, and I shook my head. I still had more than half of what he'd poured for me in my glass. "As for Michael, I never told him. He does know that he's adopted, but since the adoption was handled legally through an agency, he has no reason to think there was anything strange about the circumstances of his adoption. The agency told him the files were sealed, and that his birth mother didn't wish to be found. He never tried to seek her out. Why, I'm not sure. Possibly he did not wish to upset his adopted family."

"God." I set down my glass on the small marble-topped table next to the chair where I sat. Already I felt rather swimmy, and I thought it was probably better if I slowed down a little on the drinking. How would Silas react when he found out? Because I had to tell him. He needed to know that Michael was no ordinary vampire.

A *gula* with a vampire brother. Lucius did like his little jokes.

"That's why Michael was in the cellar when the Watcher SWAT team arrived," Lucius said. "He says he tried to stop them, but no one vampire, even with our not-inconsiderable powers, can hope to prevail against three *gula*. I suppose we should all count ourselves lucky that Silas' rescuers were more concerned with getting him out than stopping to check that the blow with the wooden stake had actually finished off their target. It went through his chest, but not through his heart, which is why he will survive their cowardly attack."

Three against one definitely wasn't a fair fight, but then, Lucius had set four of his semi-vives against Silas when he came to rescue me. At this point, I'd have to say the score was pretty even. I kept that thought to myself, though. I only made what I hoped were sympathetic sounds.

"So," Lucius continued, "now all we have to do is wait for Michael to fully absorb the blood he took in, so that he is able to finish his recovery. I've sent the call out to Tristan and Leticia, telling them to come home. While I know the

Watchers in general prefer to avoid doing anything that might call attention to them or their activities, they may be feeling bold right now and may attempt another attack. It's safer if we're all here together."

I didn't like the way he said "we." He didn't mean that I would have to stay here, too, did he? But I realized it would be strange if he didn't make the request. After all, it was much more likely that Silas would attempt to retrieve me if I was back at my condo, rather than locked up here in this mansion.

My fears were borne out, for in the next moment, Lucius said, "I know we agreed that it would look better to your family if you stayed at your condo, but after what's happened tonight, I don't think it's a good idea for you to be there. You're far too exposed. I'll have Brian bring some of your things over."

Damn. I wished I could think of a realistic protest, but it seemed as though no matter what I came up with, any reason I might give for going home sounded like a weak excuse at best. All right. I'd stayed here before and lived to tell the tale; one more night wasn't going to make that much of a difference. "Sure," I said, hoping I sounded completely unconcerned by the prospect of spending the night in Lucius' mansion. "I don't think it will look that strange for me to be staying over on my birthday."

"Excellent."

"But…."

"But?"

"What happens tomorrow? I mean, with your semivives gone, there won't be anyone here to protect me during the daytime."

A frown creased Lucius' pale forehead. "I will have to make more. It is a bother, because they always take a little time to get used to their new routines, but I fear I don't have any choice."

Oh, hell. While somewhere in the back of my mind I'd understood that eventually he would cook up a fresh batch of mindless servants, I really hadn't expected him to move on the project so quickly. And after knowing what had happened to the poor man Michael had used as a revivifying tonic, the last thing I wanted was for more innocent victims to get sucked into Lucius' orbit. But again, I knew I couldn't argue against his plan. I had to let him think I was okay with all this.

"I will wait until Tristan and Leticia get here, of course," Lucius told me. "I couldn't leave you here alone."

I nodded. The last thing I wanted was the gruesome twosome to be my babysitters, but the idea had some logic. You didn't leave your girlfriend unattended when her former lover was suddenly free and, no doubt, extremely pissed off. "I think I'll stay in my room," I said.

"Excellent idea. I know you have no love lost for the pair, and I cannot blame you. But with them here, you should be safe."

Unless one of them wants me for an after-dinner morsel, I thought. No, the two vampires were bloodthirsty and ruthless, but they weren't stupid enough to have their boss's best girl as a late night snack. "And Brian will be coming by with my things," I offered.

"Yes," Lucius said, and hesitated. It was clear enough to me that he didn't think Brian could do much to protect me, should the Watchers return to finish what they'd started. "Yes, it will be good for you to have a friend here."

"Should I make a list for him?" I asked.

"That's not necessary. He'll know what to get."

Of course he would, since he was the one who'd taken all my things from my condo when Lucius first kidnapped me. I didn't bother to point that out. Now everything was supposed to be fine between me and Lucius. After all, just an hour or so earlier, I'd agreed to become his wife.

Footsteps echoed in the corridor outside, and a moment later, Leticia and Tristan appeared in the doorway. They both wore expressions of extreme irritation, but that was nothing new.

"What's this about Michael?" Tristan demanded. "Is he all right?"

"He's fine. Or rather, he will be fine, when he awakes tomorrow evening. For now, I will need you to stand guard. Serena will be going to her room shortly, as I want her to stay here tonight. The semivive Brian will be here soon as well. I need to go out to claim more semivives, as we will need to make sure we have sufficient guards here before the sun comes up."

Neither of the two vampires appeared terribly startled by any of this information, although I noticed the way Leticia's hard blue gaze slid in my direction and then back toward her master. She didn't appear thrilled by the revelation that I would be back in the mansion once again. Or rather, I thought, since I realized she hadn't been looking at my face, but somewhere a little lower down, she'd seen the big diamond on my finger, the one that hadn't been there before. It wasn't that Leticia had any claims on Lucius herself, but she probably hated the idea of a mortal hooking up with her master.

Well, I wasn't thrilled about it, either, but I had to go along for now and seize whatever opportunities might present themselves.

"Do you want me to check on Michael when

I go upstairs?" I asked, and Lucius sent me an approving smile.

"Yes, that would be a very good idea. Why don't you look in on him now? I will be going very soon, since Leticia and Tristan are here."

"Of course, Lucius." Ignoring the glares from the two vampires, I went over to him and gave him a quick kiss on the cheek. "And Brian can just meet me in my room when he gets here?"

"Certainly." The master vampire touched my hand briefly, a gesture of reassurance, but also of dismissal.

Fine by me. I was all too happy to get out of there. I murmured, "Be careful," and then fled the salon, hurrying to the staircase so I might go up to Michael's room.

Of course, on my way upstairs, I thought of the man Michael had just fed on. Would his body still be there, lying on the bed next to him? Or had Lucius thoughtfully stuffed the poor guy in a closet?

If he's still there, just deal with it, I told myself as I mounted the steps. *Better yet, make yourself useful and check his pockets for identification. If you manage to survive this, then you can pass that information on to Detective Ortiz or someone else in the Pasadena P.D.*

That sounded very noble, and practical as well. I just had to hope I wouldn't throw up during the process. I'd never been around a dead body before.

Well, unless you counted seeing Lucius Montfort hold my sister's corpse in his arms.

I swallowed, and continued up the stairs. When I got to the top, I paused to take off my shoes. Those things had been killing my feet for the past hour. Now that I was inside — and away from Leticia and Tristan — I figured it was in my best interests to remove those torture devices before they gave me a blister.

After setting them off to one side from the staircase, I continued down the hall to Michael's room. Lucius had left the door partially ajar, so I pushed it open a few more inches and squeezed inside.

Michael lay on the bed, alone. His hands rested at his sides, and his mouth was closed. However, I could see the line of blood that trailed from the corner of his lips, across his cheek, and down his neck. I forced myself to take a breath and move closer. Lucius hadn't bothered to get him out of his stained shirt, probably because he'd known there was a very good chance that any fresh clothes would get blood-stained as well.

A healthy flush touched Michael's cheeks. In fact, he looked healthier than I'd ever seen him before, probably because Lucius had instructed his vampires to avoid any fresh kills for a while, and therefore they'd all been subsisting on bottled blood. Maybe it was the color in his face, or maybe simply that I knew the truth about him now, but for the first time I could see something of a resemblance between Michael and Silas, in the sensual curve of the lower lip, the same straight, expressive eyebrows. And the long black lashes, now lying against his cheeks.

I didn't think I'd made any sound, but all the same, those lashes flickered open. Dark eyes caught mine.

A harsh whisper. "Serena?"

"I'm here," I said.

"Silas…." he began, and then stopped, as though he didn't have the strength to say anything more than those two syllables.

I couldn't tell him. Not now, not as weak as he was. Maybe soon I'd have the chance. Anyway, I knew that wasn't what Michael had been asking me. "He got away."

"Good."

My eyes widened in shock. I'd already known that Michael St. John could be contrary and slightly quirky, but I really hadn't expected him to be happy that his master's prisoner had managed to escape. "Excuse me?"

One corner of his mouth twitched. "Crazy, I

know." He huffed out a breath that seemed to rattle at the back of his throat. "Tired."

"Sleep, then. I'll be here."

He nodded, and his eyes shut again. Within a few seconds, his breathing became even and deep, without a trace of the rattle I'd heard a moment earlier.

Sleep was what he needed…or the vampire equivalent of sleep, anyway. I still didn't know exactly how that worked. Usually a vampire wouldn't be in bed at this time of night, nocturnal creatures that they were, but it seemed obvious enough to me that Michael's need to heal had overcome his usual instincts.

I stepped away from the bed and glanced around the room. No sign of the man who'd just contributed to Michael's healing process. Pulling in a breath, I went over the the walk-in closet and opened it up. No body inside there, only neat racks of dark clothing, and a shelf at the far end, obviously custom built, that held three guitars.

Lucius had said Michael was a musician back before he'd been turned, but I'd gotten the impression he didn't play anymore. Obviously, I was mistaken. In a way, it comforted me to know that he still had an outlet for those creative energies, even though his life had been so irrevocably changed.

After shutting the closet door, I turned back toward the room. Michael seemed down for the count. Possibly he'd only wakened to see who was invading his personal space, and, once he'd assured himself that I was no threat, had allowed himself to fall into the deepest of healing slumbers.

Across the room was another door, probably to the bathroom. While I hated the thought of going in there—because it was becoming increasingly likely that the victim's body had been disposed of in that room—I knew I needed to check.

I pushed open the door and looked inside. Like the rest of the suite, the bathroom was clean and spare, with white subway-style tile on the walls, gray granite countertops, black towels. The shower was enclosed by glass blocks.

They blurred what was inside, but couldn't entirely hide it.

A tile bench had been built into one wall. The drug addict Lucius had kidnapped was propped up in the corner, his head lolling to one side, his skin nearly as white as the tile on the wall behind him. The puncture marks in his throat, livid red, were the only thing of real color about him.

My hand went to my mouth, but I didn't make any sound. I knew I couldn't. And terrible as the sight was, the expression on the man's face shocked me even more. I'd been expecting a look of horror, eyes bulging from their sockets, mouth open in a silent scream. Instead, his eyes were shut, and he looked peaceful, as though the death Michael had given him was the release he so desperately sought.

Or maybe I was simply trying to rationalize the man's murder.

I wiped my damp palms on my dress, then made myself step into the shower enclosure. The man was wearing filthy jeans, and I hated to touch them. But I forced myself to move closer, to reach inside the front pocket of his pants.

Nothing there.

All right. I tried the other front pocket. Nothing there, either. Gritting my teeth, I reached around him and felt for the edge of his back pocket. No wallet, but I did find a piece of folded paper. I drew it out, saw that it was a picture of a woman around my age, blonde, pretty. His girlfriend? Sister? Wife?

I didn't know. The picture was a piece of evidence, though, and so I transferred it to my left hand, freeing up my right to check the final pocket. It was empty. I supposed it was somewhat silly of me to expect a guy like this to be walking around with a wallet. I had the impression that people who lived on the street didn't worry too much about having the proper I.D.

What did Lucius plan to do with the man's body? Have one of his newly minted semivives dig a grave somewhere out in the yard? That seemed like the most obvious plan. I wondered how many of the vampires' other victims had been buried in unmarked plots in the mansion's extensive grounds.

A shudder went over me, and I pushed the gruesome thought away. There wasn't anything I could do to help this man now, except murmur a few words under my breath and hope the look of peace I'd seen on his features wasn't a lie.

I went back out into the main room. Michael still slept, and so I walked carefully past him — glad that I'd removed my clacking high heels — and on into the corridor. No sound from downstairs, which seemed to indicate that Lucius had left on his semivive-acquiring expedition. If Tristan and Leticia spoke to one another, their conversation was quiet enough that I couldn't hear it from up here.

Good. I didn't know how keen vampire ears were, but I had to hope they couldn't hear me, either. I picked up my shoes with my free hand, then headed down the hallway toward the wing where my bedroom was located.

It didn't look as if anything had been touched since the last time I was here. No dust, though, so someone must have cleaned the room. I hurried over to the dresser and slipped the photograph of the blonde woman into one of the drawers, then went to the closet and set my shoes down on the floor.

Just in time, too, because as I emerged from the closet, I saw not-Brian enter the room with several of my suitcases. "Hi, Brian," I said brightly, although I wanted to frown at the amount of luggage he was carrying. It seemed like rather a lot for just an overnight stay.

"Serena."

He didn't seem like his normal chirpy self— or at least, the semi-normal, sometimes-chirpy semivive he'd become. I had to ask. "Is everything okay?"

"Of course. Why wouldn't it be?"

Hmm. "Well, I know it's upsetting, to have the *gula* break in here like that, but Michael is going to be fine—I just saw him—and Lucius seems to be handling everything just fine as well, so—"

"It's not that." He dropped the suitcases near the dresser where I was standing, then went into the bathroom and set the smaller bag I used for toiletries on the countertop there. "No, it's only that Lewis couldn't quite understand why I had to go to your apartment and get your things, then bring them over here. I said I was doing a favor for a friend, and he said it seemed more like I was your errand boy. I've tried very hard to avoid arguing with him, because I know Lucius wouldn't like it, but this time it was...difficult."

"I'm so sorry," I said. "I can try to patch things up with Lewis the next time I'm home—"

"No," Brian cut in. "That would just make things worse, I think."

He was probably right. Lewis and I had always been friendly, but it was Brian I was really close to. Every once in a while, I got the impression that Lewis was slightly jealous of the time I spent with his partner, just because the two of us worked from home while Lewis had to go downtown to work each day. None of that was my fault, of course, but....

I didn't bother to argue. "I can see that. Then I guess you'd better get back before he really blows a gasket. Tristan and Leticia are here, so I'll be fine."

The real Brian might have seen something strange about me saying I was "fine" with being alone in the house with the people who'd murdered my sister. Despite the flashes of his former self that I'd seen, this Brian showed no reaction to my comment. Obviously I was safe, since two of his master's fledglings were here.

"Yes, that's probably a good idea." His gaze

moved to my hand. "Congratulations, by the way. We're—well, I'm very happy for you."

I wanted to ask him if he'd felt his fellow semivives being murdered, but no, it was probably better if I left that subject severely alone. He had to know he was the only one left...at least for now. I doubted Lucius would be able to get his semivive complement up to full strength in only one evening. How many lives would he subvert tonight? Three? Four?

Pushing those thoughts away, I smiled at Brian. "Thank you. We don't know when exactly yet, but if all goes well, hopefully it will be soon."

A nod. "Something to look forward to. Good night, Serena."

"Good night."

Brian let himself out, and I went and closed the door behind him. The wood was far too flimsy to keep out a vampire, but I wanted the illusion of privacy. At any rate, I had to hope that Tristan and Leticia were busy drinking blood cocktails, or whatever it was they did to keep themselves occupied when compelled to stay home.

Home. I'd had a few precious days in my own place, but now I'd been forced back here.

Hopefully, not for long, I told myself. *Just until Silas and the gula can figure out how to get you away.*

Problem was, the last time it had taken a week, and Silas still hadn't been successful. I had no desire to go through that again.

I looked down at the suitcase Brian had brought. The thought of unpacking it and putting everything away didn't appeal at all, probably because doing so would feel like an admission that I wouldn't be getting away anytime soon.

Then my gaze traveled to the door on the opposite side of the room…the door that led into Lucius' suite. I crossed over and reached out to test it, even as I told myself that of course he wouldn't have left it unlocked.

The knob turned in my hand.

My heart sped up, although I knew that the room beyond had to be unoccupied. Lucius was out hunting for more semivives, and the half-living servant who'd guarded this chamber for him was now dead. There was no one around to see me enter.

Still, I hesitated. Was I worried that Lucius might return unexpectedly, and catch me snooping? Of course. I somehow doubted my ability to lie my way out of that situation, although I'd been doing a serious amount of lying over the past week, and so far Lucius hadn't caught me out.

This might be my only chance.

I pulled in a breath and then pushed the door open. The room beyond wasn't completely dark, since two of the old-fashioned brass sconces on the walls had been left illuminated. They showed what I had seen before — the large space with the crystal chandelier overhead, the heavy, ornate furniture, oversized to match the scale of the room. And the large black-hung bed that dominated the chamber, although now I knew it would be empty, the equally oversized semivive who'd kept watch here now gone.

Still, I peeked past the black curtains that hung from the canopy, just to be sure that the bed really was unoccupied. My heart slowed a little as I saw that the silk coverlet lay smooth and flat, with no sign that anyone had lain there anytime recently.

Well, then.

I glanced down at my watch. It was nearly ten, and Lucius had been gone for about forty-five minutes. That couldn't be enough time to subvert one semivive, let alone a group of them. If I was lucky, he would be gone for at least three or four hours. However, that wasn't reason enough to linger.

Where to look first?

The nightstand was closest, so I opened the top drawer and peeked inside. I wasn't sure what I'd find, but the contents of that drawer almost made me smile, they were so prosaic—a couple of boxes that contained his cufflinks, a spare brush and comb, a packet of Kleenex. Did vampires even get runny noses, or were the tissues there for some other reason?

I'd probably never know, since I couldn't exactly expect Lucius to explain the items I'd found while snooping through his belongings.

The bottom drawer contained socks. Again, I wanted to laugh. Yes, vampires wore normal clothes like regular people, but for some reason, I never really thought about them wearing socks.

The lack of incriminating evidence was a little annoying. Then again, I didn't know exactly what I'd expected to find. A diary with all his plans for world domination written down so I'd have proof of his perfidy, once I was released from this place? That would have been nice, but real life was rarely that convenient.

When I went to the other nightstand, I saw that it was empty. Had it always been that way, or had Lucius cleaned it out in anticipation of my joining him here in this room in the near future?

I didn't like that idea at all.

Mouth set, I went over to the large marble-topped dresser placed up against the wall opposite from the bed. The top drawer there held undershirts, the one below that, underwear. I closed that drawer so hastily it made a distinct bang, and I winced. While neither Tristan nor Leticia had shown any inclination to come upstairs and check on me, I knew I needed to be more careful than that, even if I did find the idea of snooping around in Lucius Montfort's under-wear drawer just a tad distasteful.

All right. I moved down to the next drawer and slid it open.

Inside lay the sketchbook and notebook Brian—or possibly Lucius, since I really wasn't sure who'd taken those items—had stolen from my condo.

I froze. Things had been so chaotic that I hadn't had much of a chance to even think about my notebook, or the sketchbook. And if I had stopped to think about it, then I probably would have realized that it made sense for Lucius to have taken them, because within those pages he might have found some additional clues regarding the future I'd described to him in my visions.

Right then, I didn't care about sense, or logic. Those books were mine, filled with things I'd seen, even if only in the context of a vision. Lucius didn't have any right to even look at them, let alone steal them from my house.

Fingers shaking, I pulled out both books and hugged them to my chest. I knew I should have put them back, so Lucius wouldn't know I'd seen them, but I needed to look at them. Now that I'd gotten a sense of the bigger picture, I had to know whether I'd overlooked an earlier detail that might have told me where I would end up.

Not in here, though. The room next door wasn't really mine, either, but it felt like a sanctuary compared to the gloomy grandeur of Lucius' suite.

I shut the dresser drawer and went back into my room, closing the door that connected the two chambers. A glance at my watch told me it was ten after ten. Still early enough that I should have plenty of time to look through the notebook and sketchbook, and put them back. Lucius didn't need to know I'd ever had them. I wasn't too worried about him dusting for fingerprints. He'd never find out.

Unless, of course, vampires had some sixth sense when it came to people rooting around in their things. It was a risk I was willing to take.

I sat down on the bed, and opened the sketchbook.

CHAPTER FIFTEEN

Felix had left, after once more admonishing Silas to stay put and not do anything stupid. He would have argued, but really, the other *gula* had a point. By charging into Lucius Montfort's mansion right away instead of waiting for backup, Silas had done something sort of spectacularly stupid.

On the other hand, sitting here and waiting around while Serena was still in the vampire's hands didn't seem like a very good idea, either.

All the same, Silas had promised that he would behave himself, and Felix took off. Where to, Silas didn't know, but he had a feeling he'd join the other two Watchers in staking out Montfort's property. Would they attempt an extraction on their own? Maybe, if they thought they had a decent shot at it. Serena clearly had been going along with Montfort in an effort to keep Silas from harm, but now that he was a free man, she should have been free, too. That she was still caught in the vampire's clutches more than rankled; it made him rage.

Restless, he roamed around the house, taking note of the entrances and windows. He'd been here once before, right when he came to Los Angeles, but it had been years since he'd visited. No need—the safe house was precisely that, a place of refuge. Up until now, he'd been safe enough in his loft near downtown. But the vampires knew he lived there, and since Silas guessed that Lucius would be all too happy to rid himself of his *gula* rival, it was too risky to stay in the place that had been his home for the past three years.

This house definitely was an upgrade, he had to admit. If he'd been able to bring Serena here so they could sit by the pool and watch the lights of L.A. while they drank wine and talked about their shared future, Silas would have been happy to be here. Now, though….

He opened the door that led from the kitchen into the garden, and walked out into the darkness. It wasn't truly dark, of course, not with all those city lights bouncing their careless illumination every which way. Not dark like the forests outside Fortuna, deep in Humboldt County, where there weren't enough houses to dispel the primordial darkness of nighttime there. Still, it was dim and secluded enough that he could feel some of the tension leave his neck and shoulders. Not all; he wouldn't be able to truly relax until he had Serena back in his arms. Nevertheless, the world looked a little brighter than it had this morning, when he'd still been chained in Lucius Montfort's wine cellar.

Now would have been a good time to strike, to get Serena back, since all the vampire's semi-vives had been killed in the raid. However, that hadn't happened, and Silas could guess why— Lucius would have called his other vampires to him, and set them to guard the mansion. Three vampires against three *gula* wasn't good enough odds to take the risk, though, which was probably why Silas was sitting here. While he would have protested that he was in good enough shape to join in such a mission, thus improving those odds a good deal, he knew better. Those days of being chained up and given just enough food to keep from starving had taken their toll. Every inch of his body ached, and he was hungry.

Well, he could remedy that issue at least. Safe houses always had a decent store of frozen and canned food on hand, just because you never knew when you might need to take refuge there. And in the morning he could probably go to the local store for some fresh items. He wasn't too worried about Lucius Montfort or his slaves tracking him down here—this safe house had never been discovered, so the vampire master wouldn't think to look so far afield for his escaped prisoner.

Silas headed back inside. Sure enough, there was a good supply of frozen items, mostly from Trader Joe's, based on the packaging, but a few national brands were represented as well, like the breakfast burritos. It would be enough to keep him going.

He nuked some chicken tikka masala and rice, then dished it all onto a plate that he took with him out to the living room. A plate glass window occupied most of one wall, revealing yet another view of L.A.'s lightscape. Not very defensible, but then again, the sorts of enemies the Watchers had to worry about weren't the type to stage a commando raid and break in through the windows. No, the vampires and their servants preferred to work in stealth.

After he was done with his food, Silas set down the empty plate and headed toward the garage. He hadn't thought to ask what had happened to his Jeep, which he'd left parked down the block from Lucius' mansion. No doubt it had been towed, since Silas couldn't imagine anyone in that neighborhood putting up with an abandoned vehicle. His *gula* compatriots had probably left it in the impound yard, as they wouldn't want to be so obviously connected to him. There had to be some kind of vehicle here at the house, though. They wouldn't have left him stranded.

Would they?

All right, no *gula* could be said to be truly stranded, not when he could shift forms and use his wings to take him where he wanted to go. However, performing that kind of a maneuver in such a highly populated area was certainly not recommended.

When he opened the door to the garage, he saw it was nearly empty, missing most of the detritus of an occupied house. No boxes of holiday decorations, no peg boards with tools hanging from them. And no car.

However, in the middle of the space sat a motorcycle. Not just any motorcycle, either, but a night-black Ducati. Its key sat on the middle of the seat.

He wasn't so stranded after all. As he gazed at the motorcycle, an idea began to take form in his mind. The other *gula* would be furious, no doubt, but he didn't intend to sit here in luxury when he should be helping to get Serena away from Lucius Montfort.

All he had to do was wait a little while, until the dawn came….

～

When I'd drawn this picture, I hadn't known what it meant. Even now, I had to sort of squint to make the connection, because the reality wasn't quite the same as my vision. That happened sometimes…details would be blurred, slightly off. The gist of it was accurate, just not the fiddly bits.

This sketch, one of the first I'd drawn, was of Michael St. John. I realized that now as I looked down at the drawing. He was in profile, and his hair in the sketch was shorter than it actually was in real life, and so I hadn't made the connection. Oftentimes when you'd only glimpsed someone in profile, you didn't always see the resemblance when you were able to look at them full on. And there was the difference in the hair. I'd drawn this a while back, though, and so maybe his hair had been that short then, and had grown out in the intervening time.

Why I'd seen him, I didn't know, unless it was the visions already drawing the connection amongst all of us…Silas and Michael and Lucius and me. I hoped I'd have a chance to speak to Michael alone at some point, but I couldn't count on that. He might never get the opportunity to learn that Silas Drake was actually his younger brother.

And this other sketch. Now as I looked at it, I realized it must be the interior of the warehouse I'd seen in the first vision I'd had here in Lucius' mansion. It looked like something out of a thriller about contagion, or maybe a Red Cross evacuation center gone wrong. Rows of people lying in cots. No detail about any of them, just all those people in makeshift beds. Standing against the far wall was a row of men in dark clothes. Again, no real detail, but they had to be the guards I'd glimpsed in that same vision. Now I knew they were there to make sure the donors did their duty and provided the unending supply of the necessary blood factors to keep those future vampires happy and day-walking.

Another sketch of what clearly was the garden here. No people, just the pond and the stone bench and the clumps of trees. It hadn't rung a bell for me, because really, the garden wasn't all that distinctive, was fairly typical of the sort of thing you'd see in any house of this vintage.

These were interspersed between sketches of visions I did recognize—the house in northeast Pasadena where the little girl had been kidnapped, the two men loitering near a car that turned out to have a body in the trunk. Clearly, there hadn't been any rhyme or reason as to when the visions that affected my own future appeared. They hadn't been strung together in a coherent narrative like the series of visions I'd been forced to endure here in Lucius' home. For some reason, he had the ability to make my visions obey him. Up to a point, though, or at least only until he had no further need of them. Once he'd understood what the visions were trying to tell him, he'd let me alone.

I thumbed through the notebook quickly, finding more of the same. Buried far back were some brief notes about a vision where I'd seen two men in silhouette, one dark, one fair. I guessed those two men must be Silas and Lucius, rivals as to who would possess me.

No, that was wrong. Silas didn't want to possess me. He loved me, wanted to be with me, but I wasn't property to him, wasn't a prize or something to be exploited.

I saw the face of the little boy in my mind... our little boy. Tears pricked at my eyes, and I blinked them away. I had to be strong now, so that little boy had a future.

And that meant being careful.

I picked up the two books and took them back into Lucius' room, then stowed them in the same drawer where I'd found them, in the same order. After that task was done, I took a quick look around to make sure I hadn't disturbed anything during my hasty search. All seemed to be in order, so I returned to my bedroom and closed the door that connected our two suites.

The suitcase Brian had brought sat by the dresser. I still didn't feel like unpacking it, but I knew I might as well, if for no other reason than if Lucius came back while I was engaged in that activity, then he'd be pleased to see me settling in, and maybe wouldn't wonder whether I'd done anything I shouldn't during his absence. I had to make sure he had no reason to be suspicious.

I went over and opened up the suitcase, then put everything away. It really wasn't all that much—enough clothes for four or five days, certainly not my entire wardrobe. I refolded the jeans, and slipped the photo I'd gotten from the dead man's pocket into one pair of them. By the time I was done, it was almost eleven, and I wanted out of that cocktail dress. I got out some yoga pants and a T-shirt, deeming that outfit handy for either sleeping or talking to Lucius, whichever happened first. Afterward, I went into the bathroom and washed my face and brushed my teeth.

The Jane Austen books Lucius had provided for me still sat on a shelf in the closet, so I got out

Mansfield Park—my least favorite, and so the one most likely to put me to sleep—and settled into bed with it. Whether I'd be able to stay awake until Lucius got back was debatable. It was now nearly eleven, and while I usually stayed up later than that, my days generally didn't include getting marriage proposals from a vampire, or rifling the pockets of a dead man. The weariness that settled over me now was bone-deep, although I knew I'd do my best to ignore it.

I managed to struggle along until around midnight. Eventually, though, my eyelids kept drooping, and at last I succumbed, my eyes closing even as the book slipped from my hands and fell onto the mattress.

Back in the meadow, the cool breeze catching at my hair. This wasn't a vision, though, but only a dream. A child's laughter echoed in my ears, and I ran toward it, even though I couldn't seem to locate its source. "Where are you?" I called out.

More laughter, coming from somewhere within the trees. I plunged into them, felt the air immediately grow colder as the shadows of the pines surrounded me. In my dream, I wore the same T-shirt and yoga pants I had on now. My feet were bare, fallen pine needles rough against my toes.

I veered to the left, following the sound of the boy's laughter, ignoring the pain in my feet as they pounded against the hard forest floor. And then I came to an abrupt halt, for standing in front of an enormous redwood tree was Lucius Montfort, his pale hair glowing in the dimness of the encroaching trees.

In his arms was the boy. My son. My son with Silas.

Lucius grinned, showing his sharp canines. "You don't need him," he said. "You and I will have our own."

Then he bent and sank his teeth into the boy's neck, blood spraying everywhere, bright red, drops of scarlet painting the trees around him, spattering warm against my face.

I screamed, and someone's hands were on me, taking me by the shoulders. "Serena!"

My eyes blinked open, and I saw Lucius leaning over me, his fingers digging into my flesh. I recoiled, and he frowned. "S-sorry," I gasped. "I'm sorry. I was having a nightmare."

"Obviously." The silver eyes bored into mine. "A nightmare...or a vision?"

"Definitely a nightmare," I said, gradually returning to myself as I realized that was only the truth. A nightmare born of my anxiety, of my fear that the vision I wanted to come true never would, but that's all it was. I took a gulp of air and added, "I'm so glad you came home."

His expression warmed, and he reached up to brush a strand of hair away from my face. "I am glad, too. I'd intended to check on you, but then I heard you screaming—"

"Not the best way to introduce your new semivives to the household, that's for sure," I said.

"They were downstairs in the other wing, and so didn't hear you."

So he'd done it. While I didn't want to think about the lives he'd ruined while I was asleep, I had to ask. "How many?"

"Only two. But that will be enough to keep watch over the house tomorrow, and then tomorrow night, I will add to their number. It has to be done carefully, with none of them disappearing too close to any of the others. Otherwise, their absences, clustered together like that, will raise too many questions."

I nodded. Thank God for those logistics, because it meant the house would be sparsely guarded tomorrow. This wasn't like suborning Brian, who was allowed to stay in his former life because of the façade required to make it seem as though everything was normal. No, these men— I assumed they were men, because I'd never seen any female semivives—would be taken completely from their lives so they could be stationed permanently here.

However, I couldn't let Lucius see that I was happy he'd only been able to procure two of his slaves. "You're sure that will be all right?" I asked.

He leaned down and kissed me on the forehead. "Quite sure. I will have Brian come over as soon as his partner leaves for work, and so you will have three guardians for most of the day. Between the three of them and the security system, I know you will be well protected."

Damn. That wasn't so good. If I was going to make a break for it, I'd have to do so in the early morning. Evading two semivives was bad enough, but three? I doubted I could pull that off.

As for the security system, well, I'd worry about that later. I really didn't care if I was caught on camera, as long as all the camera caught was a view of my back as I got the hell out of there. If I managed to get away, then Lucius would realize this was all a sham.

If he didn't already. I still wasn't quite sure if he'd completely bought into my act. Yes, he'd given me a engagement ring, had basically pledged his undying love to me. That didn't mean terribly much when you got right down to it. Lucius Montfort was the sort of person who'd continue to play the game as long as he could get something useful out of it.

For now, though, I need to smile up at him tremulously, to tell him that I was sure I'd be fine, although I'd be happy when he awoke and could make more of his guards. He kissed me again. "I know you will. And I'm sorry this wasn't much of a birthday for you. I'll try to make it up to you when things settle down."

"It was fine," I said. "I got to spend it with you, didn't I?"

"Oh, Serena," he said, his silvery eyes lighting up, "I cannot wait for the day when we can be truly together."

This kiss was far more passionate than the last. I submitted to it as best I could, responding with as much fervor as I was able to summon. Inwardly, though, I could only hope that it would be the very last one I'd have to share with him.

I'd tried to escape before. This go-'round, I'd have to hope that second time was the charm.

On Friday, the sun would rise at 6:22 a.m. Silas didn't need to look up the exact time; the *gula* always knew when the sun rose and set, because those times were so crucial when one's life work included hunting vampires. In general, though, a vampire would be safely bedded down in his blacked-out bedroom at least ten minutes earlier than that in order to avoid any painful and possibly deadly mistakes. Older vampires such as Lucius would be even more cautious. Sometimes when a vampire was first made, he would flirt with the coming of day, would try to see whether he might risk staying awake long enough to see the forbidden sun...and learn a painful lesson. Scars from sun exposure would eventually fade, although the process could take years.

Lucius wouldn't take that kind of chance, however, and Silas wouldn't take any chances here, either. He'd wait until exactly 6:22, and then he'd make his move. Good thing he was alone, that Felix trusted him enough to leave him on his own. Silas disliked breaking that trust, but he couldn't wait for permission that might not even be granted. He had to do this, and now.

At five o'clock, while the world was still dark and even most of L.A. still asleep, he got up from his borrowed bed and took a shower, then had coffee and two breakfast burritos. At a quarter to six, he went out to the garage and powered up the Ducati.

It had a throaty sound, not as deep as a Harley, but enough that you could tell it meant business. A remote for the garage had been left on a shelf next to the door, and Silas activated it now, then tucked the device into his jacket pocket. That was the other thing—he'd found clothes in the dresser in the master bedroom, jeans and T-shirts in various sizes, underwear still in its packaging. And this leather jacket, which fit him almost as well as the one he'd been forced to leave behind at Lucius Montfort's mansion. No helmet, though. He liked the feel of the wind in his hair, and besides, he knew he was safe enough. Even in the unlikely event of an accident, he wouldn't suffer any kind of major injury. It took more than a spill from a motor-cycle to permanently damage a *gula*.

He backed out into the driveway, then paused to close the garage door. A glance up at the dark sky told him it was low and gloomy, reflecting the odd pinkish-orange illumination from the sodium vapor streetlights. Hard to tell whether those were real rain clouds, or merely the low clouds and fog of Southern California's "June gloom," come a little early. It didn't matter, though. Let it rain. The skies could open up, and they still wouldn't deter him from the path he'd chosen.

Even at this early hour, there was a lot of traffic on the streets of Hollywood. Luckily, though, he was heading away from most of it, cutting up past the Hollywood Bowl, on through Universal City, and through the hills past Forest Lawn. At last he was able to get on the 134 Freeway and head east, toward Pasadena.

Midway through Glendale, a sharp, irritating drizzle began to fall. Silas ignored it, continued at a precise sixty-five miles per hour until he got to the San Rafael exit. There he slowed, and pulled off into the wealthy neighborhood he'd come to know all too well. With any luck, this would be the last time he came here.

He slowed down as he came to the block where Lucius' mansion was located, then parked the Ducati a few doors away on the opposite side of the street. The drizzle had turned into a cold, thin rain, beginning to dampen Silas' hair. He lifted one hand to push the wet strands away from his face before taking a quick look in either direction. Several of the houses had begun to show some signs of life—yellow lamplight behind closed curtains and blinds; sprinklers turning on, their timers oblivious to the rain that now fell. Since it was now after six, it would be safe to leave the motorcycle parked here without worrying about some over-zealous policeman writing a ticket for violating the overnight street parking rules for the neighborhood.

It was still dark and gloomy, though, the clouds overhead taking on a slightly lighter shade of charcoal gray as the sun began to rise. He was glad of the rain and the clouds, because they would help to obscure his movements. Although he hadn't gotten a good look at the security system Lucius Montfort had deployed on his property, Silas was fairly certain it used regular CCD cameras, nothing fancy like infrared. In the semidarkness, it would be very difficult to see him moving around...and because there was no way the vampire could have gotten his complement of semivives up to full strength yet, the enslaved guards should be easy enough to avoid.

Silas glanced up and down the street, making sure no one was around to see him cross over to the property that belonged to Montfort. Because of the foul weather, people seemed to be staying indoors. Good. The last thing he wanted was to encounter an eager early-morning runner or gardener.

Since the coast remained clear, he jogged over to the property line, carefully avoiding the driveway and its security cameras. At the corner of the lot, where the fence that surrounded the yard joined up with the fence from the adjoining property, he reached up and grasped the wrought iron and pulled himself over, doing his best to avoid the pointed fleur-de-lis that topped each fence pole. This task would have been easier if he'd taken on his *gula* form, but Silas didn't dare risk being seen. Just because the neighborhood streets were currently deserted didn't mean they'd remain that way.

He dropped down in the narrow space between the fence and a hedge of arborvitae. So far, so good. Actually, the hedge would provide some handy cover, since it followed the fence around the perimeter of the property, and he could lurk behind it until he got to the side of the house where Serena's room was located.

Assuming she was in that same room. Lucius might have moved her. It wasn't as though there was a lack of empty rooms in the enormous house.

...which he realized now appeared to him in its true state, gray and looming, with the towers at its corners and stained-glass windows on the ground floor. Why he didn't see the illusion of the Mediterranean home that Montfort used to disguise the place, Silas wasn't precisely sure. Perhaps it was merely that he'd already pierced that illusion, and therefore it no longer had any power over him.

At any rate, better to start from the known quantity of the room Serena had previously occupied and move out from there if necessary. Silas hurried along, pausing for a moment to check his watch. Six seventeen. Very little chance of Lucius being up and around at that hour, or his fledglings. Briefly, Silas wondered how Michael was doing. The wound from the wooden pole Felix had flung at the vampire must have hurt a good deal, although Felix had purposely aimed to injure, not to kill.

Even a vampire took a little while to bounce back from that kind of injury and blood loss. No doubt Michael was already asleep, too. The only beings capable of movement in the house would be however many semivives Lucius had managed to rustle up, and Serena.

To Silas' surprise, a faint light showed behind the curtains in her room. Was she awake already? He'd never gotten the impression that she was an early riser, but....

Or perhaps she had her own escape plan in place, had realized that she would never have the opportunity after today, when the place was so ill-guarded.

The thought spurred him to action, and he came out from the cover of the hedge to move quickly through the rain and the gray, lowering light. A quick glance from side to side told him that no one was around, so he continued on his course, heading straight for the wing where Serena's room was located.

Nothing so handy as a ladder, or a trellis with climbing vines. He didn't really need either of those things, though — here he was out of eyeshot from the street, so shifting forms wasn't a problem. Pausing, he quickly drew off his leather jacket and T-shirt and tucked them behind a rosebush, hoping the plant would provide enough cover that the garments wouldn't get soaked. At once the cold rain stung his exposed flesh, but he paid no attention to the discomfort. He had more important things to do.

Out came the wings, propelling him upward to the second floor. Since it seemed that Serena was already awake, he decided to knock on the window rather than burst right through it. At least, he hoped it was Serena who had turned on that light, and not one of Lucius Montfort's newly minted semivives. But if it turned out enemies lurked behind that window, Silas would handle them. There couldn't be more than two or three at the most, and since they wouldn't have been enslaved to the vampire for very long, they no doubt would be clumsy, easy to defeat.

His wings beat against the wet air. He lifted his hand, and rapped lightly at the window.

The heavy curtains parted slightly. In the gap he could see Serena's pale face, her eyes widening as she realized who was hovering outside her room. But, bless her, she didn't hesitate. At once she pushed the curtains out of the way, then unlatched the window and opened it.

Silas climbed in as she stepped off to one side to allow him room. "Are you alone?"

"Yes," she replied. He noticed that she was dressed in jeans and a long-sleeved T-shirt, wearing tennis shoes instead of her usual flats. Clearly, she'd been planning to make a break for it. "The vampires are all sleeping, and there are only two semivives guarding the place. I figured this was my only chance."

"My thought as well." He paused so he could shift back into his human form, then reached out for her. At once she went into his arms, let him pull her against his chest. He was damp with rain, but she didn't seem to mind. She hugged him fiercely.

"God, Silas, I was starting to worry that I'd never get to hold you like this again. But we need to go."

He agreed with her, although it was difficult to let her go, to allow her to step away. She looked pale but determined, her warm brown hair pulled back into a ponytail, not a speck of makeup on her face. And she was the most beautiful thing he'd ever seen.

"I packed my stuff, but I couldn't decide whether to take it with me."

His gaze moved away from her to a suitcase and oversized cosmetics case that sat by the dresser. "We'll take it," he said. "I'm bringing you to a *gula* safe house, so it would be better if you had your things with you." He crossed over and picked up the suitcase and cosmetics case, handing the latter item to her. That way, each of them had a hand free...just to be safe.

"Okay," she said. Her gaze shifted toward a door on the opposite side of the room.

"Is he in there?" Silas asked in a murmur.

She nodded.

"It's all right," he told her. "Once a vampire has passed into day sleep, nothing will wake him until the sun sets. You could set off a bomb outside his window, and he'd never hear it."

"Well, that's good to know, but we should still get the hell out of here. I don't know where the semivives are—it's possible that Lucius has them standing guard right outside my door."

"In which case I'll make sure to take care of them if they try to interfere," Silas said. To tell the truth, he would take a grim pleasure in dispatching the slaves. Doing so would mean that the vampire household would be completely unguarded, a perfect opportunity for the rest of the *gula* team here in Los Angeles to come back and smoke out the nest once and for all.

Serena's mouth tightened, but she didn't argue. No point in telling her that there was little chance of saving those semivives, even as newly made as they were. With rare exceptions, once a semivive was enslaved, there was no coming back. Killing them would be a mercy.

"How are we getting out?" she asked. Clearly, she knew there was no point in pushing him on the subject of the semivives, so better for them to focus on the practicalities of the situation. "Back through the window?"

"That was my plan," he said. "It is still dark enough that no one would see us, especially with this rain."

"Then let's get going. I know you just told me that vampire sleep like the dead...or the undead, as the case may be," she added with a quick grin. "But I'll feel a lot better getting the hell out of here."

He couldn't agree more. A quick breath, and he began to summon the change that would alter every cell in his body, turn him into what some people might call a monster.

But before he could shift, become his *gula* self, the door flew open, tearing the hinges right from the wall. There stood Michael St. John, apparently recovered, hands planted on his hips.

"I thought I heard voices in here."

CHAPTER SIXTEEN

I GASPED. HOW COULD I NOT, WITH MICHAEL St. John standing in front of me and Silas, looking extremely pissed off?

"The sun will be up in only a few more minutes," Silas said. His expression was so calm, he might as well have been inquiring as to what Michael wanted in his coffee.

"I know that," the vampire said. "But I can accomplish a lot in a few minutes. You just couldn't stay away, could you?"

"Not when you're holding the woman I love hostage."

Michael's mouth twitched in a sardonic smile. He looked so completely recovered that it was hard to believe he'd been lying on the floor of the cellar, drenched in his own blood, only a few hours earlier. "Oh, but Lucius claims to love her, too. So you could say you're just as big a kidnapper and a thief. He told me last night that he planned to ask her to marry him."

"Ridiculous."

"No, it's true," I said in a very small voice. "He did, over dinner."

"And you said?"

Silas' voice was so tight, I could barely recognize it as his. Damn it—this was not how I wanted to tell him. Anyway, that promise meant nothing. Only another lie I'd told to trick Lucius into thinking I cared. "I said yes!" I burst out. "What the hell else was I supposed to do? I'd tell him anything he wanted to hear, as long as he kept me in this house. But if I really wanted to marry him, do you think I would be dressed and trying to sneak out at the first opportunity?"

No reply for a moment. Silas' dark eyes flashed with anger, although I couldn't say for sure whether that anger was directed at me, or at Lucius, or even at Michael St. John. I hoped Silas wasn't angry with me; I'd only done what I had to, nothing more. "I suppose you have a point," he said at last, still in that taut, flat tone. He glanced over at the vampire. "You heard her. She doesn't love your master. She never did, and never will. We're leaving. You can tell him what you like."

"Oh, sure. I'm going to love delivering that

news to him. He's not going to be very happy when he learns I didn't even try to stop you."

"It's better if you don't."

No way anyone could misconstrue the threat in that statement, and clearly Michael realized that. His eyes narrowed as he appeared to take in the measure of the man who stood before him. "I'd say we're evenly matched."

"Stop it," I broke in. I couldn't stand this anymore. I wanted to go—but I also wanted Michael to get safely back to his room before the sun came up. There was so little time left. Even so, I knew what I had to do.

I had to tell them the truth.

"You can't fight," I went on, the words tumbling over themselves in my haste. "You can't be at odds because—well...you're brothers."

Both men turned incredulous dark eyes on me. "What?" Silas demanded.

"That's ridiculous," Michael said.

"No, it's not," I countered. "Lucius told me. He said that Michael is your older brother, Silas, sent away and adopted by a family here in Southern California because he doesn't have the *gula* blood. Lucius thought it would be amusing to turn him into a vampire."

"'Amusing,'" Michael repeated. His hands clenched into fists. "That bastard. That *fucking* bastard."

Silas was quiet, staring at the other man. I had a feeling he was cataloguing his features, comparing them to his own, trying to find the similarities, the telltales that would provide the visual evidence he needed. I knew he was doing exactly that, because I'd done the same thing.

"Yes," I said. "He is a fucking bastard. A manipulative bastard. And the best way to get him back is to let us leave now...and for you to get to your room before the sun comes up. Act like nothing happened. It'll drive him crazy."

"You're right—it will." Michael smiled, his gaze moving to where the diamond engagement ring Lucius had given me sat on the nightstand. The message couldn't be more clear. "Come tomorrow night, he's going to be one seriously pissed-off vampire. So I will go to bed now, because I want to make sure I'm in perfect health tomorrow to watch the fireworks. Have a good life, you crazy kids."

He turned then, going past the broken door as it sagged on its hinges. How he'd explain that, I wasn't sure, although I guessed he'd probably blame the damage on Silas.

"You heard him," I said. "Let's go."

He scrubbed a hand over his face. "My brother."

"Yes. And we can talk about it when we're safely away from here. Okay?"

His jaw set. "Okay."

And then I watched the transformation steal over him, watched his skin darken, his eyes turn amber, the enormous bat-like wings sprout from his back. I wasn't afraid, though. I knew this part of him. I knew it intimately. It was him, just in a different shape.

He held out his arms and I went to him. As they closed around me, though, he let go with one arm so he could scoop up my luggage in his free hand. Then we were out in the cold morning air and the rain, which was falling heavily now, soaking my hair. I didn't care, though. All that mattered was being with Silas, getting away from this place.

We landed on the soggy earth, and he set down the suitcases. A second later, he was his human self again, bending to retrieve a damp T-shirt and leather jacket from beneath one of the rosebushes. "Let's go. I'm parked on the street."

I followed him toward the fence that encircled the property. No sign of the semivives so far. The sky had begun to lighten a little, just enough to show that the sun had indeed come up, somewhere far from this wet landscape. We hugged the wall as we headed toward the street, although Silas didn't take me to the gate. No, he stopped at the southwest corner of the property, where it butted up against the next-door neighbors' wall, and gave me a leg up so I could climb over the fence. After that he picked up my two cases and threw them over as well, and finally clambered to safety.

For a second, we just stood there, staring at one another. I couldn't quite grasp that I had gotten away. True, the house was right there, but I wasn't trapped inside. I was standing on a sidewalk, in a public space, not locked in my room, no vampires breathing down my neck. What I wanted to do was run to Silas and have him hold me for roughly a hundred years, but we didn't have that kind of time.

"Let's get going," Silas said. "My motorcycle is partway down the block."

I stopped, staring at him in consternation. "Motorcycle? How the hell are we going to get these suitcases on a motorcycle?"

"It's not a problem," he replied. "We'll manage. But we have to go."

I couldn't argue with that. Trying to blink the rain out of my eyes, I followed him half a block down from Lucius' property to a sleek and wicked-looking black motorcycle that had been somewhat sheltered by a sycamore tree.

"Get behind me," he instructed as he swung his leg over the seat. "Put the larger case between the two of us, and sling the cosmetic case over your shoulder."

That might work. It wouldn't be very comfortable, but luckily both pieces were soft nylon and therefore easier to manage. Thank God Brian hadn't packed my things in the hard-sided rolling suitcase I'd used back in the day when I still flew.

"Do we have far to go?" I asked as Silas started up the bike. It rumbled beneath us, a live thing.

"Far enough," he said shortly. It seemed obvious to me that he didn't want to mention our destination out loud, even though I saw no signs of pursuit, or even any of the neighbors out and about. The hour was still early for people to be leaving for work, and, like good Southern Californians, they seemed to be doing their best to stay inside and out of the rain. "Hang on."

We began to roll. I clung to Silas, the suitcase smashed between us. Away from Lucius' house, down through San Rafael's quiet streets, following Colorado Boulevard through Eagle Rock. I noticed he took a lot of surface streets, avoiding the freeway. Was he worried about early-morning commuters, or did he simply think it was safer to drive at lower speeds, considering that he had me on the seat behind him, weighed down with these bags?

I really didn't care. The important thing was that each mile put me a little farther away from

Lucius Montfort, from the mansion that had been my prison for too long. It didn't matter that I was soaked to the skin, my wet hair plastered to my cheeks.

The only thing which mattered was that I was free.

We came through Hollywood and headed west on Franklin, then jogged up a side street whose name I didn't catch. This was the true Hollywood Hills, though—the street sloped sharply upward as we passed Italianate mansions and Frank Lloyd Wright-inspired mid-century homes, all of them worth millions. How in the world had the *gula* managed to secure a safe house in this neighborhood? Did they really have that much disposable income?

Silas slowed down, then turned into the driveway of a low-slung house whose outlines I couldn't make out that well because of all the trees crowding around it. Secluded, and private. I liked that. I needed a chance to hide for a while.

The garage was nearly empty. I supposed that made sense, since no one actually lived here full-time. As soon as the garage door closed behind us, Silas killed the engine. With a sigh of relief, I eased the cosmetic bag off my shoulder and let it drop to the ground, then climbed off the bike, taking the larger bag with me.

After he got off the motorcycle, he reached for the bag and tilted his head at the smaller one on the ground. "Go ahead and take that one."

Since it was a far lighter burden, I wasn't about to argue. He led me into the house through the laundry room, which was actually quite small, just a stacked washer and dryer and a cramped countertop with some built-in cupboards above it. Then we emerged into the kitchen, which was a decent-sized space, with newer stainless appliances and dark green tile counters. The walls had been painted a warm yellow, the combination lively and fun, especially on such a dark, dank day.

Silas set the bag he carried down on the tile floor, then took the smaller one from me and put it next to its mate. In the next instant, he reached for both my hands and pulled me toward him, his mouth descending on mine.

Oh, dear God. I was damp—well, all right, basically soaked—chilled to my bones, and in that moment my whole body was on fire. I hadn't realized how much I needed him until he held me in his arms again.

Eventually he pulled his mouth from mine. "Hungry?" he whispered.

"For you," I replied.

That was all the encouragement he needed, apparently, because then he gathered me up in his arms and took me out of the kitchen, and down a hallway. I didn't get much of a chance to look at the room where we ended up, only noted that the walls were a rich terra-cotta shade, the prints on the walls reproductions of Frida Kahlo and Diego Rivera pieces. Silas grabbed the patchwork-silk quilt that lay on the bed and yanked it to one side, and we were falling, hands scrabbling for damp clothes, shirts and jackets and jeans flung away with abandon.

And oh, God, at last it was his skin against mine, warm, burning with his own internal fire. His hands cupped my breasts, and I reached down to take him into my hand, so hard, so ready. He moaned, even as he bent to touch his tongue to my nipple, and then it was my turn to moan, to give voice to my aching need for him.

"Warm me, Silas," I whispered. "Make me yours again."

He didn't need any more encouragement than that. A slight shift, and my legs wrapped around him, driving him into me, our bodies joining in a way that I knew could never be matched. There could never be anyone besides him. I hated the thought of every kiss I'd shared with Lucius Montfort, but at least those had only been kisses, had never progressed to something more.

After that, I didn't think of anything else, only the sensation of Silas moving in and out of me, every driving stroke bringing me closer and closer to climax, just the feel of him, the scent of him, his damp hair falling against my face, until at last the orgasm burst through me, a rush of exquisite agony, my entire body and soul coming alive for him. He climaxed a moment or two later, another groan torn from somewhere deep in his throat, our bodies locked together as we clung to one another, needing to feel skin to skin, flesh to flesh, to take away the pain of the separation Lucius had inflicted on us.

Eventually we unlocked our bodies, but we didn't move any further than that, still held on to each other, as though letting go might risk another unwanted separation. "I love you," Silas whispered.

"I love you," I replied. "I always did. I never stopped. I never gave up hope."

He ran his hand over my rain-washed hair. "I know. I just—"

A slight chill ran down my spine. I moved so I could sit up, the sheets clutched against my naked breasts. "You just what?"

"Why did you tell him yes?"

"Because I had to, Silas. I told you why.

You'd gotten away, but I still wasn't safe. Not really. I had to keep playing the game until I knew it would be safe to let Lucius know how I really felt about him."

Silas also sat up. His expression was hard to read. On the one hand, he looked far more relaxed than he had only a half hour earlier. Even so, there was a tightness to his mouth that I didn't like.

"You saw that I was leaving," I went on, pressing my case. "If I'd had any feelings for him, I wouldn't have done that. But I had that one chance and needed to take it."

"I know," he said quietly. "It's the same reason I was there. Lucius wouldn't allow himself to be so unprotected for very long. And I understand intellectually. It's just—I suppose I'm trying to get my gut to understand as well. I hate the thought of you being with him, on any level."

"I wasn't too thrilled about it, either." I reached over and laid a hand on Silas' arm, knowing that I had to clear the air between us. While I didn't completely understand his anger, I wouldn't be doing either one of us a favor by trying to ignore it. "I'll be honest with you, Silas. Lucius did kiss me…multiple times. I endured it because I had to. But it never went any further than that. He wanted to wait."

"Why? That is, I'm very glad he was so

restrained, but that doesn't seem very much like him."

No, I supposed it didn't, not in a man like Lucius Montfort, who was used to taking what he wanted. "He wanted to wait because he was hoping the serum my brother's researchers are working on would become a reality." I paused then, realizing Silas probably didn't know anything about that. "I had a vision about it. Lucius saw that as a guarantee. The serum would—"

"You don't have to explain," Silas cut in. "Felix told me about it. So Lucius Montfort wanted to wait so he could be with you in a more normal way."

"Yes." I decided it was probably better not to mention the comment Lucius had made about wanting to have children with me. The mere thought made me feel slightly nauseated. "He believed it would happen because I'd seen it in a vision."

"Not that strange…your visions do have a way of coming true."

"Sometimes."

Silas reached over so he could take my hand in his. "Most of the time. Which is why I'm still worried. You saw a future in which vampires could walk in the sun."

"A possible future," I protested. "One I'm

beginning to think will never happen. I'm here with you, and I'll contact my brother soon to let him know he doesn't have to continue with the research. I'll tell him the truth about Lucius Montfort."

"What about your niece?"

The question caught me off guard. I had to remind myself that Silas had been free long enough to talk to Felix and get filled in on what had been happening over the past few days, so he would be privy to information that I hadn't personally shared with him. Also, I'd been so focused on making sure Lucius never got the vampire paradise I'd seen in my visions, I hadn't wanted to think about what cutting off the research might mean for Addison. "I don't know," I said, my voice barely above a whisper. "I hope they can continue with that line of inquiry, and let the rest of it go. I'll have to wait to talk to Jackson."

"He's back in D.C. right now, isn't he?"

"Yes. But he'll be coming back to California as soon as he gets his business wrapped up. Actually, he could be flying here today, for all I know. Yesterday was a little chaotic, and I wasn't in touch."

Silas' fingers tightened on mine. "You've had a lot to juggle. It's understandable." He paused for a moment, then went on, his tone much more brisk, "How about a hot shower and some food? You'll be in better shape to face the rest of the day."

The suggestion sounded heavenly, especially since this morning at Lucius' mansion I'd basically rolled out of bed and gotten dressed, and prepared to run. I figured I could deal with showering and all that once I was a free woman again.

I recalled how Silas and I had shared a shower at his loft. That had been heavenly, too—the feel of the hot water beating down on us as he ran his hands over my body. A flare of desire flashed through me again. We might have just had sex, but that didn't mean we couldn't go for round two.

Slanting a look over at him through my lashes, I asked, "Is your shower big enough for two?"

"Only one way to find out."

His hand still on mine, he pulled me over to him, kissing me strong and hot, right before he scooped me into his arms and took me into the bathroom. And yes, that was a nice big shower stall, tiled in a warm biscuit beige tone.

Smiling, Silas shut the door and turned on the water. Its heat flowed all over me, but it was nothing compared to the heat I felt inside. He kissed me, over and over again, his hands on my body. Yes, this—this was exactly what I wanted, what I needed.

I had to make sure it would never end.

She sat across from him at the dining room table, her hair forming itself into fascinating waves and ripples as it dried. Her eyes shone, and her full mouth was still rosy from his kisses.

Truly, she was the most beautiful thing he had ever seen.

He had to remind himself that she was real, and not another daydream. Memories of her had been all he could hold on to while locked up in Lucius' cellar. This was the real Serena, every exquisite inch of her.

While Silas would have been happy to simply sit here and look at her, drink her in, he knew there was still much to be resolved. They could take this small breathing space this morning, but sooner or later he'd have to let his *gula* brethren know what he'd done. Felix and the rest of the Watchers here in Southern California probably wouldn't be thrilled by his latest escapade, but the important thing was that Serena was here with him now, and safe. Silas' higher-ups on the Conclave might have a few choice words for the way he'd gone off half-cocked for yet a second time. However, being in the Watchers wasn't like being in the army. They couldn't exactly kick him out. The most they would do was retire him from field duty, which was fine by him. He had Serena, and the two of them could go to Humboldt and live a quiet life there, try to start a family.

Well, that was what he wished for. He thought her feelings ran along similar lines, but he didn't know for sure. The chance to speak together on such topics had been stolen by Lucius Montfort.

Temporarily stolen, Silas reminded himself. The vampire would no longer be able to possess her, control her.

Serena set down the English muffin she'd been eating, then reached for her mug of coffee. "You're very quiet."

"Just thinking."

"I suppose there is a lot to think about." She sipped some coffee, shut her eyes as she appeared to savor the rich taste. The house had a very good coffeemaker, as well as a supply of interesting blends in the cupboard. The batch he'd brewed up this morning had been Sumatran. "I actually had a vision of us a few days ago."

His heart beat a little more quickly, but Silas forced himself to stay calm. Serena's visions could mean a number of things, not all of them good. "You did?"

"Yes." She smiled and flicked a lock of semi-damp hair over one shoulder. "Later on I discovered it was up somewhere near your compound in Humboldt, although at the time I wasn't entirely sure. A green field, with an evergreen forest all around it."

"That does sound like my home," he said. "What did you see?"

"I saw us," she replied. "And our son."

Silas went very still. How he wanted to believe it was the future she'd seen, but hope could be a very treacherous thing. "Our son? You're sure?"

"Well, he looked like you, except he had my eyes. He was around four years old, I think. He was flying the fanciest kite." Her smile didn't exactly fade away, but it did diminish somewhat. "I have to believe he was ours. Why else would we be out in the woods, flying a kite with a little boy?"

Why else? Perhaps they were watching one of the *gula* children, although Silas didn't know why her visions would show her such a scene. It made far more sense that she would have been offered a glimpse of her own offspring. "I don't know," he said slowly. "That is quite a vision. Do you think it will come true?"

"A week ago, I would have said no." Her hands wrapped around the coffee mug, although she didn't lift it. Perhaps she wanted to feel its warmth against her fingers. "But I'm here with you now. I think it's more that I was offered a look at a possible future, one with as great a chance of happening as the terrible future I envisioned with Lucius." A shake of her head, and she tapped a finger against the warm celadon-green glaze of the coffee mug. Outside, rain beat against the windows. "This is the first time I've ever had competing visions of the future, so I'm not sure exactly what to make of it. But I'm going to hope for the best. That's the only way to move forward, I think."

Silas reached over and touched her free hand with his. Her skin was warm; clearly, she hadn't taken a chill from their rain-soaked motorcycle ride to get here. "I think it's a very good sign. And…is it a future you want to see happen?"

Her hazel eyes met his. In contrast to the purple top she'd slipped on after the shower, those eyes looked almost pure green. "More than anything, Silas. Lucius tried to convince me that being with him was the right thing, that he could give me the kind of life I deserved. Problem is — aside from the fact that I was already in love with you, and nothing was going to change that — I had no desire for that kind of life. I could have had it already, because of the family I was born into. I didn't want it. I want you, and green forests, and that dark-haired little boy. Something quiet, and precious, and nothing I could have here in Southern California."

Silas didn't recall rising to his feet, but in the next moment, he stood, and pulled Serena up from her seat so she could face him. She smiled, and he bent and kissed her, tasted the richness of coffee on her lips, and her own sweet savor, something that was uniquely hers. God, how he wanted her, needed her.

And the miracle was, it appeared that she felt exactly the same way about him.

CHAPTER SEVENTEEN

AFTER WE'D FINISHED BREAKFAST, AND SILAS was rinsing off our plates and mugs so he could put them in the dishwasher, the phone rang. An actual landline phone, hanging from the wall in the kitchen. I supposed that made sense, since any phone Silas would have had with him when he was captured would be long gone, and I didn't think he'd had time to replace it.

Frowning, he rubbed his hands on his jeans and went to lift the handset from the receiver. "Hello?" A pause, and he said, "Yes, I got her. She's here with me." Another long pause, during which his frown only deepened. "I realize that, Felix, but in this case I'd say the ends justify the means. Now we just have to plan our next step. Senator Quinn—" Silas stopped there, as though Felix had cut him off.

I could see how that formidable-looking *gula*—the one who wouldn't have appeared out of place in a Viking horde, if his hair was a little longer—might have been annoyed by the way Silas had swooped in and snatched me up. Not that I was about to complain about his methods. He looked over at me, hand over the mouthpiece to the phone. "Serena, do you have your cell phone?"

I actually did, since Lucius had returned it to me once he thought I was securely on his team. It was shoved into the larger of my two suitcases, along with my purse. I nodded.

"Please text your brother and see if he really is on his way back to California. We need to meet with him as soon as possible."

"Sure," I responded, and left the kitchen to go back to the bedroom where my luggage had been deposited. When I'd gotten my clean clothes out of the suitcase, I'd set my purse on the dresser. I went straight over to it and dug my phone out of the bottom, then checked my messages. A birthday wish from Candace, along with a promise to get together once she had her current case out of her hair. I felt a little guilty that I hadn't gotten back to her on the day itself, but since she was clearly swamped at work, I wouldn't let myself stress about it. I typed out a quick reply, letting her know that I understood and that I had tons to tell her, so I hoped we could meet for lunch at some point.

A voicemail from my mother, with more birthday wishes, and a hope that I'd had a nice dinner. And an invitation for Lucius and me to come to the house for dinner this coming Sunday. Oops. I'd have to let my parents know about the change in my relationship status…and figure out a way to do so that didn't involve telling them that Lucius actually happened to be a vampire and that I'd never really been in love with him.

These things could get so complicated.

That was it for messages, though, which was a relief. My hermit-like existence had shrunk my social circle down to almost nothing, but people did have a tendency to come out of the wood-work when it was your birthday.

I sent a text message to Jackson, telling him it was urgent and that I needed to hear from him ASAP. For a moment I'd wondered whether I should try calling instead, but figured a text message was a little less intrusive, especially if he happened to already be on his flight back to Los Angeles. After I was done with that, I headed back to the kitchen, taking the phone with me so I wouldn't miss any texts or calls. Silas seemed to be done with his own phone call from Felix, since he was in the middle of rinsing out the carafe from the coffeemaker when I came into the room.

"I sent a text," I said, and set the cell phone down on the counter at a safe distance from the sink.

"Good."

"I hope Felix didn't chew you out too much."

That comment elicited a reluctant smile. "Felix actually isn't my superior. The Watchers don't have ranks, per se, although seniority does afford some privileges. But because he's in charge of the current operation in Southern California, and therefore is the one who'll have to answer to the Conclave when all this is over with, he would prefer to avoid any more unauthorized missions like the one I undertook this morning."

"Ah." I watched him as he fetched a dishtowel from one of the kitchen drawers and began drying out the carafe. "So why didn't you ask for their help? I mean, clearly they weren't averse to staging a raid on Lucius' house, since they did that very thing when they came and got you."

"I wasn't sure they would have agreed. In their eyes, you weren't in any immediate danger. Also, they would have wanted more time to plan, since extracting you would have required a slightly different methodology. I didn't want to wait. Lucius was weak. Or rather, his ability to protect his house or the people in it was severely reduced because Felix's team had already wiped out all the semivives. The timing was right. I couldn't afford to get into a back-and-forth with Felix. Besides…." He let the words trail off, then shrugged as he returned the carafe to the coffeemaker.

"Better to ask forgiveness than permission?"

"Something like that." He came over and bent slightly so he could press his lips against the side of my head. "There is that very short, precious moment when the world hasn't quite woken up, before dawn has truly taken hold, when a vampire is forced into his daytime sleep. I knew that was the best time to come get you. If I'd waited another day, Lucius would have had time to make more semivives, and the chance would have been lost."

"Well, it makes sense to me," I said, glad of his closeness. Even when he wasn't holding me, I was so very aware of him, of the strength of his body, the warmth that seemed to emanate from his very being. "Even if Felix doesn't quite get it."

"Oh, I think Felix does. He just doesn't want to admit it. But now that he's told me it was a stupid idea, and that I probably will still have to answer to the Conclave when this is all over with, he can let it go. He's done his work.

Anyway, he's coming over so we can plan our next move."

"Which is dealing with Jackson."

"Yes." Silas paused then, keen dark eyes studying my face. "Are you going to be okay with that, even acknowledging the repercussions a change in plans might have for your niece?"

What could I say? I'd never been a confrontational person, especially when it came to my godlike—or so he'd seemed to my eyes when I was younger—big brother. But this was too important to let go. Anyway, once he understood that Lucius was not the sort of person he would wish to be associated with, he'd have to back off. If he wanted to continue the research on the healing benefits of vampire blood for humans, fine. However, he'd have to swear that the other aspect of the project would be forever abandoned, even if he'd agreed to do one in exchange for the other.

"I'm not sure if 'okay' is the right word," I said slowly. "More like...I understand what needs to be done, and I'm not going to back away from that."

His eyes warmed. "I love you."

"I love you, too," I replied. Those words seemed so inadequate to express how I really felt about him, though. I wanted him and needed him...and trusted him, and admired him. He wasn't like anyone I'd ever known, and I desperately wanted to deserve him. I let out a breath and said, my tone quite different, "What time will Felix be here?"

"Soon. I don't know where he's staying, but from the way he talked, it sounded as if it wasn't too far away from here."

"How many safe houses do you guys have stashed around L.A.?" I asked. I'd halfway meant the question as a joke, but Silas appeared to take me seriously.

"Several. This one, and another over in Santa Monica somewhere. Maybe more that I don't know about. It's also possible that Felix isn't staying in any of those places, but is using a false profile to stay at an Airbnb, or a local hotel. We do our best to change our methodologies so it's difficult to track us."

That made sense. I waved a hand at the kitchen. "And this house? How did you end up with such a prime spot?"

He smiled then, looking much more relaxed than he had a few minutes earlier. "I'd say it was luck, but really, it's just the result of our agents keeping an eye on the local market and taking advantage of timing. This house belonged to an artist of some note. She didn't have any children, so when she passed away, her younger sister, who lives on the East Coast, had to handle the sale. Apparently they weren't very close, because the sister didn't want to travel to Los Angeles to take care of the transaction. We offered to buy the house complete with furnishings, and she jumped at the chance, since that meant she wouldn't have to deal with any of the physical details of settling her sister's estate."

"No wonder," I commented, looking around. The house did have a lot of very personal touches, an artsy but welcoming vibe. Not really the sort of décor one would expect of an unoccupied safe house intended for an all-male secret society, but if the Watchers had bought it lock, stock, and barrel, that made a lot of sense. "Should we set out some water, or a pitcher of tea or something? It's too late for breakfast and too early for lunch, so I don't know about snacks, but…."

"Water will be fine," Silas broke in, but gently, still with that smile on his face. I supposed my hostess instincts amused him. I couldn't really help myself—no matter how much I wanted to deny it, I was still very much a product of my mother's upbringing. "This is a business meeting, nothing else."

"Got it." I started going through the cupboards and found a pitcher of heavy, bubbled greenish glass, and some glasses to match. Since I didn't really trust L.A. tap water, I filled the pitcher from the door in the refrigerator, since at least that had to go through a filter. No ice, though; the day was too gloomy and chilly for that. The rain didn't show any sign of letting up, which wasn't that unusual for March. Still, I wished I had a better idea as to whether the storm was going to clear out today. The little of the backyard I'd seen so far looked inviting, and it would have been nice to be able to sit out there and try to get my thoughts together.

After this visit, of course. I took the pitcher, and Silas picked up the glasses, and we both went out to the living room. Even on such a gray day, the view from the window there was nothing short of spectacular, taking in everything from Hollywood all the way out to Century City.

Silas must have noticed me looking out the window, because after he'd set down the glasses, he asked, "Like it?"

"Oh, yes. This place is amazing."

He smiled slightly at the compliment, but didn't say anything else. I thought I understood the reason for his reticence. The house might be awesome, and I might be currently occupying it with the man I loved, but this was only a way station, a temporary refuge. Sooner or later we'd have to decide where we wanted to end up, and I very much doubted that would be anywhere in Southern California.

The doorbell rang, and Silas went to answer it while I waited in the living room, wondering whether I should remain standing or go ahead and sit down on the oversized couch, covered in cheerful yellow linen. I decided to hover near the arm of the couch, figuring I could sit on it or lean against it, or simply remain standing, depending on what Felix and Silas did.

They entered the room, Felix ruffling some damp from his close-cut hair. He wasn't wearing a jacket or coat, but I realized he'd probably taken off his outerwear in the entry and hung it in the closet there.

"Hi, Felix," I said cheerily. Judging by his expression, he was still less than thrilled with Silas, but I figured it couldn't hurt to forestall any recriminations by acting as if everything was normal.

"Hello, Serena," he replied, voice smooth, not missing a beat. "You're looking very well."

Was that some kind of subtle dig, a hint that he knew exactly what Silas and I had been up to in the hours since he'd rescued me from Lucius Montfort's mansion? Possibly; I didn't know Felix well enough to guess whether he was the sort of person who'd comment on such a thing. I thought it was probably better to ignore any subtexts, and said, "Thank you, Felix. Would you like some water?"

A corner of his mouth lifted slightly. "Sure."

I poured water into one of the glasses and handed it to him. He took it, murmuring a thank-you, and then settled himself into the armchair placed to the right of the couch. Good. That meant Silas and I could occupy the couch. I sat down, and a second or two later, Silas took a seat next to me. He seemed tense, even though only a few minutes earlier he'd been reassuring me that Felix wouldn't waste time with any more scolding.

Well, whether or not Felix was still annoyed with Silas, he definitely didn't intend to dawdle. Hands clasped on one jean-clad knee, he asked, "Have you heard anything from your brother?"

Even though the situation was deadly serious, I had a hard time keeping myself from smiling at his "get down to business" attitude. "Not yet. I only texted him about ten minutes ago, though. And he could be in a meeting or something."

"He's not," Felix told me. "I checked his schedule—that's public record, you know."

Even as the *gula* spoke, I knew I should have thought of that. Most of the time, you could go to a senator's or congressperson's website and look at their schedule for the week. It seemed more helpful to stalkers than anything else, but if you were in Washington, D.C., and really wanted to know what your representative was up to, then I supposed it was valuable information. Anyway, as scattered as I'd been lately, the thought of looking up Jackson's schedule had completely slipped my mind.

"Traveling?" Silas asked.

"Yes. He was present for a vote yesterday, as Serena said, but his schedule shows him as coming back to California for the weekend. Next week only says 'TBD,' so it seems that he's not yet certain what he plans to do."

That didn't surprise me. After all, he'd want to check in with Shelby Gutierrez to see how the research was faring, and, depending on the news he received, he'd either feel confident returning to Washington…or would want to stay here and spend as much time as he could with his daughter.

That thought made my throat constrict slightly. I didn't want to face the possibility of losing Addison. I'd been there at Huntington Memorial when she was born, had seen her christened, watched her smear rainbow cake all over her face at her first birthday party. She was family. She had her whole life ahead of her.

"If he's on a flight out here, then eventually he'll check his messages," Silas said. "We just need to be patient."

Felix shrugged slightly, as though he wasn't

overly thrilled by the prospect of having to practice patience. "I suppose so. In the meantime, we
need to formulate our strategy."

"Which is?" I asked, not sure I liked the
sound of that.

"That we need to convince your brother the
research needs to be stopped."

I sent a wary glance at Silas, who was
watching Felix, brows pulled together. "Stopped
altogether? Because I don't see why they can't
continue with the work of looking for a cure for
Addie. There's nothing harmful in that, is there?"

"Unfortunately, there is." Felix shot a troubled glance at Silas. "Didn't you explain it
to her?"

"Explain what to me?" I really wasn't liking
this, especially since Silas remained silent, as
though loath to tell me what Felix—and, by
extension, the rest of the *gula*—had in mind.

"We haven't had a lot of time," Silas said at
last. His gaze was fixed on Felix. "And besides, it
sounds as if you and the Conclave have been
discussing this without my input."

"Yes, because clearly you were otherwise
occupied." Felix shifted in his chair, returning his
focus to me. "It's really very simple, Serena. I
know by getting the blood samples from Lucius
Montfort, you were doing your best to keep him
happy, distracted, anything to prevent him from

causing harm to Silas. Your motivations were completely understandable. However, that blood is dangerous. It could provide a cure for your niece—but it also could be used to create biological enhancements for human soldiers. It could be weaponized. I'm not saying your brother intends to do anything of the sort, but there's no guarantee that someone working for him might not eventually see its potential and decide to sell it on the black market. That would be...unfortunate. For centuries, the vampires and the *gula* have maintained a very delicate balance. If the vampires' blood and the components that can be synthesized from it are let loose in the world, then I fear the changes it might wreak would be catastrophic."

I wanted to protest, to say that Felix was imagining worst-case scenarios and that everything would be fine. But even as I opened my mouth to speak, I stopped myself. After all, I didn't know who Shelby Gutierrez had hired to work in her labs; I also didn't know much of anything about Shelby herself. I wanted to think they were all stand-up people who could be absolutely trusted, but the truth was, I had no way of knowing that was the case. Corporate and scientific espionage were very real things. If someone leaked even a bit of information about what was going on that lab, then it might reach interested parties who were willing to pay a high price for that kind of research.

The two men were watching me, clearly waiting for me to respond. Silas' expression was grave but sympathetic, while Felix wore a formidable frown that made him appear even more like a Viking about to go on the rampage.

I cleared my throat and wished I'd paused to take a sip of water. "I guess I can understand some of those concerns," I said at last. "But do you really expect me to go to my brother and tell him to put a stop to everything when he's only gotten started? Leaving aside the very real worries about what that will do to Addison, he's just hired a bunch of people. He's supposed to lay them all off after less than a week?"

Felix shrugged. "Start-ups fail all the time, sometimes in that short an amount of time. It's unfortunate, but wouldn't it be better to pull the plug early on before they've all gotten used to those paychecks?"

Something in his logic seemed faulty, but right then I couldn't get my racing brain to slow down enough to tell me what it might be. I sent a beseeching look at Silas, and he said, "In addition to those concerns, Jackson Quinn must have laid out a significant amount of capital to lease that building, procure the equipment, pay the staff. You expect him to walk away from all that?"

"I do," Felix said imperturbably. "My best estimate is that his losses would be somewhere around a million dollars. To someone with his fortune, that amount is lunch money."

I thought that was being a little dismissive. If we'd been talking about my father, sure. But while Jackson had his own wealth from investments and so on, in addition to his senatorial salary, it wasn't as though he had access to the kind of money my father did. One day Jackson and I would have to split that enormous fortune —a day I prayed would be very far in the future —but in the meantime he could only be counted as very wealthy, not super-rich like our parents.

Silas must have noted the look of distress on my face, because he responded, "I'm not sure that's exactly the case, but we'll leave that aside for now. I think the important thing to do here is to impress on Senator Quinn the implications of this sort of research, and give him a better idea of the sort of person Lucius Montfort really is. Appealing to his better nature is probably the best way to approach this. What do you think, Serena?"

I'd been in the middle of taking a sip from my glass of water, so I had to wait a few seconds before I could reply. When I was ready, though,

I said, "I agree. Jackson isn't going to want to be in a business arrangement with Lucius once he realizes what a criminal he is. He was a little reluctant from the beginning, but I reassured him that it would be fine. He went along with the whole thing because he wants to save his daughter, and because he didn't think I could possibly be with someone who wasn't on the up and up."

"You're that close?" Felix asked. He didn't sound very convinced.

"No," I said frankly. "We're not. But he knows me well enough to know that I'm very careful in my relationships. That's what gave Lucius an in, more than anything else."

"And now you're going to reverse course. How will Jackson respond to that?"

"I don't know." I glanced over at Silas, who was watching me carefully. Something about the solemn regard in those dark, dark eyes made me feel far braver than I knew I was. Being back with him was a miracle, one I didn't intend to take for granted. "I want him to meet Silas. And I'll tell him the whole story. That should help to convince him that Lucius Montfort is bad news."

"What if your brother doesn't agree to stop the research?"

"Well, I—" I floundered for a moment, because I honestly didn't know what I would do if Jackson proved to be stubborn. But he wouldn't. My brother — unlike a lot of politicians — really did strive to do the right thing. I couldn't imagine him staying in a partnership with someone he knew to be a bad person.

Apparently Felix had been expecting that kind of non-reply, because he gave a grim nod and said, "Don't worry, Serena. If your brother doesn't shut this thing down, then we'll do it for him."

"What's that supposed to mean?" I demanded, even as I shot a worried look at my *gula* partner. "Silas, what is he talking about?"

"When the Watchers make a plan, they very rarely stray from that course," Silas said. Now his attention was fixed on his fellow *gula,* the set of his jaw telling me that he knew exactly what Felix had meant. "It seems word has come down that the research must be stopped, one way or another. If you can't convince Jackson to end the research, close down the facility, then they'll destroy it."

"You can't do that," I protested. "I thought you were supposed to be observers. So now you're domestic terrorists?"

Felix's eyes narrowed at the word "terrorists," and the glare he shot me was as bright and focused as a blue laser beam. "I'd be more likely to call your brother a terrorist if he tries to continue this research. Its consequences will be far more dire than a wrecked lab, I assure you."

But…. I couldn't believe what I was hearing. Or rather, I didn't want to believe it. Surely he couldn't really be serious about destroying the lab. He was just trying to scare me, to make sure I would be as persuasive as possible when I spoke to Jackson.

I sent a frantic look at Silas, and he responded with a barely perceptible lift of his shoulders. Clearly, he believed Felix, knew his fellow Watchers would do whatever was necessary to make sure the vampire blood and any of the components it contained never made it out to the general population.

And I also thought of my vision, of that warehouse in the middle of nowhere. The sketch that matched it, with its rows and rows of hospital beds. If I allowed any of this to go on, then who was the terrorist?

CHAPTER EIGHTEEN

Felix left not too long after that. Probably he didn't see any reason to linger. He'd said his piece and made his intentions known. At that point, it was up to me.

At least the rain had stopped sometime during our conversation, and the sun looked as if it was trying to come out, although its presence didn't do quite as much as I'd hoped to improve my mood. I checked my phone, but I didn't have any missed texts or calls.

"He'll contact you," Silas said as he rubbed my neck. With Felix gone, the two of us could sit closer to one another on the couch and share displays of affection I was certain the blond *gula* wouldn't have appreciated. "I'm sure he's just waiting for the right opportunity. If he's on a plane surrounded by people, he's not going to make what could be a highly charged call."

"You're probably right." I was quiet for a moment, letting Silas' powerful fingers knead some of the tension from my neck and shoulders. Right then, it was enough to enjoy his touch, the palpable sense of love and comfort that seemed to flow from his fingertips. "It just feels like he's been in the air forever."

"Well, it's not a short flight, and you only texted him a little over an hour ago." He lifted his hands from my shoulders, and I turned around so I could face him. Although his gaze was serious enough, one corner of his mouth quirked slightly. "Maybe we should go out for a while, get some air, have some lunch."

"Are you sure that's safe?" I looked from him to the still-dripping garden outside. Now that the sun was out, its rays caught the drops of rain on the grass and leaves, turning them into a constellation of shimmering diamonds. I didn't know what I was expecting to see out there, but all that time as Lucius' prisoner had made me more than a little paranoid.

"As safe as it can be," he said. "It's daytime, and the vampires are asleep. All of Lucius Montfort's semivives are dead, so who would even be able to track us down?"

"They're not all dead," I said gloomily.

"There are the two semivives he made last night. Also, Brian wasn't at the mansion during the raid. He was at home, pretending to be normal."

Silas touched my hand. "Do you really think he would venture all the way out here to Hollywood?"

"I don't know." Actually, I hadn't stopped to think what he'd be doing. During the day, he could come and go as he pleased, since Lewis was at work and not around to see what his partner was up to. I wondered if Lucius had contemplated having Brian come to the mansion for guard duty after all the other semivives had been destroyed, but that wouldn't have been a very good idea. All of Lucius' semivives looked as if they had been chosen because they would make good bodyguards, whereas Brian had the slightly flabby physique of a stereotypical geek. In a fight, even I, with my yoga-trained muscles, might have beaten him. Anyway, he would have been hard-pressed to come up with a reason for being away from home all night. "I doubt it. Even if he did come wandering around here for some reason, what would be the chances of him running across us? L.A. is a pretty big place."

"Yes, it is," Silas agreed. "But if you're not comfortable leaving the house, I understand. It was just a thought."

I looked over at the window again. Something in me yearned for fresh air, for a chance to wander around in a part of town I didn't know very well. However, I could feel it somewhere deep inside, a little niggling voice that told me, *Don't do it.*

"We should probably stay here," I told him. "But maybe we could get some food delivered for lunch? That would be fun."

"There are a lot of places down on Hollywood Boulevard and Sunset. I'm sure some of them must deliver to this area."

"I'll check Yelp."

I picked up my phone and started thumbing through the offerings. That was when it *bing*ed, indicating that a new text message had come in. At once I abandoned my Yelp search and went to the messages app. Sure enough, there was something from Jackson.

I'm about an hour out from LAX. What's going on?

I'd rather talk in person, I typed. *Are you going straight home from the airport?*

Yes. Bethany took the kids to Disneyland, since Addison was feeling better today.

Crappy day for it, I thought. *All that rain.* But the storm was already clearing out, and a gloomy start to the day meant the amusement park probably wouldn't be as crowded. And with Bethany and the kids miles and miles away in

Anaheim, Jackson would be available for an in-person meeting.

Can you let me know when you're on your way to Claremont? I responded. *Then we'll head out around the same time and meet you at your house.*

"*We*"? he typed back. *Who? It can't be him, because....*

The text trailed off there, but Jackson's meaning was clear enough. He knew I couldn't be coming with Lucius because it was still broad daylight, barely noon. *A friend,* I responded. *Just please text again once you're on your way.*

I will. Talk to you soon.

Thanks.

We ended the convo there, since we didn't have anything else that could be said right then. I closed the app and set my phone on the coffee table. Silas looked at me expectantly. "Well?"

"He'll be at LAX soon, and he'll text once he's on his way home. I assume he's having a limo take him or something."

"And his Secret Service protection?"

I'd forgotten all about that. Jackson was still a working U.S. senator, but he was also a candidate for President. He probably had some agents traveling with him, helping to clog up first class.

"I guess so," I replied. "But when Jackson and I went to meet with him earlier in the week, they didn't come inside. So I don't think you need to worry about them overhearing anything we might say."

"Good." He lifted an eyebrow at me. "What are you going to tell him?"

"Everything," I said simply. "I have to. The only way to get him to believe me is to not hold anything back." I thumbed back over to the Yelp app and scrolled down the results of my search. "So, do you want Thai, or Mexican?"

Silas could tell Serena was anxious, although she did her best to hide it. But he saw, from the way her gaze would shift away from his, or how her fingers were clenched a little too tightly on her fork as she lifted some refried beans to her mouth, that she was not looking forward to this interview with her brother at all. She would have to reverse all the things she had told him just a few days earlier, and it was not in her nature to take back her word.

He loved her for that, but he also knew the upcoming conversation was necessary. No, that was too weak a word. It was imperative. Although he hoped there would be some way to save Serena's niece, the risks were too great to allow any of this to continue.

The weather had cleared out enough that they were able to open the windows in the dining room, to let a mild, damp breeze enter the house. Silas could see that Serena enjoyed it here, and he wished the house could be something more than merely a way station, a place to take shelter for a day or two. But as soon as this situation with Jackson Quinn—and Lucius Montfort— was resolved, he and Serena would have to find their own resolution. He would be sent back to Humboldt.

The question was, would she come with him?

That she'd had a vision of them together in the future, their child with them, should have reassured him. But she'd also had visions of a future with the master vampire. Which one was real?

There was also a third possibility, that she would reject both of them, and continue her life here in Southern California, alone. He didn't want to believe that. He had never been with a woman before Serena and so had no basis of comparison, and yet he still couldn't imagine how someone could be so open with him, so loving, only to walk away from him in the end.

Her phone buzzed, and immediately she set down her fork and picked it up, then tapped in the code to unlock the screen. Her eyes scanned the message she found there. "Jackson says the limo just picked him up. He should be at the Claremont house by two-thirty at the latest."

Silas glanced past her to the clock of recycled tin that hung on the wall opposite him. "How long will it take us to get there from here?"

Her shoulders lifted, and she reached for her glass of water before replying, "A little over an hour? It's a bit early for the traffic to start getting really bad, so I think if we're on the road by one-thirty, we should be okay."

Which left them approximately twenty minutes to finish their meal and get out the door. They were nearly done, so it shouldn't be a problem. And neither should traffic, if they did encounter any, since they would be riding the motorcycle and could split lanes if they did hit any congestion.

"That should work."

Serena nodded, then pressed her lips together, as though wrestling with an unpleasant thought. "I don't quite know how to explain you, though."

"What's to explain? Tell Jackson the truth."

"And you're okay with that? I thought the Watchers were all about keeping their identities secret."

"We are, but in this case, you can't avoid the truth. It will be easier to convince Jackson of what he needs to do if he understands that the people who have been keeping guard on the vampires for centuries know what a terrible danger this vampire blood—and its resulting serums—might pose."

His words seemed to reassure her somewhat, because she relaxed against the back of the painted wooden chair where she sat. "I hope so. At least I know that Jackson isn't the sort to go blabbing to anyone. He won't betray your secrets."

Silas wasn't sure if he could be quite that confident, but he also knew that in this case, discretion was also self-preservation. Trying to tell the world that shape-shifting monsters walked amongst them seemed like a very quick route to being kicked off the campaign trail. He didn't mention any of that, however, but only said, "I'm sure he won't."

She gave him a half-hearted smile and returned to the food on her plate, although he noticed that she only took a few more bites of enchilada before she set down her fork once again. "I think I'm done. I want to go brush my teeth and fix my face before we head out. Is that okay?"

"Of course," he replied. "I'll finish mine, and then clear the table. We have time."

Another smile, and she got up from the table and headed down the hall toward the master suite. Silas ate the rest of his carne asada burrito, then picked up his plate and Serena's. Rinsing the dishes and putting them in the dishwasher only took a few more minutes, and soon enough he had joined her in the bathroom. Apparently she was done with brushing her teeth, because she had a tube of lipstick in one hand and was scowling at her reflection in the mirror.

"Is something wrong?"

She startled, then shook her head and put the lipstick down on the tiled countertop. "No. I was just thinking that I look like about fifty miles of bad road. All this sleep deprivation is doing nothing for the circles under my eyes."

Silas looked into the mirror and stared at her reflection for a moment. "I have no idea what you're talking about. You look beautiful, as always."

That comment made her chuckle. "If you say so. But thank you."

He honestly couldn't see any faults in her lovely face, but he'd heard that women could be odd about such things. Deciding it was probably best to let the matter go, he squeezed some toothpaste onto his toothbrush and took care of scrubbing away all the flavors of burrito and beans and rice. After he was done, he put away the brush and toothpaste, and looked over at Serena once again. She'd been busy with pulling her heavy hair back into a thick ponytail. He liked it loose better, but knew her hair would survive the motorcycle trip better while confined in such a way.

"Ready?" he asked.

She drew in a breath, then nodded. "As I'll ever be."

This trip to Claremont couldn't have been more different from the last one I'd taken. Then it had been dusk, and I'd sat in the back of a Mercedes sedan with a vampire at my side. Now I clung to Silas as he maneuvered the Ducati along the 210 Freeway, and a bright sun shone down from overhead, warm and innocent, as though it had absolutely no recollection of the rain that had fallen only a few hours earlier.

I couldn't feel the wind blowing in my hair, however, because Silas had produced a helmet when we went out to the garage, and told me I needed to wear it. Although I wondered why he was worried now, when we'd both been helmet-less when he stole me from Lucius' mansion, I didn't argue. The last thing I needed was to tumble off the back of the motorcycle and cave my head in.

Because it was so early in the afternoon, the

traffic wasn't too bad yet. Some clogginess where the 134 and the 210 met in western Pasadena, but Silas deftly maneuvered the Ducati between lanes until we were clear from the thicket and then back up to speed. We passed the exit for Allen Avenue, and I felt an odd twinge inside. That was the exit you'd take if you were headed down to my parents' house in San Marino, but of course we weren't going that way.

I didn't know if I'd ever go that way again.

As we got off the freeway in Claremont, I felt my phone buzz in the pocket of the loaner jacket Silas had also given me. Since we'd slowed down to take the turn, I figured it was safe enough to reach in and retrieve the phone. A brief message was displayed on the home screen.

I'm here, it read. *Come over when you can.*

Since I couldn't take my left arm away from Silas' waist to type out a reply, I just tucked the phone back into my pocket. Obviously, Jackson was waiting for us, so an answer wasn't strictly necessary.

We drove north on Indian Hill, then jogged over on Baseline so we could continue north on Mills Avenue. The houses got larger and more expensive as the elevation climbed, and then we were at the gated complex where Jackson's home was located.

As we pulled up to the guard shack, I could

see the man inside step out into the bright
sunlight and squint at us. His expression wasn't
entirely welcoming, and I thought I could guess
why. The Ducati was an expensive bike, but it
didn't exactly rate the same kind of respect as
Lucius' S-class. And Silas, who hadn't been
wearing a helmet, looked windblown and rather
rough, with his shoulder-length hair and a scruff
of beard on his cheeks and chin.

"I'm Serena Quinn," I told the guard. "I'm
here to see my brother Jackson."

At once the man's face relaxed. I didn't
recognize him, so he must be new. Clearly he
recognized Jackson's name, though, because he
said at once, "Of course, Ms. Quinn. He called
ahead to say you were coming. Go on in."

He went inside and touched the controls for
the gate, which began to slide open for us. As
soon as there was enough room to squeeze the
motorcycle past, Silas started moving forward
again.

"Down this street, and then jog to the left.
It'll be the last house on that side, up against the
boundary wall."

"Got it."

We moved slowly and sedately, but even so I
was all too aware of the low grunt of the motorcycle's engine. This thing felt too damn conspicu-
ous, but there wasn't much I could do about that.

At least it was the middle of the day, and so most of Jackson's neighbors should be off at work. *Or golfing,* I added mentally, thinking of my father's favorite pasttime. Anyway, as long as the neighbors weren't home, I really didn't care what they were doing.

The same Secret Service agents who'd been here the night I'd come with Lucius stood in front of the garage. They didn't move as Silas brought the Ducati to a halt in the section of driveway nearest the path to the house. Maybe they blinked; I couldn't see behind the dark glasses they wore.

"Hello, Ms. Quinn," said one of them. "You can go on in."

"Thank you," I replied, wishing I'd learned their names. Then my reply wouldn't have sounded so truncated. Since it was too late to do anything about it now, I gave a mental shrug and pulled off my helmet, then set it on the motorcycle's seat. Silas had already gotten off the bike, so I gestured for him to follow me.

As we approached the front door, my stomach did its best to knot itself up, not exactly the most appealing sensation when you've just had an enchilada plate for lunch. I swallowed and told myself this had to be done. Once we'd explained everything, surely Jackson would understand.

I rang the doorbell, acutely aware of the man who stood next to me. The other thing I just wasn't sure of was my brother's reaction to Silas. The last time I'd come here, I'd been with someone entirely different. It wasn't like me to flip-flop between two men, and I knew my brother would find it strange.

The door opened, and Jackson looked out at the two of us. For just the briefest second, his brows drew together, as though he was trying to figure out who this scruffy-looking stranger might be. Then he seemed to shrug, and said, "Come on in."

We went inside. It seemed that one of the first things Jackson must have done on his arrival home was to open the windows, because a fresh breeze blew through the house, playing with the filmy curtains.

"Do you mind going outside?" he asked. "Seems a shame to waste a day like this, especially after being cooped up in an airplane for hours."

"No," I said, then added hastily, "Oh, and Jackson, this is Silas Drake."

"Very nice to meet you, Senator," Silas said, and my brother shook his head.

"Jackson is fine, Silas. So you're a friend of Serena's? It seems as though she's picked up quite a few new friends lately."

That remark made me frown, and I could tell Silas wasn't too pleased by it, either. But he didn't react, only said, "Yes, I've been acquainted with Serena for quite a while, although this is the first time I've had a chance to meet any of her family."

Which I supposed was true enough. He had been a part of my life for more than three years now. I just hadn't known about his existence until a few weeks ago.

But Jackson only said, "Ah," and led us to an outdoor living set of wicker and glass, placed under a pergola covered in climbing vines. Bougainvillea, already thick with riotous fuchsia blooms. They provided shade from the sun, which now felt almost hot. California weather, almost as fickle as the entertainment industry that made its home here.

My brother had set out acrylic glasses and a couple of bottles of Perrier. He cracked open one of the bottles, then poured sparkling water for everyone. Once he was done, he settled himself on the love seat and shot a quizzical glance at Silas and me. "Serena, do you want to tell me what this is about? Your initial text sounded very urgent."

I looked over at Silas, who sat on the couch next to me. The corners of his mouth turned up slightly, as if he wanted to give me an encouraging smile but knew it probably wasn't appropriate to the moment.

"It is urgent," I said. "I know this is going to sound crazy, but I need you to hear me out."

"Crazier than bringing a vampire to see me?" he returned, then looked over at Silas. "Obviously, this one isn't a vampire. Not with that blazing sun overhead."

"No, I'm not a vampire," Silas said politely, but he didn't elaborate.

I reached over and picked up my glass, drank some Perrier. It fizzed at the back of my throat and seemed to do little for the dryness there. After swallowing, I blurted out, "Actually, Lucius Montfort is a very evil man. Erm, vampire. Whatever."

My brother's eyebrows lifted again. "Excuse me? I thought you two had a thing."

"No, I was faking so he wouldn't kill Silas."

That remark made Jackson swivel his head toward the man who sat next to me. "Lucius Montfort wanted to kill you?"

"I believe that was his ultimate goal," Silas replied. "He had me locked up in his wine cellar. Serena pretended to be with him, to go along with plans, in order to save my life."

Had I ever seen Jackson look so bug-eyed? I didn't think so. Usually, my brother was the unflappable type. But clearly stories about being locked up in wine cellars were outside his usual range of experience.

"You're not in the wine cellar now," he said. "Why aren't the police dealing with this?"

"The police would not be able to help. But yes, I was able to escape, with some assistance. "

"So Montfort no longer has any leverage."

"Sort of," I broke in. "That is, by the time Silas was free, Lucius and I had already come and talked to you. You'd started the ball rolling on the research project, one that could benefit Addison. It wasn't like I could just end things."

"Then why are you here?" My brother sipped some Perrier and set down his glass. "No offense, Serena, but it's not really like you to drop everything just so you could welcome me home from Washington."

That was true. My brother and I lived separate lives. We saw each other during the holidays, a few other times during the year when Congress was on vacation. And Jackson hadn't made the comment with any kind of reproach — he'd only been pointing out an obvious fact. "Well, I didn't think there would be a problem with you continuing the research that involved Addison's illness. But...."

"But unfortunately, there's a very large problem," Silas put in. He had to have noticed the way I hesitated, and decided he should come to my rescue. "While vampire blood may hold a cure for leukemia and other diseases, it's too intrinsically dangerous a substance to be investigated."

For a few seconds, Jackson didn't respond. He regarded Silas with slightly narrowed eyes as he leaned against the back of the love seat where he sat, his expression almost blank. I noted how my brother's gaze shifted to me for the barest of seconds before returning to the *gula*. "Excuse me, but who are you exactly? Why does this concern you?"

"Jackson—" I began, angry that he would talk to Silas that way, but my lover only touched my arm briefly, letting me know that he would handle this.

"Valid questions, Senator Quinn. I can't give you all those answers, because I'm not at liberty to do so. Let's just say that I'm affiliated with an organization that has spent many years tracking vampires, taking note of where they make their lairs, doing our best to ensure that the vampires don't abuse their powers, or take too many victims. Because of this background, I can tell you with all assurance that vampire blood is a very dangerous compound. If any of it should go missing from your lab—if it should fall into the wrong hands—then the consequences could be disastrous."

"'Disastrous'?" my brother repeated, sounding skeptical. "That seems a bit melodramatic. And what exactly is this 'organization' you belong to?"

"He can't tell you that," I said. "They need to keep their identities secret."

"Secret identities? Do they wear tinfoil hats, too?"

I opened my mouth to tell him what an asshole remark that was, but Silas forestalled me. He didn't look particularly offended; in fact, his expression was almost amused, as if he'd expected this kind of pushback. "No tinfoil hats. No chem trails or alien invasions or anything like that. But you know that vampires are real, because you've met Lucius Montfort. I assume he did something to prove his supernatural status."

"Yes," Jackson said, his face suddenly sober, as if he was recalling how he'd watched Lucius go upstairs and back in what felt like the blink of an eye. "He's...very fast."

"That he is," Silas agreed. "So if you can understand that Mr. Montfort is a vampire, then you can also understand that the blood which flows through his veins is entirely unnatural, and not something to be trifled with. Serena did not fully understand the ramifications of offering up his blood for research. Do you think you're the first person to be tempted by such a thing? Do you think Lucius Montfort is the first vampire to seek a cure for his own unnatural state? Such ventures have been attempted before, and failed utterly. Vampirism is a contagion, Senator Quinn. It can be held in check now, because we make sure that it doesn't spread too far, but can you vouch for every single person your project manager has hired? Do you know for a fact that none of them will try to sell this volatile compound on the black market?"

"I don't know that for a fact," my brother said, clearly annoyed by the implication that the people at the research facility hadn't been properly vetted. "But I'm sure Dr. Gutierrez has done her due diligence, and I trust her judgment. Anyway, what precisely are you asking me to do here?"

"You have to stop the research," I said earnestly.

As Jackson began to frown, Silas added, "And destroy all the samples of vampire blood... and make sure that any tests done on those samples are also destroyed. There can't be any trace left of the research. Nothing."

My brother ran a hand through his hair. In that moment, I noticed the dark circles under his eyes, the way the vertical line between his brows appeared more deeply etched than it had been even a few months ago. I wondered how much he'd been sleeping.

At length he said, "You're asking a lot of me. What about Addie?"

"I know," I said miserably. "I wanted a way out of this, but…."

"But there isn't," Silas said. "None of us wish to cause you any hurt, but the harm done to many, many others far outweighs the concerns of a single person."

"Even if she's my daughter?" The words came out tight, controlled, but I saw how Jackson's hands clenched on the knees of his khakis.

"Even then," Silas replied, his tone sad and quiet.

Jackson was silent for a moment. "And what exactly is this 'harm done'? Right now all I have is your word to go on. Beg my pardon, Silas, but I don't know you from Adam."

"No, you don't," he said gravely. "But I love your sister, and want only the best for her and her family, which includes you and your family, Senator Quinn. However, I also know that Serena has seen a very dark future if this research continues—vampires in positions of power, common citizens treated like cattle. And you at the very top, Senator, glad to take their bribes, to allow them to curry favor by selling immortality. Is that really the legacy you want to give your country?"

Again my brother was quiet. Then he looked over at me. "You saw this?"

"Yes."

"You saw that I was President?"

I nodded. "Yes."

"And you didn't say anything?"

The anger in his voice was obvious. I flinched, partly because I hated to be at odds with him, and partly because this wasn't a Jackson I'd seen before. He usually did a much better job of hiding his emotions. "Well, considering neither you nor anyone else in the family ever seemed to have much interest in my visions, I figured it was better to keep it to myself. Besides, when I first had those visions, I was Lucius Montfort's prisoner and not in much of a position to talk to you or anyone else."

That revelation seemed to take him aback. "Wait—you were his *prisoner?*"

"For a while, yes. Then I managed to convince him that I was attracted to him. I'm sure he thought it was Stockholm syndrome, or maybe just his own vanity." I shrugged and reached for my glass of Perrier. "Or maybe he convinced himself, simply because I had something he wanted—access to you. Anyway, it doesn't matter now. Silas broke me out of Montfort prison early this morning, and now I'm a free woman again. But I really do need you to stop the research. It's too dangerous. Believe me, you don't want the future I saw to come true."

My brother's face had gone poker-still... never a good sign. He got up from the love seat and walked out into the sunshine, and stood at the edge of the pool. It had been built with a fountain at one end that fed into the spa area; the splashing of the water sounded very loud in the stillness.

Silas laid a hand on mine and spoke in a murmur. "Should I go speak with him?"

"No," I said at once. "He's processing. The best thing to do now is let him work it through himself. He's heard what we have to say. If you push him too hard, he'll just dig his heels in."

A reluctant nod, and Silas settled back against the couch, a frown pulling at his brows. For myself, I could feel my heart beating nervously as I waited. It was harder to follow my own advice than I'd thought it would be, but I knew I didn't dare approach my brother. As I'd said, he needed to come to his own decision. Any attempts to cajole him into doing the right thing would only backfire.

At last Jackson turned away from the pool's edge and walked back to the pergola. He stopped just within its shade and crossed his arms. "No."

I blinked up at him, my entire body going cold even though it was quite warm out there. "What?"

"I'm not going to do it. I'm not going to stop the only thing that might keep my daughter alive. All you've given me is visions and maybes and vague warnings. That's not good enough."

Silas stood up, although he didn't move toward my brother. "The cure for your daughter isn't a sure thing, either."

"I know that. But right now it's the only chance she has. I'm willing to take the risk."

"A risk that might one day endanger the entire world?"

"I don't believe that."

I rose from the couch as well. Silas slipped his hand into mine, his fingers warm and somewhat reassuring. "Jackson, please —"

"No. I've got to stay the course on this one." His eyes met mine, hard, unflinching. "If you had a child of your own, you'd do the same thing."

Would I? Right then, I couldn't think of how to respond, because I didn't have a child. I could imagine, but I couldn't know for sure how I might have reacted if I'd been put in the same situation. Voice cold, I said, "I guess I have to hope that having a child wouldn't blind me to the consequences of my actions."

A muscle twitched in his cheek. "I think you'd better go."

I wanted to protest. Problem was, when Jackson looked like that, sounded like that, there wasn't much you could do, except wait for him to cool off. "All right. But—" I stopped myself. If I kept arguing, I might say things that it would take a long time for him to forget.

"We're leaving," Silas said. "Very nice to meet you, Jackson."

"Wish I could say it was mutual."

Holding Silas' hand, I walked away from my brother. I didn't bother to say anything else. There was no point. We went through the house, and on out to the driveway, where the two Secret Service agents still stood, apparently keeping watch on the Ducati. Neither Silas nor I spoke. In silence, we got on the motorcycle and drove away.

It wasn't until we were back on the freeway that I allowed the tears to come.

CHAPTER NINETEEN

SERENA'S CHEEKS WERE DRY BY THE TIME Silas pulled into the garage at the house in the Hollywood Hills, but he could tell from her reddened eyes that she'd wept on the drive back here. He couldn't blame her; that had been a dreadful interview.

They went inside, and he headed to the kitchen so he could fetch her a glass of water. He handed it to her, and she gave him a watery smile.

"Do you have anything stronger?"

"Unfortunately, no. In general, if you're staying at a safe house, there's a good reason for you to stay away from alcohol."

She nodded, then sipped at the water. "I suppose that makes sense. It's just…."

"I know." He touched her shoulder briefly,

hoping the contact would give her some comfort. "Why don't we go sit out in the garden? It should be warm enough now, even this much closer to the ocean."

Her eyes wouldn't quite meet his, but she still responded in the affirmative. "That would be nice."

They went outside. The grass smelled warm and damp, very alive. Luckily, the sun had been out long enough that all the moisture left behind by the rain was now gone. Silas pulled out one of the chairs at the patio table for her, and she sat down, then set her glass on the tabletop.

Her gaze moved to the vista beyond the backyard, to the high-rises of Century City out toward the west. The sun had moved in that direction as well; in only a few hours, it would set, and Lucius Montfort would wake to find his prize gone. Silas somehow doubted the vampire would be pleased.

"I can't believe he said no."

Serena was still looking away from him, out toward the skyline. Was she ashamed of her brother? Was that why she couldn't meet his eyes?

"I can," Silas said gently. "His first thought is for his daughter. I'd hoped we could persuade him, but remember that we are not entirely without options."

"You're going to call in the *gula* squad."

"I have no choice."

She crossed her arms, hugging herself as though she was cold, although the sunny afternoon was very warm and mild, the soft breezes like a caress against the skin. "If we do this, he'll never speak to me again."

Should he be relieved that she had said "we"? After all, Serena herself had nothing to do with the team of Watchers who would make sure the lab and the samples it contained were destroyed. But with that simple word, it sounded as if she had aligned herself with them.

With him.

"You don't know that."

"Well, I know that he's going to be seriously pissed off, and Jackson never forgets. He may act polite in public—after all, he's a politician—but he doesn't forgive easily." Her hands wrapped around the glass of water Silas had given her, but she didn't lift it to her lips to take another drink.

He had to ask, even if the question was painful for her. "Can you live with that?"

Serena's eyes met his. Most of the redness from her weeping had disappeared, but she still looked tired. Beautiful, but tired, as if she needed to lock herself away for a long time to restore some of the sleep she'd lost over these past few weeks. Gold and green glinted in her gaze, reminding him of the forests he'd left behind in northern California. "I guess I'll have to. It's...." She let the words trail off. Her chest rose and fell with a heavy breath, but he couldn't hear her sigh. "Silas, tell me what you want."

"What I want?" he repeated, puzzled by the shift in her tone.

"Yes, what do you want from all this? Pretend there's no Lucius, no lab, no argument with my brother. Just the two of us. What are you hoping for?"

They'd confessed their love for one another, but the future had been like a forbidden land, one whose border they dared not cross. He knew he had to speak now, or risk losing her, despite the love they shared. "I'm hoping for the future you saw in your vision. You and I, and our son. Far away from here, from all this." He gestured toward the skyscrapers in the distance, now somewhat hazy in the afternoon light as the city's smog blended with the fog that had already begun to move in off the ocean. "It's a simple life, but I pray that you'll discover it's a better life. I've watched you, Serena. I've watched you for a very long time. You could have had everything the world has to offer, and yet you never seemed happy. Not really. I suppose in my heart I hoped it was because you didn't want this world, wanted something different. I know you said earlier that you did want to come to Humboldt. But…are you sure? Really sure?"

Her hazel eyes blurred with tears. "Oh, yes, I'm sure," she said in a near-whisper. "You know me better than I know myself. I don't want to be here. I want you to take me far away. Promise me that you will."

"I promise," he said, then got up from his chair so he could fold her in his arms, hold her against him, feel the slenderness of her body, so fragile-seeming, and yet with true steel at its heart. She had survived so much.

She only needed to survive a little more.

We went inside. I was drained, and yet somehow content. Jackson would be so very angry with me—and so would my parents, and Bethany, and so many others—if they ever found out. But I couldn't let that terrible future come to pass. We had the means to stop it.

I didn't want to hurt Addison. With every fiber of my being, I prayed there might be some miracle, that the experts at UCLA might find something they'd missed. But while I understood why my brother had chosen as he did, I couldn't let those considerations sway me. The *gula* had been fighting vampires for a very long time. If they said that blood was a danger to the future of mankind, then I believed them.

Silas spent a long time on the phone with Felix. I purposely didn't eavesdrop on their conversation, partly because it would have been rude, and partly because I wasn't sure I wanted to know everything they had planned. It was one thing to feel noble, as if you were doing the right thing, but if I heard the details of their operation, that would make it all too real. Right now, the whole venture felt terribly abstract. As soon as I knew exactly how they planned to attack the lab, it would all come home to me, and I'd realize that I'd sentenced my niece to death. Guilt washed over me. Maybe I wasn't doing the right thing at all. Maybe Felix was just fear-mongering. No, I couldn't say I knew him well, but I could tell he was clearly the unflappable type. He wouldn't have told me that destroying the samples was urgent unless it truly was.

I went back outside to breathe the fresh air, to try to calm myself. My phone was still inside, sitting on the kitchen counter where I'd left it. I didn't want to look at it, didn't want to see if I'd missed any messages from Jackson, or Candace, or my parents. Right now I floated in a bubble of my own making. Easier to hide in here until it was all over, and then I could emerge and figure out what to do next.

Whatever happened, though, I wouldn't face it alone. Silas would be there with me, and he would take me away from here. A coward's choice? Maybe. I only knew I was tired. Tired of the burden of my visions, tired of not being what my family expected me to be. Up in Humboldt County, in a compound outside a little town called Fortuna, I could start over.

Maybe then I'd finally figure out who Serena Quinn was supposed to be.

The sun dipped toward the horizon, and the warm breeze grew cooler. Silas came up behind me and dropped a sweater around my shoulders.

"You looked cold."

"Thank you." The sweater had been hanging in the closet along with the rest of the clothes I'd unpacked. I'd known where it was, but I didn't think Silas had paid much attention to how I disposed my meager travel wardrobe.

I should have known better. Silas noticed everything.

"Do you have it all worked out?" I asked.

"Yes. The team will meet at the lab at eleven o'clock tonight."

"I suppose they want you there."

"We need everyone we can muster, just in

case Lucius somehow gets wind of what we're planning and brings his fledglings to stop us."

I pulled the sweater more tightly about me and looked up at Silas. His expression was serious, but not terribly worried. "Do you really think that's a possibility?"

"Everything is a possibility, just some things more than others. But Lucius is canny. I know you weren't followed, that no one knows we're here. And yet...."

"Your spider sense is tingling?"

"Spider sense?"

"From *Spider Man?* The comic books? The movies?"

His shoulders lifted in a shrug. "We don't follow popular culture all that closely."

Apparently not. Plowing ahead, I said, "It just means that you're getting a hinky feeling about something, that you can tell something isn't quite right."

"Oh, well, in that case...yes." Silas was quiet for a few seconds, fine profile painted in the rays of the setting sun. "I feel—and Felix believes as well—that we need to be prepared for some kind of defense of the lab facility, even if that defense only comes from the security detail I'm sure your brother has assigned to the building."

I didn't like the sound of that. Kicking vampire ass was one thing. But going after a bunch of innocent security guards just because they happened to be in the wrong place at the wrong time? Not good.

Although I didn't say anything, Silas clearly noticed a shift in my expression. "We won't hurt them," he said gently. "The security guards, that is. We *gula* have many nonlethal means to subdue people, if it becomes necessary."

"Well, that's something, I guess."

He tilted his head at me. "Are you seeing anything? A vision would be helpful right about now."

"No." The word came out flat and tired, which was basically how I felt right then. "They don't come on command. And I don't know...I saw so many visions while I was trapped at Lucius Montfort's mansion, maybe I burned myself out or something."

"Well, don't fret over it. I only thought I'd ask."

His tone was soothing, an obvious effort to comfort me. I didn't feel terribly comforted, though. I just wanted this over with so I could face the aftermath and get on with my life.

Our lives. The life I wanted to share with Silas.

He seemed to understand that I didn't feel like talking anymore, because he touched my arm and guided me inside, out of the increasingly chilly wind. I sat in the living room while he made another call to Felix. At some point after that, Silas suggested that we head out, get something to eat, maybe go see a movie to fill up the time. Eleven o'clock was a long ways off, after all.

I agreed because I knew I'd fall asleep on the couch if I tried to stay in the safe house and watch TV until it was time to leave. Possibly Silas and I could have made love during part of that time, but I wasn't in the mood right then. I wanted the next time we slept together to be after all this, when we could truly commit to our future together.

We came down the hill and went further into Hollywood, decided to kill two birds with one stone by having dinner at the café at the Arclight and then seeing a movie there. That would get us out a little before ten, giving us plenty of time to head east to Rancho Cucamonga and the lab.

As much as I wished for a glass of wine with my meal, I told myself that wouldn't be a very good idea. I was already wearier than I wanted to admit, and the wine would make me sleepy. And I'd chosen the latest installment of a super-hero franchise as our movie of the evening, partly because it wouldn't require me to engage my brain very much, and partly because I hoped the explosions and the other loud sound effects would keep me from falling asleep with my head on Silas' shoulder.

The ploy did seem to work, or maybe it was the bottomless iced tea I'd had with my burger. Either way, I was awake enough as we went to the parking structure to retrieve the Ducati. We both climbed on, and I slipped the helmet over my head. Silas never wore one; I'd forgotten to ask why. Maybe the *gula* didn't have to worry about head injuries the way regular humans did.

Regular humans. Silas seemed so real to me, so very human himself, that sometimes it was hard to remember he wasn't quite human, that he came from a race some might call monsters.

The night wind was cold on my face, further helping me to stay awake. Then again, if I got sleepy and loosened my grip on Silas' waist, I'd be in a world of hurt, which only provided an extra incentive to stay alert.

Traffic at this time of night was light, almost nonexistent. We'd reach our destination long before we had to at this rate. The exit we would have taken to get to my condo flashed by, and I hardly noticed. Whatever happened next, I didn't think I'd be returning there, except to pack up my things.

If all went well.

When we got to Rancho Cucamonga, Silas pulled up to a Denny's on Foothill Boulevard.

"We're early," he said. "And I want some coffee. You?"

"More iced tea, I think."

We went inside and ordered our drinks, and decided to split a plate of fries, just to help keep us going. Both of us were fairly quiet, simply because we didn't think discussing our upcoming confrontation was a very good idea with so many listening ears around. Even though it was past ten-thirty, the diner was more crowded than I'd anticipated, people out after seeing a movie, or maybe just wanting to prolong their evening. With an odd sense of detachment, I realized it was Saturday night.

After a rowdy group of high school kids vacated the booth behind us, Silas said in a murmur, "Are you ready for this?"

"Probably not," I replied. "But I haven't been ready for any of the shit I've had to deal with lately, and yet here I am. I won't let not being ready stop me. I just have to...do what needs to be done, I guess. Although in this case, I suppose I'm mostly going to stand back and watch, right?"

"Right." Silas lifted his cup of coffee to his lips and drank. "I don't want you involved at all."

"Then why am I here? Shouldn't I have stayed back at the safe house?"

Not that I would have done such a thing. No

way would I have let Silas go off and put himself in harm's way without me there to have his back if necessary.

"That might have been the sensible thing to do," he said. "But I couldn't have allowed you to stay there alone. After having Lucius steal you from me, I find I don't want to let you out of my sight. We've spent too much time apart as it is."

Wasn't that the truth. Less than two weeks, but still, those were weeks that Silas and I could have spent getting to know one another, learning more of each other's rhythms and moods. I didn't dare let myself wander too far down the path of what if?, however, because that would only start me thinking about what would have happened if Lucius Montfort had never interfered with my life. For one thing, my sister would still be alive.

Even that thought was enough to make my throat tighten. I reached for my iced tea and drank, glad of the extra little charge of caffeine it provided. "I know," I said. "And I'm done with that. We can be joined at the hip from here on out."

He smiled. Not a big grin, but a reassuring little twitch of his lips that brought some light to his dark eyes. Just seeing the shift in his expression made me feel better, told me that he was perfectly fine about being inseparable from now on. He pulled his phone out of his pocket, checked the time. "We should get going."

My stomach clenched, but I told it to stop being such a baby. Since the waitress had already dropped off the check, Silas picked it up and took it over to the cash register. A minute later, and we were back outside, the cool night wind catching in my hair. Which reminded me — I reached in the pocket of my borrowed jacket and got out an elastic band, then pulled back my hair once again. I'd let it down while we were eating, but I knew it would turn into a tangled mess if I didn't confine it for the motorcycle ride.

We headed east on Foothill Boulevard, then zigzagged into the office park where the lab was located, a few blocks east of the 15 Freeway. All was quiet, although once Silas turned off the motorcycle's engine and we began to glide toward the prearranged meeting place, I thought I could hear the *chugga-chugga* sound of an automatic sprinkler system off in the distance.

The *gula* had chosen as their gathering place a spot behind the building next to the one the lab occupied. They hid in the shadows of the trees, and only came out when they saw us approaching. I recognized Felix because even in the darkness his fair hair glinted, pale and ghostly.

His gaze shifted to me for a moment, and I thought I saw his brows pull together. He didn't say anything, though, or at least, when he spoke, he ignored my presence.

"There are two security guards making the rounds, but they seem to be sweeping the entire office park. As far as we've been able to tell, there aren't any guards assigned specifically to the lab."

"That seems kind of odd," Silas remarked. "You'd think that Senator Quinn would make sure to protect his prize better than that."

"Possibly. On the other hand, too heavy a security presence would only make it more obvious that there was something in that particular building which needed to be protected. It's a toss-up. Also, we did detect cameras at all the corners of the buildings, but they shouldn't be a huge deterrent. We prepared ourselves for that." He gestured to a wad of dark cloth around his neck that I'd thought was a scarf, but realized must be some kind of combination of ski mask and muffler, ready to be pulled up to hide his features.

Silas nodded. "So what's the plan?"

"Aaron and Micah will cut the power to the building. That'll give us access to the automatic doors. It should also disable the alarm system momentarily, but we're fairly certain it has a battery backup, so we can't count on it being offline for very long. Not that we need it to—I'm confident we should be able to gain access to the lab and destroy the samples within a few minutes."

"The data on the computers?"

"We have a virus ready to introduce to the system. It's designed to wipe out all the hard drives and any tape backups they might have."

Thorough. I supposed I should be surprised that the *gula* had access to all that technology, but then I remembered how Felix had been able to tunnel through my VPN and still contact me despite all the safeguards I had in palace. The Watchers might live in a compound out in the middle of nowhere, but that obviously didn't prevent them from being at the top of their game when it came to that sort of thing.

"What if they've stored some of their data off-site? Or in the cloud?"

Felix's mouth thinned slightly. "It's a possibility, but, considering how eager Senator Quinn was to keep this project on the down-low, I'm not anticipating that he would have done so. The more places information is stored, the more opportunities exist to hack into it. No fear, though—if he did create a backup somewhere outside this lab, we'll track it down and destroy it as well."

Apparently his fellow Watcher's answers

were enough to satisfy Silas, because he nodded. "Ready?"

"Yes. The security guards are on the opposite side of the complex. Best to go now." He gestured toward Micah and Aaron. In response, they pulled up their ski masks, hiding their faces. Felix did the same, while Silas tugged at the bandana he'd knotted around his neck, loosening it so he could draw it up to cover his mouth and chin and nose.

I watched them, knowing that I didn't have any way to hide my own identity. Silas appeared to note my unease, because he touched my arm and said, "Serena, you'll need to stay back in the cover of the trees. Best not to get close enough that the cameras have even a chance of catching your face."

"It doesn't matter," I replied, my tone subdued. "As soon as Jackson gets wind of this, he's going to know it was me, or at least people working for me or with me."

"Probably," Silas agreed. "Still, it's better if you try to remain anonymous."

Since I couldn't really argue with that, I murmured a "yes" and then followed the group as they headed toward the building that housed the laboratory. While I stayed back in the trees, they began to move toward the front door.

Only to halt in the middle of the parking lot

as a man stepped forward from the shadows, his hair even paler than Felix's, although it lay loose on his shoulders rather than being cut short. However, I barely noticed that minor detail.

Cold surged through me as I realized he wasn't alone. His arm was hooked around the throat of a woman with blonde hair, someone whose face was nearly as familiar to me as my own.

My friend Candace.

CHAPTER TWENTY

AN INCOHERENT CRY OF DENIAL BURST FROM my lips. This was what I'd worried about when Lucius first mentioned my friend—that he'd somehow find a way to use her to hurt me. I began to surge forward, only to have Silas' hand clamp down on my forearm.

"Hello, Serena," Lucius said, his tone almost conversational. "I had a feeling you might try something foolish like this, so I thought I had better give myself an insurance policy."

"Let her go," I told him fiercely, at the same time wishing I had a useful psychic power, like being able to reach out and choke him with my mind. "She has nothing to do with any of this."

Candace's wide blue eyes met mine. Although I knew she had to be scared out of her wits, she sounded calm and in control when she spoke. "It's all right, Serena. He hasn't hurt me."

"Oh, no," Lucius said, as Tristan McVey and Leticia Carver also emerged from the shadows to flank him. I spotted more movement as five men I'd never seen before came forth to take up protective positions around the vampires. Lucius' new semivives, no doubt. To either side of Silas and me, the *gula* were still and quiet, clearly assessing the situation, trying to determine their best plan of attack. "I haven't hurt her...yet. In fact, I must admit she is a worthy specimen, full of fire and determination. Perhaps she's a likely candidate to walk the otherworld and survive and return changed. What do you think, Serena?"

I guessed all too well what he was hinting at. For all I knew, Candace was tough enough to survive the transformation into a vampire state. However, I couldn't allow Lucius to do such a thing to her. She needed to stay here, among the living. "I think you're just trying to get a rise out of me, Lucius," I returned, my voice level. "You'd think that someone who's survived for more than three hundred years could do better than resort to cheap tricks."

He laughed then, but I thought I detected something forced about the sound, as though he'd made himself laugh in order to prevent me from seeing how angry he really was. "Oh, I don't think it's a cheap trick. But perhaps you're only trying to suppress a certain level of jealousy?"

Silas made a low growling sound in the back of his throat, but I could only offer Lucius a pitying smile and a shake of my head. "Hardly. Are you still trying to flatter yourself that I wanted you, Lucius? I would have thought that my escape this morning—and the engagement ring I left on the nightstand—would be enough to erase any doubt."

The vampire master's mouth tightened. "That was rather declassé of you, Serena. One would think that someone with your background would behave better."

Maybe he'd been attempting to wound me with that comment, but I couldn't have cared less what he thought of me, or my background. I held his gaze, even as I felt rather than saw the tension of the Watchers who stood around me, ready to pounce. Four of them, if you counted Silas, against three vampires and five semivives. Not exactly an even fight, although since those semivives were new, and possibly not fully accli- mated to having someone else in control of their minds, it might very well be that they wouldn't put up much of a fight.

Silas stepped forward. "You've been outmaneuvered, Lucius. You thought you could reshape the world the way you wanted it to be, but you should have known that we would never allow you to do such a thing. Just as you should have known that Serena could never love you."

"Love me?" Lucius' lip curled, and he shot a contemptuous glance at Silas that seemed to take me in as well. "It didn't matter whether she loved me or not. I certainly cared nothing for her. All I cared about was gaining access to her visions. They were what was truly valuable, for they told me what my future would be. And that future does not include you or your fellow goons destroying the research being conducted in this building."

Although I didn't love Lucius Montfort—the exact opposite, actually—his words still felt like a slap in the face. All the time I'd been acting, he'd been acting as well. I had been stupid enough, and naïve enough, to believe that he'd somehow found it in his black heart to harbor a little bit of affection for me.

I should have known better. Lucius Montfort never did anything for anyone except himself.

"Enough," Felix growled. He'd been standing off to one side, listening to this exchange, but clearly he was done listening. "The future is not yours, vampire. It never was."

If he gave a signal to the other *gula,* I didn't catch it, but somehow they got the message, because in the next instant they all began to transform, dark wings sprouting from their backs and tearing the garments they wore. In response, the semivives moved forward, shifting positions so they could protect their vampire master and his fledglings.

Besides me, Silas murmured, "I must go to their aid," even as he pulled off the leather jacket he wore so it wouldn't get destroyed during his transformation.

As much as I hated to let him go, I couldn't stop him. He loved me, but he was one of their brethren, sworn to protect all his kind...and mine as well. "I know," I said. "Be careful."

He didn't answer, but began to transform as well, skin darkening, his frame growing larger as those enormous bat wings protruded from his back. Even though I'd seen him make this change before, witnessing it again brought home to me just how alien he was, at a cellular level I couldn't quite understand.

And yet...I loved him. I needed him more than I'd ever needed anything in my life.

One of the other *gula*—Micah? It was almost impossible to tell, once they were in their gargoyle forms—reached with clawed hands for a semivive, catching him by his shirt and tossing him against the side of the building, which he hit with an audible *crack*. I winced, even though I knew the *gula* had no choice. They had to get inside the lab, destroy the blood samples and everything related to them. It still hurt, though, because I knew that semivive was blameless, had been innocently living his life before Lucius descended and transformed him into a slave.

From somewhere behind me, I heard the roar of a car's engine, followed by a squeal of brakes. I whirled, expecting to see one of the office park's security officers pulling up in his patrol car, but instead I realized the vehicle that had just arrived was the dark green Range Rover my brother Jackson drove while he was here in Southern California. He got out of the SUV and ran forward, shouting, "Stop this! Stop it!"

A distracted part of my mind wondered how he'd managed to ditch his Secret Service detail. But that was as far as I got, because another of the *gula* hurled one of the semivives aside and charged for the front doors of the building. Almost at once, Tristan McVey moved forward in a blur, hands outstretched so he could grasp the *gula* by one of his wings and tear at it, partly wrenching it from his back. The Watcher—not Silas, thank God, although otherwise I couldn't tell who it was—let out an unearthly howl and staggered backward, dark blood pouring down from the wound.

At the same time, Leticia Carver darted sideways in a blur, heading for a *gula* I was fairly certain had to be Felix. Her hands were curved into claws, and I worried that she was about to attempt the same maneuver with him, rendering him incapable of flight and leaving him badly wounded. However, he seemed to see the attack coming, and backhanded her with a blow that made her fly backward at least five feet, where she landed with a heavy thud on the sidewalk in front of the building.

Jackson stopped beside me, chest heaving, his eyes wide, as though he couldn't quite take in the scene before him. "What—what *are* they?"

I knew he wasn't talking about the vampires. They looked more or less human. "The Watchers," I told him. "The ones sworn to protect humanity from the vampires. They couldn't let you do it, Jackson."

"I—"

He stopped there and looked away from me, toward Lucius Montfort and the woman he still held captive. Candace's eyes were wide with terror, but she wasn't trying to get away. How could she, when the vampire master held her with a grip of iron? I knew all too well how impossible it was for a mere human to try to escape a vampire's grasp. Thank God Candace was the type to stay calm in a crisis situation — she seemed to realize that struggling with Lucius would be pointless, or downright dangerous.

Hands balled into fists at his sides, Jackson called out, "Stop it, Montfort. You have no right to drag Serena's friend into this."

"Rights mean very little to me, senator," Lucius replied calmly, as though oblivious to the battle going on around him. "We had a deal. I am only trying to protect my part of the bargain."

Jackson's jaw tightened. I could tell he was wrestling with himself, trying to decide whether it was worth it to keep arguing with the vampire, or whether he should take more direct action. If Lucius had been an ordinary man, the two of them might have been evenly matched. My brother was tall and worked out regularly to maintain his athletic build, was in fact a good bit bulkier than the vampire. But mere muscles weren't of much use here. Right then, I wasn't sure what any of us could do to prevail against Lucius Montfort and his minions.

All around, the *gula* and the semivives went still, watching the exchange between the two men. Leticia Carver pushed herself to her feet, blood dripping from a cut along her cheek. Her eyes were narrowed with rage.

Lucius went on, his voice soft and insinuating, "You must think of your daughter, Senator Quinn. If you allow these monsters to destroy the samples and the research, then all hope for her is gone. Will you be able to sleep at night, knowing that you had the cure within your grasp and you still threw it away?"

Jackson's head went up, eyes blazing. "I know my daughter," he said clearly. "I've been thinking ever since I talked to Serena earlier today. And I realized that Addison wouldn't want this. She wouldn't want the world put at risk just so she could live."

"You expect me to believe that a nine-year-old can be so noble?"

"Not really," my brother replied. "I doubt you're able to see nobility in anyone else, since you obviously lack it in yourself. All the same, this is my facility. I pay the bills. And so I'm the one who has the final say in what happens here." He shifted slightly so he could look look over at me. "I don't want to continue. This needs to end."

"Thank you, Jackson," I murmured.

"I'm glad I have a little sister like you who can keep me on the right path," he said. Then he transferred his gaze from me to Silas. How he was able to pick out my lover from the rest of the *gula*, I didn't know, but Jackson always had been perceptive. Raising his voice, he went on, "The security code is 79437. Here are the keys." And he lobbed a plain metal ring with a set of three keys on it to Silas, who caught it in midair with one clawed hand.

Even as Silas began to hurry toward the front door of the office suite, Lucius spat, "You wish to betray me? I'll make sure you're incapable of ever doing such a thing again."

With a shove, he pushed Candace away so she stumbled and fell to her knees on the concrete walkway. In a blur, he was moving toward my brother, reaching for him, fangs bared. For a second I couldn't figure out why he'd give up his hostage, but then I realized what he intended.

If Lucius couldn't get Jackson to cooperate, he'd turn him into a semivive, incapable of doing anything except his bidding.

"No!" I screamed, and hurled myself between them. The vampire crashed into me, knocking me to the ground. Grit from the walkway stung my palms, while the shock of the impact sent a searing flash of pain through the leg with the pin in it, but I ignored the throbbing in my thigh, pushed myself to my feet. I had to stop him, although I had no idea how.

I wasn't given the chance, because in the next moment Silas launched himself at the vampire master, the impact when he plowed into him so fierce that I could hear it from where I stood. Lucius let out a whoosh of a breath, but clearly the blow wasn't enough to stop him, because he reached for my lover, hands ready to tear. I'd already seen how the wings seemed to be the *gulas'* one vulnerability, and it seemed that was where Montfort planned to strike.

A dark blur seemed to come from nowhere, and I realized, in my shock and fear, that the blur was Michael St. John, who'd been conspic-uously absent up until that moment. I began to move toward Silas and Lucius, thinking for sure that Michael must have come to assist the vampire who'd made him.

But then his fingers wrapped around Lucius Montfort's neck, and he yanked him backward, pulling him away from my lover. Lucius writhed in his fledgling's grasp, but Michael held firm.

"Traitor! You cannot go against your master!"

"Watch...me," Michael grunted, eyes slitted with the strain of holding the older vampire back.

From the corner of my eye, I saw Tristan and Leticia turn and begin to run toward him, clearly intent on helping their master. They weren't given the chance, however, because the *gula,* even the wounded Micah, blocked their way.

And Silas, seeing his chance, grasped a branch from a nearby tree, breaking it off so one end formed a sharp point. Muscles bulging in his arms, he flung the branch at Lucius Montfort.

It drove through his dark shirt, directly into his chest. Blood, an oily reddish-black under the illumination from the sodium vapor streetlights that lined the streets of the office park, sprayed outward, hitting Michael in the face, some of it even spattering against the leather jacket I wore.

The master vampire collapsed, slipping from Michael St. John's grasp like a pile of limp laundry. For one second the vampire's silver-bright eyes caught mine, angry, confused. "You... should...have...chosen...me," he gasped.

And then he was gone, body dissolving into dust. Leticia and Tristan both cried out then, guttural cries that sounded more like they should have emerged from the throats of wild animals. Nothing else from them, however, because as they stood there in their shock and dismay, the other *gula* descended on them with their own makeshift stakes and drove them through the vampires' hearts. Before I could blink, the two fledglings were gone, dwindling into the same sooty gray dust as their master.

At the same time, the semivives blinked, as

though waking from a nightmare. The man who'd been thrown against the wall pushed himself to his feet and rubbed his shoulder. Thank God. At least he hadn't sustained any lasting injuries.

"What the—?" said one of them, glassy eyes focusing on the monstrous forms of the four *gula*.

Immediately, all of the Watchers transformed, shifting into their human selves. Felix bent and picked up his own discarded jacket and shrugged into it as if there was nothing particularly strange about the sudden alteration in his appearance. "Are you all right?" he asked the semivive who'd spoken. "Do you know where you are?"

"No," said the man, who looked to be in his mid-thirties, brawny but already balding. "Weren't you…?"

"We work security here," Felix said. "Someone reported a group of men wandering around, looking drugged. I think someone's played a cruel trick on you."

The former semivive blinked and glanced back at his compatriots, all of whom appeared equally disoriented. Like the first semivive, they appeared to be in their thirties, athletic in build. Well, I supposed Lucius wouldn't have bothered with specimens who couldn't hold their own in a fight. "Drugged?" the man said. He put a hand to his head, as if it hurt him.

"Yes, I think so," Felix told him. "Let's call the police, see if we can get this straightened out...."

He led the semivive away, while Micah and Aaron did the same with the men who remained. The wound on Micah's back appeared to have healed, or at least had stopped bleeding, because once he put his jacket on, I couldn't tell that he'd been hurt at all.

Candace came up to us, rubbing at her elbow. "Well...that was different."

"Are you okay?" I asked.

"I'm fine. Some bumps and bruises, that's all."

"I'm so sorry about this—"

She held up a hand. "It's okay. The most exciting Saturday night I've had in a while, that's for sure."

Silas looked over at his brother, who stood a few feet away from us. "Why did you do it?"

Michael's shoulders lifted slightly. As usual, his expression appeared vaguely ironic, as if he didn't want anyone to guess at what he might be truly feeling. "He might have made me, but you're my brother. Besides, once I knew what he was up to, I realized he had to be stopped. We vampires are powerful enough without getting all those extra advantages."

My brother had been listening to all this with a mystified expression on his face. "Wait—you're a vampire?" he asked Michael. "And you're also Silas' brother?"

"It's a long story," Michael said. "One I don't feel like telling right now. Anyway, don't you still have work to do?" He looked over at the building that contained the lab.

"You're right." Jackson's gaze moved to me. "We need to end this."

No alarms went off. No armed guards came to ask what they were doing. But why would they? Jackson Quinn had the codes, and the keys to the office suite. There was no reason for anyone to raise the alarm.

As Candace and Michael and Serena waited in the lab's break room, Jackson and Silas went to the refrigerated storage area and methodically destroyed the samples one by one. The senator's expression was blank as the vampire blood swirled down into the drain, gone forever. Was he regretting his decision? Or was he simply trying very hard not to think about the future to which he'd doomed his daughter?

Silas didn't know the man well enough to ask, and so he remained silent until the task was complete. After the last vial had been dumped and rinsed out, he said, "Can you get us into the computer systems? I can wait for Felix to come back—he's our expert on that sort of thing—but if you have access...."

"I do," Jackson said.

"Good. Then let's take care of it."

The senator nodded, and led Silas out of the storage area and down the hall to a office with "S. Gutierrez" stamped into the plastic name-plate affixed to the door. Using one of his keys, Jackson Quinn unlocked the door and went inside, then sat down at the desk there and booted up the computer, a thin, elegant iMac with an enormous screen. After typing in the password that would allow him access, he got up from the chair and said, "Your turn. I wouldn't know what to look for."

Silas took the seat and pulled a jump drive from his pocket. On that drive was a copy of the program Felix had created to search out every file related to the program and zap them all into nothingness. How it all worked, he didn't know for sure; that wasn't his field of expertise. But Felix had yet to let the *gula* down when it came to technical matters.

"Would your project manager have made

backups?" he asked as he shut the computer back down.

"I'm sure she did. She's very thorough. I'll request those when I talk to her first thing tomorrow morning."

"What if she asks why you wanted the research shut down?"

"She won't." Jackson offered Silas a thin smile. "I pay her very well to do what I ask. She'll take care of it, especially once I offer to give her a sterling recommendation for her next position."

"Ah." Yes, Jackson Quinn did have the resources to make sure Shelby Gutierrez was very happy, and unlikely to ask too many questions. For a moment, Silas wondered what that would be like, to have the money and power to know that people would do precisely as you requested, no questions asked. But then he realized he wouldn't want to be in that position, wouldn't want to have the means to make the world do as he wished. Far too much temptation to do the wrong thing.

For a moment Jackson was silent. Then he gave Silas a long, penetrating look. "Do you love her?"

"More than anything."

"Then I won't blame you."

"For what?"

"Taking her away from us."

~

Silas and Jackson emerged from Shelby Gutierrez's office, both of them grave-faced and not speaking. I got up from the couch where the rest of us had been waiting, but Jackson held up a hand. "Do you all mind if I speak to my sister in private?"

"Of course not," Candace said at once. She rose from her own chair, and after a brief hesitation, Michael got to his feet as well.

"I think my work here is done," he said. His gaze shifted to Candace. "Need a ride back to Pasadena?"

Now it was Candace's turn to hesitate. Usually she was not one to be diffident, but I could see why Michael's question might have given her pause. "Uh...aren't you a vampire?"

He grinned. "Yeah, but I don't bite."

"It'll be all right," Silas said. His dark eyes, so like his brother's, fastened on Michael. "Won't it?"

"Of course."

Candace looked at me. "I guess...call me when you can?"

"Absolutely," I assured her.

"Okay," she said, and turned to Michael. "So you live in Pasadena, too?"

"Yes." Michael stopped there, a frown pulling at his brows. "Or at least, I guess I do. I'm not really sure what happens next, except I'm sure the neighbors are going to wonder why the Mediterranean place they lived next to suddenly turned into a faux-gothic mansion."

Of course. Once Lucius was gone, the illusion that had shielded the house would have disappeared with him. That would take a bit of explaining. And had the vampire master even left a will? It would be just like him, to set his fledglings adrift to fend for themselves in the unlikely event of his true death.

"But that's to worry about later," Michael went on. "In the meantime, I have a car, and you need a ride. Shall we?"

Even my hyper-competent friend appeared a bit flummoxed by Michael's comment. After another pause, she shrugged, then offered him a reluctant smile and gave a half-wave to me as she followed him out of the room. Silas went after them, leaving me alone with my brother.

"Well," he said, and paused.

"'Well' is right." I looked up at him, trying to detect some clue as to how he felt about what had just transpired. He appeared weary but calm, as though glad that he'd faced his fears for

Addison and had managed to come out on the other side. "I'm sorry."

"*You're* sorry?" A shake of the head, and he came over to sit next to me on the sofa. "You don't have to be sorry. I'm the one who should be sorry."

"Considering the circumstances, I think you're forgiven."

He ran his hands over the knees of his khakis. "I let myself be blinded by my worries for my child. And I'm running for President? Someone who wants to be the leader of the free world can't allow himself to be swayed by personal issues."

"Again, Jackson...I don't think too many people would blame you. I certainly can't, since I'm the one who brought the idea to you in the first place." Prodded by Lucius Montfort, but still. My mind flashed back to the terrible pile of gray dust that lay on the ground in front of the building. I still wasn't quite sure what to feel about that. Yes, the world would be a safer place with the vampire master gone, and I could only be glad that Tristan and Leticia had faced justice, but it had all happened so quickly that my mind hadn't quite processed everything yet. Aware that my brother was watching me closely, expecting me to say something else, I added, "I'm certain that in the future you'll be sure to examine all the ramifications of a decision before you make it."

A silence. Then, "Do you think I should withdraw my candidacy?"

What a question...and one I couldn't possibly answer for him. "That's up to you, and Bethany, and Addison," I replied. "I can't tell you what would be best for all of you. I do know that you did the right thing here. In my book, that makes you a great candidate for President."

His eyes met mine. "And what about you, Serena?"

I hesitated. In my mind, I saw a green field, and a small dark-haired boy laughing as he pulled a kite nearly bigger than he was. "I don't think my place is here anymore."

"I'm sorry."

"Sorry for what?"

"Sorry we couldn't be a better family for you. Sorry that we really didn't try to understand what you were going through."

He looked so troubled, so overcome by self-recrimination, that I had to move closer and put my arms around him, give him a fierce hug. "It's not your fault," I told him. "It's just...life."

"I suppose," he said. He touched my arm. "Then go make your own, and don't worry about us."

~

That night Silas and I slept in the safe house, wrapped in one another's arms. Candace had texted me to say that she was home and she was fine. Michael clearly had been on his best behavior, not that I doubted he would be. After all, Silas knew where he lived...for the moment, anyway.

The next day we went to my condo so I could begin to pack up my things, although I knew the bulk of the furniture and household items would end up being donated to charity. There were some personal items I wanted to take with me, though, things I didn't want to leave behind, books and clothes, a few pieces of jewelry, an album of pictures from my childhood...possibly all I'd have to remind me of the family I would leave behind.

My mind was as at peace as it could be, since Felix had called Silas early that morning to let him know that he'd just had word of a new experimental program at Loma Linda University Hospital, one he was sure Jackson hadn't heard of because it was so new. I passed the information along to my brother, and he had an appointment set up for Addie for the following afternoon. No promise of a cure yet, but I allowed a little hope to bloom in my heart. After all, I'd had my own personal miracle in surviving Lucius Montfort and finding the man I loved. Maybe Addison would have her miracle, too.

And Silas had contacted Detective Ortiz, had told him as much as he dared of what had happened with Lucius Montfort, just so the detective's mind could be somewhat at ease, now that the loose end of my disappearance had been cleared up. He also passed along the photo I'd found in the pocket of Michael's victim. With any luck, the police would be able to find the dead man's family, give them as much closure as they could. I didn't have to worry about the police connecting Michael to that death, however, because he'd sent a note to us soon afterward, saying he hoped the best for us, but that he needed to disappear for a while. While I hated the idea of the two brothers being sepa- rated yet again, I thought I understood. We'd all been through a great many changes in the recent past, and he needed time to come to terms with the shift in his circumstances. I did hope he wouldn't disappear forever, though. Vampire or not, he was family, too.

As Silas and I were coming back upstairs after putting some suitcases in the back of my Mercedes SUV, Brian came out of his place and paused on the landing, staring at the two of us with some of the same fuzziness I'd seen in

Lucius Montfort's newly minted semivives the night before.

"Are you going somewhere, Serena?"

At least he still remembered my name. "Yes, Brian. Silas and I have decided to move in together, so I'm getting some things packed."

"Oh." His gaze shifted to Silas. "Have we met?"

"Not formally." Silas extended a hand, and Brian took it.

"I could have sworn you were someone else, but my brain hasn't been itself lately. Distracted by work, I guess."

"It happens to the best of us," I said with a smile. "I'm sure it'll pass."

"Probably," he agreed. "Well, back to work. 'Bye now."

He closed the door, and I looked up at Silas. "Will it pass?"

"I think so," he replied. "In the grand scheme of things, he wasn't enslaved for very long. Not many semivives can return from a vampire's mind control, but Montfort's grip on him was lighter than it was on his other slaves, probably because Brian had to function in the real world. It may take a few more days for him to return completely to himself, but in the end, he'll do all right. Lucius Montfort will just be a memory of a bad dream."

"Like he is for me," I said, and Silas bent down and kissed me gently on the cheek.

"Yes. And I'll make sure you'll never have to worry about bad dreams again."

Another kiss, this one warmer and deeper. After everything we had been through, I was ready to take him at his word.

I knew that would be enough.

EPILOGUE

THE BREEZE WAS COOL, BUT THE SUN WARM, glinting on Silas' hair as he leaned back on the plaid blanket and lifted his face to the light. Summer was only a few weeks old, but already he'd become browned from the sun's rays, since we'd tried to be outdoors as much as possible to enjoy the delicious weather.

This was my home, so far away from everything I'd known and loved. The *gula* were now my family, a family who saw my visions as something to be welcomed and embraced, not hidden. I'd left much behind, but I had far more to look forward to.

"Mommy, look!"

There was the sun warming Zachary's hair as he ran as hard as his little legs could carry him, the kite's string tugging at his hand. Streamers of red and gold flowed away from the tail of the kite, which Felix had painted with a fanciful dragon — because, as he'd pointed out, a little boy with the last name of Drake needed a dragon on his kite.

"That's amazing, Zach!" I called out. "Be careful it doesn't lift you right off the ground."

"It's all right, Mommy. If I go up in the air, my wings will come out."

Which they would. He was growing fast, our little Zach. Precocious and already learning how to manage his transformations, even at barely four years old.

Four years. The country was looking forward to another four years with President Jackson Quinn at the helm, just as Silas and I looked forward to each and every day with our precious boy. Hard to believe that Addie was now in junior high, bright and beautiful and healed.

That was all of us. Moving forward, enjoying our day in the sun. In that world, the unending night of the vampire was only an uneasy dream, one dispelled with the rising of the dawn.

I leaned my head against Silas' shoulder, and was content.

The End

Defender

Bad Blood (August 2017)

Deep Magic (October 2017)

THE DJINN WARS

(Paranormal Romance)

Chosen

Taken

Fallen

Broken

Forsaken

Forbidden

Awoken (July 2017)

THE SEDONA FILES

(Paranormal Romance)

Bad Vibrations

Desert Hearts

Angel Fire

Star Crossed

Falling Angels

Enemy Mine

TALES OF THE LATTER KINGDOMS

(Fantasy Romance)

All Fall Down

Dragon Rose

Binding Spell

Ashes of Roses

One Thousand Nights

Threads of Gold

The Wolf of Harrow Hall

Moon Dance

The Song of the Thrush (November 2017)

THE GAIAN CONSORTIUM SERIES

(Science Fiction Romance)

Blood Will Tell

Breath of Life

The Gaia Gambit

The Mandala Maneuver

The Titan Trap

The Zhore Deception

Refugees (September 2017)

ABOUT THE AUTHOR

Christine Pope has been writing stories ever since she commandeered her family's Smith-Corona typewriter back in the sixth grade. Her work includes paranormal romance, fantasy romance, and science fiction/space opera romance. She fell under the Land of Enchantment's spell while researching her Djinn Wars series and now makes her home in Santa Fe, New Mexico.

www.christinepope.com